WICKED SENSE

Fabio Bueno

Booklings Publishing

Booklings Publishing

Wicked Sense
Copyright © 2012 Fabio Bueno

Cover Design by Martina Elise Dalton

First Printing, 2012

ISBN: 098587791X
ISBN-13: 978-0-9858779-1-0 (paperback)

To

Daisy

Chapter 1: Drake

I don't buy into the high-school-is-hell theory. To me, it's more like this joyless limbo most of the time, utterly boring, with the occasional humiliation and the rare thrill.

The new girl is a fine example of the latter.

"Drake's got a crush," Sean taunts.

Not yet, but I'm... intrigued. She's different. Alluring. Sitting at an outside cafeteria table twenty yards from ours, absorbed in a small hardcover black book, she remains oblivious to the darkening skies above us and to the Greenwood High crowd watching her.

"You're staring too, moron," Boulder says, shoving Sean playfully. Kind of. "But I don't blame you guys. She's hot."

Sean chuckles. "An R-rated body."

My eyes stay on her. "What are you talking about? She's petite," I say before my brain can stop me. Oh, man, they've suckered me into one of these testosterone-fueled talks again. With a heroic effort, I take my eyes off her and look at them. "Are we talking about the same girl?"

"Yeah, the new chick. The brunette chick." Boulder, the paradigm of subtlety, points to her. "Don't sweat it, D-Man. Sean is just messing with you. She's pretty, but she's no Priscilla. And, for the

1

record, I don't think you should call *anyone* petite." This from the guy who just used a fowl-related word to describe a human being. Twice.

My head turns to her again, as if a pulled by a magnetic force.

She peeks over at us. It doesn't fool me; I've been burned before by mistaking a furtive look for something else. Just an involuntary, split-second, rest-my-eyes-in-a-random-direction kind of glance. I know it means nothing.

"Did you see that? She looked right at me!" Sean says, chuckling once again. It must be nice living inside his head.

His reward is another of Boulder's trademark shoves. "Yeah, right," Boulder says. "With this male specimen here?" He taps his own chest.

I shake my head. These talks always end in—

"I'm going over there," Boulder says. For a built seventeen-year-old linebacker with a square jaw and an above-average vocabulary, Boulder has an alarmingly high strikeout rate with the ladies. I don't know why; he seems confident. Over-confident. Maybe that's it. Boulder is over-everything.

"No," I say, stealing some of his surplus confidence. "My turn."

My brain is definitely taking the day off. I'm never that bold. Sean snickers, predictably.

Boulder, astonished at my daring, remains speechless for a few unnerving seconds. But soon he grins. He slaps me hard on the back, in what he thinks is a friendly manner, and probably damages my kidneys in the process. "Go for it! Get yourself some hotness!"

Emboldened by their approval, I get up and start my ill-advised journey to inevitable disaster. For a moment, I think the ominous gray clouds signal a bad day. But in Seattle, it just means it's another day.

I cross the muddy grass and the gravel path. In my mind, the schoolyard vanishes. There's only her, and I process every detail. The book still hypnotizes her. She wears glasses, a delicate red frame with a faint rainbow effect on the lenses. I drink her in: dark brown hair in a tight ponytail, thin nose, and pale, flawless skin. Something about her screams otherworldly—maybe the impossible symmetry of her face. It's so weird. She's not stunning, but her face is so maddeningly… attractive. She's definitely not Sean's type (bombshell), although she's Boulder's type (female).

I arrive unnoticed and say a weak "Hi." Yup, I'm that smooth.

Apparently, the book is still very interesting. Great, I'm losing to dead trees.

At last, she raises her eyes, still hidden by those weird lenses, and says, "I'm sorry. I'm sure you're nice and all that, but I need to finish this." Her manicured finger taps the book.

Love her voice—slightly hoarse, but feminine. And the accent: she must be British, maybe an exchange student. Her accent comes and goes as if she's an unprepared American actress playing a British character.

The snub doesn't shake me. I expected it, and I thought about the perfect reply on my way over. "I understand. But I'm trying to help you. If you don't talk to me, Boulder over there will try his luck with a much lamer and potentially offensive pickup line." I look over my shoulder. Boulder, typically, misreads my thumb pointing at him and does the pigeon-chest thing.

She looks at me, then at him, and then back at me. I'm feeling like part of a tennis match when she closes the book and says, "Okay. What do you want to talk about?"

Of course I haven't planned this far. I'm caught flat-footed and fumble my lines about her accent. The familiar panic starts to take over, but the least likely person saves me.

Exchange girl notices Jane arriving, as does everybody else. I mean, everybody *always* looks when Jane arrives; she's impossible to avoid. Jane is a biker chick, and she's biker-chic. She's all about leather jackets, customized helmets, strangling pants, and sexy Italian bikes with brand names that sound like dirty words.

Sean tried to ask Jane out once, and she punched him in the face. *Punched* him. A firm "no"—or even a good slap—should be enough for most people. But she knocked him down and almost broke his nose. Jane fractured her hand, but she didn't even flinch. Sean never reported her. Knowing him, I'd guess he said something inappropriate. And he probably went down laughing.

For once, it's Jane's turn to stare at someone else. She pierces Exchange Girl with demonic eyes. Everybody notices. Jane marches toward us, blood-red helmet in elbow, parting the sea of students with her commanding presence. It's as if we can *feel* her hatred for the new girl. The weather report said to expect a thunderstorm today. Maybe this is it.

The buzz in the schoolyard rises. The excitement of a new student's arrival is compounded by the possibility of an even more sensational event: a cat fight.

Chapter 2: Skye

The boy rises. I shouldn't have glanced over. I should have kept my head down! But his aura is so unusual. I don't even know how to read it.

Is he the...? No, he isn't. Don't be stupid, Skye. It can't be that simple. Besides, he doesn't radiate any energy. Follow the plan. Be ordinary. Lie low. Some contact is inevitable. I'm a little surprised, though. I thought the steroids junkie would be the one to chance it. Or maybe the stocky guy with a buzz cut and lewd eyes. I brace myself anyway.

Don't worry. Just be sulky and moody, and he'll go away.

Even with my eyes still on my book, I can sense him forcing each step, almost marching. He arrives, hovers for a second, and says, "Hi."

I give him my prepared speech; he replies with a somewhat reasonable argument. I choose the lesser of two evils—as I always do—and challenge him to say something interesting.-Besides, upon seeing him up close I notice an understated but undeniable cuteness.

That's when I feel her presence. Soon she senses me too. When she removes her helmet, the girl reveals a short, spiky, almost-military haircut that she can only pull off because of her thick dark hair. I must admit, she puts on a show, dressed in several shades of brooding and black. Her fury is palpable. I wonder—

Oh, Goddess! She's coming over. Is she insane? Everybody's watching.

I'm paralyzed, and I'm uncertain if it's her doing, or my own usual powerlessness. I just sit there, an easy target. Only one thought crosses my mind: don't break the Veil.

She goes past the boy, who looks as petrified as I am. She leans over me and hisses, "What are you doing here?"

Her magical signature overwhelms me. The tingling sensation becomes almost an electric shock.

She's tall and muscular like a fitness instructor. She may have an Athletics Charm. Her quasi-gray eyes and her crimson full lips are the only colors on her. I summon all my strength and get up, bluffing, hoping she doesn't realize my distress, but her black boots add to her height advantage, and she still towers over me.

I can feel all eyes upon us. I get in her face and do my best tough-girl impression. "Don't do this," I say. "Not here."

"*You* came here." She has a point. "Don't forget that." She scans the school grounds and realizes we have attracted an audience. Her frown gets deeper. She mercifully leaves.

I'm still recovering from all that negative energy when the boy turns to me and says, "So, old friends, you and Jane?"

"Jane?" I ask, stupidly. He looks at me in a weird way. My mistake. Another one.

I glance at her again as she leaves. Not only is she a witch, her magical energy flowing from her in waves, but the vibe she radiates is so suffocating that it feels as if I've lost a part of my soul just by standing up to her.

6

I didn't know they already had a Sister here. Maybe Jane has no connection to the Mothers. I thought Connor was the Seattle overseer. Connor. All this grief, and that's before I see him again.

That Jane girl took away my balance. I vowed I wouldn't feel sorry for myself anymore, and I stand by it. No more porcelain feelings. No moping around because nobody gets me. And certainly no supposedly amazing boyfriend who stomps on my heart.

I went through all that right after my Daybreak. It won't happen again, thank you very much. Nothing is worse than this curse disguised as a blessing. I wish it were as simple as shooting lightning from your fingertips. I can only long for bright sparkles that make everything right. Why can't magic work as it does in fairy tales?

Stop complaining, Skye. Most people would sell their souls (some certainly try) to have this gift. Don't be ungrateful.

Secretly-cute boy looks at his cell. I forgot about him.

I say to him. "That was awkward. Listen—"

Before I finish, he jumps in. "You know what? Awkwardness is one of the biggest threats to our society. We should do something about it, create an organization, mobilize people. Raise awareness, you know? I'm all for social issues. Maybe we should hang out and discuss our plan of attack?"

His words stun me. I look down at my book to gain time.

He doesn't stop. "What do you say? Should we meet and discuss the issue? I've even got a log line. 'Awkwardness awareness.' Catchy."

I'm still lost. My plan was to remain inconspicuous, quietly make a few friends , and investigate. Well, the quiet ship has sailed away after the Jane confrontation.

He's trying so hard, and I feel a speck of guilt. His enthusiasm is partly my Allure Charm's fault, after all. I wish I could turn it off sometimes.

The boy waits patiently while I try to snap out of it. Oh, okay. I just hope I won't regret it later. I tell him, "Sure."

He walks back, beaming. I just made someone's day.

I think about returning to my book, but somehow another girl sneaked up on me while I was distracted.

It's been an eventful morning. When I saw the weather, I picked this table outside to be alone, but it seems chilly winds and menacing clouds don't scare people around here.

I create a mental catalog of everybody in the parade: hoodie-jeans-sneakers boy with overdue haircut and weird speeches, psychotic biker witch, and now, in front of me, fake-tanned skinny blonde with possible posture problems in her future.

She tells me her name is Priscilla, and then she goes over the new-girl questionnaire. Her candor is disarming. Name? Skye. Senior? Yup. Where from? New York, London before that. Accent? British. Kind of trying to get rid of it. Know anybody? Nope.

Priscilla shakes her head in secretly-cute boy's direction, her heavily highlighted shoulder-length hair billowing as if out of a conditioner ad. "What did Drake want with you?" Wow, she *is* direct. And now I know his name.

"I'm not sure yet," I say. Well, I guess he wants what all boys want, but I try to give her a chance to gossip. "Do you know him?"

"Kinda. Word is he's a good kisser." She looks a little distracted.

That's not what I was expecting to learn. "Really? Well, we're not there yet." So, quiet Drake has a reputation. Were Priscilla and Drake involved? I wonder if she's here to tell me to back off. Somehow I can't picture these two as a couple, though, and I dismiss the thought.

8

Priscilla sits down and pulls down on my arm, making me sit next to her. I don't resist. Our lunch table is next to the building, and many other tables circle us. With everyone *still* staring, I feel like I'm onstage.

She lowers her voice. "Listen, I'm not going to lie to you." Her hand rests on my arm in a sisterly touch. "You need me. I don't know the school you came from, but this one is a mess: gossips, backstabbers, false friends. Luckily for you, I'm the helping type. Do you want to hang out?"

While she talks, I take a good look at her. She is wearing clothes just long enough to avoid detention. Eyebrows plucked so thinly they'd be distracting if it weren't for her big green eyes getting all the attention. Even her pouty lips seem hand-drawn. She looks like the in-crowd queen. It's hard to imagine what a drop-dead gorgeous girl like her wants with me.

Since I'm here to make friends anyway, I accept it. Besides, her aura is mostly pink. It bodes well. "Sure," I say.

The bell rings. Priscilla stands, pulling me up with her. She asks about my next class and tells me to follow her. She bosses me around in such a gentle and sweet way that it doesn't bother me.

I got three bizarre new connections in just a few minutes. A busy morning. The Mothers would be proud.

Chapter 3: Drake

As I throw my verbal Hail Mary, I already know it sounds desperate.

"Sure," she says after a while. She gives me a smile, and I want to frame it.

Daydreaming, I smile back and walk slowly to my friends.

I sneak a peek to my cell again: "ASK HER OUT STUPID." Sean uses roughly one-third of the text to offend me. However, against all odds, it turns out to be useful advice.

He is almost jumping up and down when I arrive back at our table. "So, how did it go?"

"Not bad," I say, still relishing that smile.

Sean doesn't let it go. "Do you have a date?"

"I do. I guess."

He smirks. "Hold on. You guess?"

"Well, that's the thing." I scratch my head. "I'm not sure."

Boulder hides his face behind his overgrown hands. "You're a disgrace."

Sean guffaws. Of course, I want to punch his brains out. Why is it that the closer the friend, the more you feel entitled to punch him? Reasons are aplenty: maybe he embarrassed you, or told you a hard truth, or you want *him* to see the truth. There's always a punch-worthy opportunity between friends.

"Your level of dorkiness is staggering," Boulder continues.

"I know." I feel like punching Boulder too, but that's tantamount to suicide.

Sean keeps laughing.

Boulder doesn't let go. "Your sissiness is the stuff of legend."

"I already agreed with you," I say, my teeth clenched.

Sean laughs uncontrollably, banging his fist on the table.

"Never mind," Boulder says, ignoring Sean's antics and giving me a one-armed man hug. "A win is a win. Tell me about her. What's her name?"

"I... I..."

Boulder shoves me away in disgust. "You didn't ask?!?!"

Holding his side, Sean sits on the ground. He's laughing so hard, I see tears.

Even though most students are already immunized against Sean's theatrics, his displays of hysteria still embarrass me. I look around to check if people are staring at us, but they're gawking at my perhaps-date. With good reason.

"The Predator is talking to your girlfriend," Boulder also notices.

Even Sean stops laughing and says, "Now, The Predator isn't 'petite.' Is she, Drake?"

Boulder answers for me. "Petite? Only if you spell it with double Ds."

Priscilla, The Predator, earned her nickname. In the last two years she tore through the male student body—"male" and "body" being key words here—but somehow managed to sidestep me. (That's my life in a nutshell, by the way).

Now, done with feasting at Greenwood High, she relies on a

11

strict diet of college guys.

The two girls sit close together, and Priscilla is already making friends with the new girl. The bell rings and they leave side-by-side, BFFs after three minutes together. That's weird, but not as weird as the new girl's face-off with Jane.

Poor new girl. On day one, she gets to meet The Predator, Jane, and me. Greenwood High is doing its best to make the worst first impression possible.

***

During Pre-Calc, I overhear someone saying her name: Skye.

I wish I could talk to the guys about her, but they are… Let's just say we have different sensibilities. Also, let's say that if I ever use the word "sensibilities" around them, I'll be killed. First mocked, then killed.

The rest of the school talks, though: I hear all kinds of comments about her. Most of them are rumors about her confrontation with Jane and the sudden friendship with Priscilla. People barely remember my cameo—one of the advantages of being invisible.

I spend my day as I spend most of them: unnoticed and undisturbed. It's only when I arrive at the pool building across the street from school that somebody talks to me.

"Hey, Drake. Have you thought about our talk?" Coach Summers has given me the same hello for almost two years running now.

"I thought about it, but I can't be part of the swim team. I'm against team sports." I always come up with a different excuse.

He nods. "That's because you suck at them. I saw you trying out for baseball."

"Always a motivator, Coach."

"Stop making excuses. The offer stands until you graduate, just in case you decide to grow a pair."

"Thanks, Coach. I'll let you know when they're fully grown."

We wave at each other. He doesn't smile—he never does—but I do.

I get all my laps in, at a leisurely pace. No competitions for me, not even against the clock. I don't need or want the pressure. Besides, one of the most effective ways to avoid being a loser is to avoid competition.

In the pool, I forget the world: home, school, even Skye. It's my time, all mine, only mine.

I leave the pool building renewed. It's almost dark, the dusk coming earlier because of the angry clouds, but I don't care. Even the rain doesn't bother me. I'm at peace with myself.

Then I see Skye, and my world tumbles again.

"Hey," I holler.

"Hey, you," she yells back from across the street.

I take it as an invitation and cross over to her side. She looks tired, but still radiant. Again, her unconventional beauty confuses me. She looks like an average girl—the most perfect average girl I've ever met, if that makes sense.

"What a coincidence," she says.

"Maybe it's fate," I say, and I immediately regret it. My comment is so lame the other lame comments look down on it in disgust. But she doesn't mind.

"Fate? Do you believe in fate?" she asks.

"I do now."

She blinks a few times, seemingly amused. Her glasses are gone, and I notice her eyes are a bright shade of blue I've never seen before. It's hard not to stare. For a moment, those deep pools suck me in, play with me, own me, and spit me out. She looks away, reaches into her backpack, fishes the strange rainbow glasses out, and puts them back on.

I wonder if that eye color has a name.

"So, Drake, huh?" She offers her hand.

"So, Skye, huh?" I shake it, gently, lingering for a nanosecond too long. "Nice to meet you too."

"Gossip is a popular sport here, isn't it?"

I shrug. "It wouldn't be high school without gossip."

The rain picks up. Real rain, not the perpetual drizzle we usually have. "Welcome to Seattle in October," I say, pointing toward the clouds.

"Yes, a real downer, after living in sunny London," she says, a resigned expression on her face. "What's there?" She nods past my shoulder to the building behind me.

"The pool. I was swimming."

She raises her eyebrows. "Wow, you swim? That's cool."

What an odd thing to say. I look for sarcasm in her voice, but I can't find any. She sidetracks me with her comment, and these words escape me somehow: "Are you going home? May I walk you?"

She eyes me and ponders it for a while, disregarding the rain dampening her hair. "'Walk me home?' Aren't you the old-fashioned gentleman?"

It's getting dark. The announced thunderstorm is coming. I look up pointedly.

Chapter 4: Skye

Drake sounds trustworthy. My only uneasiness is his fuzzy aura. I still don't know what it means, and it bothers me a little. Not enough to refuse his offer to become my escort, though.

"I live on Stone Avenue," I say. The rain is heavy. We start moving north.

"What were you still doing in school?" he asks.

"A bunch of paperwork. They misplaced my school records, a mess."

It's pouring, and even for us, people rained on for all our lives, it gets uncomfortable. As a good Londoner and a good Seattleite, we don't carry umbrellas. But we move faster.

"Are you north of 97th? If you are, we can take a shortcut through the park." He points to a walking trail surrounded by thick trees. In the middle of a residential area. Emerald City, indeed.

A quick thought crosses my mind: is he trying something?

He must have noticed my expression. "Never mind," he corrects himself. "Stupid idea. It's probably muddy and slippery."

The skies rumble. I want to get home soon. The darkness on the brink of overtaking us is both an incentive and a deterrent. If he has a hidden agenda, he's a hell of an actor—and I know actors. I feel safe. Besides, I'm already drenched. So, I say, "No, let's. It's okay."

15

He looks at me, surprised, and changes direction. I follow him.

It *is* muddy. The trail is mostly dirt with a layer of dead leaves. To our right, an upward slope has several trees with exposed roots, and we hold on to them when we lose balance. To our left is a downward slope, not as steep as the other side, but falling and sliding is a possibility.

My feet falter, but Drake catches me, his warm hands steadying me. He seems self-conscious and lets me go as soon as I regain my balance.

"How much more?" I ask, a little louder than I intended. The thunder and the rain hitting the canopy muffle our voices. This storm got ugly fast.

"Three blocks," he yells. He is not afraid, but perhaps a little embarrassed by his suggestion of taking a shortcut.

It wasn't a good idea. Streams of thick mud cross our path and flow down to our left. We're caught in the middle.

We hear a roar at the same time. I glance at him. He looks to his right, and then he shoves me away without warning. Before I know it, I'm sliding down the slope, grasping for plants to stop my descent, and a tree is falling over him. He tries to get out of its way. The trunk misses him, but one of the main branches hits him in the head. He tumbles over, and I scream.

Pulling myself up with the help of the vegetation, I try to get back to the path. My special glasses are gone, and I know I sprained something, but I don't care.

The falling tree slides down with Drake caught in the branches. It drags him for just a few feet. He's facedown, motionless, a little to the left of the trail. At least the tree didn't drag him down all the way. I crawl to him and call his name. I turn him over.

16

Drake's unconscious, but breathing. Under the dirt, his face is scratched, the mud making a grotesque mask. On his right temple, a big gash pours red, sticky blood.

I pull back, not in disgust, but in shock. Another roar of thunder startles me, but it also awakens me. I know any head wound will bleed profusely, even a minor cut. And he's knocked out. I reach for my cell, before remembering I didn't bring it to Seattle. I recall he received a text when we were talking earlier; he had a clip-on on his belt. I search in vain for it. It probably fell and slid down the slope, lost in the dark mud now.

Desperate, I try to clean his face with rainwater. I use my jacket's sleeve to halt the blood coming from the gash. When the fabric absorbs the thick liquid, I see the cut is deep and wide. Serious. Life-threatening.

I look around, as if the trees have the answers. *Wake up, Skye. This is real. And you can do something about it.* I focus, ignoring the storm, the thunder, the pain. I try to remember Judi's and Mum's lessons, all those words and gestures I thought would be useless. They come to me.

Still kneeling, I close my eyes and stretch out my arms to the sides, the palms of my hands facing up. Rainwater washes over me, cleansing me; the rawness of the storm helps me attune to nature. The elements and I become one.

Empowered by the Goddess, I feel my personal magic flowing inside me. With my eyes wide open now, I lean over him and remove the jacket's sleeve from the wound. I get his blood on my right hand and make a triangular shape of dark red on his forehead. I take off his sneakers and socks, arrange his body in a spread-eagle position, and draw triangles on the palms of his hands and on his feet. Without

17

my ceremonial knife, I have to improvise: my fingers dig deep into the wet dirt to make a circle around Drake. I get back to my original stance, kneeling beside him, and use the words from a language long gone.

There, in the dark, in the deluge, I say my ancient prayer. I hope it's enough.

Chapter 5: Drake

So, that's what being hit by a truck feels like, I guess.

The emergency room smells of antiseptic and boredom. The doctor, a cutie too young to be out of med school, reads my CAT scan results. She tells my father that I'm okay, but they'll be watching me overnight.

A still-soaked Skye stares at them. She's standing next to the curtain that separates me from other unfortunate people. The blue of her eyes is subdued.

"Are you sure?" Dad asks the doctor. "Skye," he continues, pointing to my savior, "said a tree fell on him. A *tree*. He's only got a mild concussion. How is that possible?"

I look at Skye. There it is, a faint knowing smile. I see it—it's not my possibly damaged brain playing tricks on me. That smile goes to the top of the pile of questions I have for her.

"He was very lucky, that's all," the doctor tells my father. She looks like a kid wearing a lab coat for Halloween. "What we see here is not unlike a football hit. They bring boys to the ER with this type of concussion all the time."

It's true. Boulder had one last year. Which is not really comforting: no way he can be called a model of a healthy mind.

After the young doctor leaves, my father approaches my bed. "You feeling better, buddy?"

"I'm buzzed, that's all. Feeling very good, actually. Please add Percocet to the shopping list, Dad."

"Okay, you sound like yourself," he says, tapping my hand, but still concerned. That's my father: concerned all the time. Adding another burden to him is almost cruel, after all he's been through. He turns to Skye, "Thanks again, Skye. I—"

She cuts him off gently. "Don't mention it, Mr. Hunter."

"No, I mean it. Anything, anytime. Just let me know."

She nods sympathetically.

Dad faces me. "It was a hell of a storm. A lot of fallen trees, mudslides, flash floods, even a blackout west of I-5. Be glad the hospital has backup energy." I can see the wariness in his eyes. "Now, Drake, I'll tell the good news to your friends. And call Mona. Be right back."

"Sure," I say. "Wait. My friends?"

"Yes," he says. "Sean and Boulder have been sitting outside for hours, but visiting time's over now. I'll tell them to go home."

That surprises me. Even though they're my best friends, I'm not *their* best friend. I mean, Sean is Boulder's and vice-versa. I'm kind of their backup best friend.

There's this unspoken pecking order among us: Boulder is the alpha-dog, Sean is his sidekick, and I'm there just for entertainment purposes. I don't complain. They hang out with me, and I'm grateful. Having them watching over me is unexpected.

I look to my right and see Skye staring at me. She comes over, puts her hand on my shoulder, and I feel a tsunami of goose bumps.

"The shortcut was a little longer than I thought," I tell her.

"Sorry."

"Don't be sorry. You saved me," she says.

I remember. I shoved her away when the tree fell. Instinct.

"Well, you saved me more." I smile.

Skye lets out a soft chuckle. "Actually, I left you and found someone with a cell phone. Not very heroic."

I know that's not all, but she doesn't mention it. I respect it. I owe it to her.

"Still," I say instead.

"Call it even?" She grins. She's so beautiful my head hurts. Oh, wait, that's not it.

Dad pokes his head in. "Drake, listen. I'm taking Skye to her house. I'll be back, all right? Mona is sleeping over at her freaky friend's house."

I'm drifting to sleep, and I try to understand what Dad says. Mona is my little sister, the world's most neurotic fourteen-year-old. Right now, she's probably thinking my near-death experience is some cheap ploy to get Dad's attention. Her "freaky friend" is most likely that goth girl who calls herself "Rain" or something. Okay, brain still works.

"I think I'm going to crash before you get back," I say, suppressing a yawn.

Skye's hand leaves my shoulder, and I miss it. I wish I could keep her touch with me the whole night. I long for a gesture of caring from her.

"Sweet dreams," Skye says as she leaves.

That will do.

***

I wake up in the morning, and I remember the year and my name.

So far, so good.

The problem is, I also remember what happened during the storm. What I didn't have the heart to ask Skye last night.

I was drifting in and out of consciousness with an excruciating pain in my head. Skye was in front me, in a yoga pose or something. Then, darkness.

My eyes opened, and there she was again, blood all over her hands, and she was... chanting, I guess. Besides my head hurting, I felt painful pinpricks throughout my body and a strange sensation of weightlessness, almost as if I were levitating. Before I could understand what was happening, I blacked out again.

When I woke up again, my whole body was hot, as if ablaze, even in the freezing rain. In my mind, I was burning alive. I wanted to scream, but I couldn't. Skye was breathing deeply, using a guttural voice, and rubbing my head, my hands, my feet. Swaying back and forth like that, she looked like a lunatic, to tell the truth.

That's the last thing I remember before the ER. I have to admit it was dark, but the night darkness was different from my lights-out darkness, and much clearer. Also, I could have been hallucinating, with my banged head and all, but it felt so vivid. So real.

So, I have many questions, and the most important appears to be: when is it a good time to ask a girl you've just met whether she's a Satanist or a nut-job?

Chapter 6: Skye

I wanted to make contacts and be discreet. And I ended up almost killing someone. On my first day of school. Good job, Skye!

My glasses are gone. Now I can't see auras anymore. And I can't disguise my weird blue eyes. I couldn't attract more attention.

I'm drinking my morning coffee when Aunt Gemma walks into the kitchen. She smiles warmly and gets a mug.

Aunt Gemma is not my aunt, but she's my host family here. She's not a witch either, but a Knowing—a non-magic user who knows about the Veil and is trusted by the Mothers. Knowings are usually friendly, which makes sense, since the unfriendly might incur the risk of being "dealt with." Some of them benefit from magic, but most of them keep quiet out of plain loyalty, like Aunt Gemma. The British Mothers arranged for my lodging here. I can't complain. Aunt Gemma is okay. As with the other Knowings, she's fascinated by us and tries to learn as much as possible.

After we say our good mornings, I ask her, "Did you know there's already a Sister at Greenwood High?"

"No." She looks surprised. "Who?"

"A girl. Jane Kaplan. Do you know her? She rides a red motorbike, er, motorcycle."

Having Jane at school is truly annoying. I can sense her energy *all the time.* It's like being back home, when Mum's energy was always around me. Only I love Mum, while Jane… I don't.

"Kaplan, Kaplan…" Gemma goes through her list of neighbors and acquaintances from church. Yes, she goes to church. I don't even ask her about it. "No, I don't know her."

"Why would the Mothers send me here then?"

"Maybe they don't know about her." She shrugs. "Connor would, though."

Argh, Connor. Golden boy, from one of the oldest magic families. The rare male witch, what people call a warlock, but nobody I know uses this term. He's a male witch.

He's also my former boyfriend.

My silence doesn't deter Aunt Gemma. "Don't be gloomy; you knew you'd have to talk to him. He's the Seattle area overseer." Gemma knows about my past with Connor. Gossip mills work as well in the witch circles as in any high school.

"It's ridiculous they chose a male witch for this position," I say, out of spite.

"He's almost royalty, you know that," Gemma says. She pauses to munch on a Milano mint. "Besides, he's not your regular witch." She points the biscuit at me.

"No, he's a world class jerk," I say. Bitter much?

Gemma shakes her head. "Now, if you don't want me to pry, why do you say such things? What happened between you two?"

I say nothing. She sighs. "Are you going to meet him?"

"I'll find him. He's at University of Washington, right? Philosophy, Savery Hall."

Gemma giggles. "People here call it U-Dub, Skye. You want to sound like a local, right?"

24

Now I'm taking hip lessons from someone forty years older than me. "Thanks," I say. She's trying to help, after all. Besides, Aunt Gemma pretty much leaves me to myself, which I appreciate. She only asks that I don't bring boys home. As if, as they say.

I kiss her and leave.

Walking around Greenwood makes me feel good. The neighborhood is filled with antique stores and thrift shops. This connection to the past somehow makes me more attuned with my personal magic. The open spaces and streets lined with trees don't hurt either.

I need some connection with nature. Aunt Gemma told me about some secluded Seattle parks, and I have to check them out sometime. Our small backyard is no substitute for a large outdoor area. I haven't performed a decent ritual since I arrived. Well, not counting the healing one I improvised for Drake.

I'm almost at the bus stop when I remember. First, I'll go to a store and get a phone. If anyone else tries to die in my arms, I'd like to be prepared.

***

The bus drops me off a couple of blocks from "U-Dub." I saw pictures of the university once before: they showed clear skies and blossoming cherry trees that revealed the spring glory of Seattle. No such scenes in the autumn. Now the only beauty is the palette on the trees and on the ground. Yellow, orange, red: the leaves in Seattle die a colorful death. I navigate the lawn and the elegant buildings until I find a directory. Resolute, I go down Memorial Way, expecting a stunning vista of Mount Rainier, but it's hidden by clouds in the distance. Oh, well.

I turn my attention to the students. Around my age, but

somehow… adults. Or maybe it's just my impression of them. Is college for me? I'm a blank canvas. I have so many interests, but nothing compels me. I'm not passionate about anything in particular. I feel disconnected even from my Sisterhood. Maybe I'm empty inside. Like Connor told me.

Connor. The Mothers chose him for the search, granted. But I know he wouldn't come here if he didn't want to. He had a choice. He chose to leave me.

What am I doing here? I could get hurt all by myself in London. I didn't need to cross the pond to feel crushed.

Yet here I am, looking for him. Well, *I* didn't have a choice. The Mothers sent me here.

I'd better find him. I try to concentrate on the magical energy— that faint signature that all magic users exude. Close to Savery Hall, I feel it. A prickling sensation all over my body. Strong. Unmistakable.

There he is, looking around. No doubt he feels my energy too, now that I'm close. But I have the True Sight Charm; I can spot him before he spots me.

When Connor sees I'm the source, though, he is stunned. He mumbles something to the three girls gathered around him. They giggle (probably his Allure Charm at work), but leave. He uses the time I take to walk over to him to recover. His pearly teeth show a big smile. Without my glasses, I can only wonder if his powerful purple aura still shines bright.

"Skye! Of all the gin joints in all the towns…" His baritone voice tries to win me over. I bet his British accent, the same I worked so hard to lose, impresses the girls here.

"Hello, Connor."

"What a surprise," he says.

26

Wait, what? Didn't the Mothers tell him I was coming to help? That's weird, but I don't want to sound more confused than I already am, so I just say, "How's the search?"

Connor scans the people around, afraid somebody will eavesdrop on us. "Don't break the Veil, Skye," he whispers to me. "Come with me." He reaches to grab my arm, but thinks better of it in mid-movement, and changes the gesture into a beckoning wave. Smart move, Connor.

We walk for a while, silent, until he says, "This is the HUB. Let's stop for coffee."

He asks for a long-named concoction. I observe him while he chats up the barista. He shows off his bulging arms. I wonder if he still rows.

With his easy smile, perfect teeth, and amazingly soft and perfumed hair, he doesn't even need the Allure Charm. He could flirt with you while he sleeps. I get a double espresso, to blend in. We walk around the campus, trying to avoid the students. We need privacy.

When we're far enough from prying ears, he says, "I knew they would send someone, but I never expected you." He sips his coffee. "Not that it's a bad thing. Did you ask to come?"

"No!" I say. "I asked *not* to come. But it's my duty."

Connor nods. "It actually makes sense. With your True Sight Charm, you can help us." He's right. My Charm not only detects magical energy from afar, it also detects traces of it.

I face him, and he examines my eyes. "Hey, where are your glasses?" he asks.

"Lost them," I say. It's so odd talking to him after two years. We didn't part on friendly terms. Okay, that's an understatement. We parted on horrible terms and never exchanged calls, texts, or emails since. However, here we are, all civilized. Inside, though, I'm a tornado of conflicting emotions.

If he feels the same way, it doesn't show. "Have you met Jane already?"

That catches me by surprise. He does know about her. "She's kind of unmissable," I say.

Connor pierces me with his look. "Yeah, she's quite a handful." He sips his coffee again. I think the cup is just a prop so he can gain time and examine my reactions. "She's independent: she doesn't answer to the Mothers, doesn't belong to a coven, and I couldn't get her to cooperate. And with her attitude and her Intimidation Charm…"

"Are you sure she's not the Singularity?" I ask.

"She isn't," he says with authority.

"That's why you need someone else at Greenwood High." I try to sound business-like, but I can see in his eyes I'm failing. I carry on. "Any news about the Singularity?"

He looks away with a concerned expression on his face. He must take this assignment seriously. "No. She is still blocking her magical energy somehow. She might have some kind of shield up. She must be even more powerful than we'd guessed, to erase her magical signature completely. I hope your True Sight can spot her. If she's around your school."

A little vulnerability shows beneath his controlled façade. He says, "We're almost out of time, Skye. The Singularity must be seventeen now. If she's living a regular life, she's almost finishing school. She might leave soon, to college, or a job. Or just to run away: she knows we're looking for her, or she wouldn't be hiding her energy. She might even already be gone."

His sincerity moves me, but then I remember his other Charm is Trust. Everybody believes him and wants to help him. It's not his fault: he can't turn the Charm off. Still, I can't help but feel manipulated a little. As I did when we were together.

We are back to Savery Hall, and I spot the girls that surrounded Connor when I arrived. They linger around, like crows that don't scare easily. "Nice harem." I jerk my chin to his gathering of admirers.

He doesn't even look at them. "Oh, jealous much?" He smiles the devilish smile I remember. "Oh, come on," he says when he sees my face. "It was a bad joke. Sorry."

Maybe he's changing. The old Connor would never say he's sorry. He never did.

I always assumed it was over between us. But his apology sparks something—something I didn't realize was still inside of me. Is there a chance of us being together again?

I don't know, and I will not find out today. I'd better leave.

Chapter 7: Drake

"Da-ad! That's so unfair!" Mona is chanting her mantra.

My sister is still in ninth grade, and I'm glad in our district this means we go to different schools. Neither of us wants the other lurking around. We have nothing in common.

Mona and I came out of different assembly lines: I'm wiry and lanky like Dad; she is round and short like our mother. The only thing Mona and I share is eye color: hazel.

She has gained considerable weight in the last few months. Since she's so sensitive about everything, neither Dad nor I have had the guts to broach the subject. We don't know if the change is caused by stress, a hormonal thing, or a natural development. Dad wants to ask her about her health and if she's okay, but he doesn't want to upset the precarious balance of Mona's psyche. Me too. I mean, of all things I could point out, I imagine this is the one of the biggest no-nos in a brother-sister relationship.

Dad and I also didn't mention the black mini-skirts. Her body changed but she still wears her old clothes, which causes the mini-skirts to look… mini-er. Nor have we asked about the excessive highlights that look more like yellow stripes than blonde, giving the impression she's going for a tiger motif. Nor the heavy make-up. Nor the oversized jewelry. But, hey, no piercings yet!

So, through the gift of silence, Dad and I keep harmony in our house.

That's why Dad is so cautious when explaining things to her. "You can't even get a permit yet, Mona," my father says patiently. "Maybe you'll get the car when Drake is done with it."

"You said we don't have money!" My sister has a point.

"I said we don't have money *to burn*," my father says and then looks quickly at me, alarmed. Any mention of fire-related words around me makes him nervous, because he thinks I'll get upset. And he's right.

I'm the reason we don't have money to... spare. About two years ago, I accidentally burned our old house down, with the help of a cigarette—my first and only. Our insurance wasn't the greatest, and Dad lost most of our savings. We rent a smaller house now.

And that's not the worst that happened: I almost lost Mona. When I realized the house was on fire, I ran to her bedroom and found her unconscious. The smoke had already gotten to her. The paramedics that ultimately saved her said I was a hero, but I knew better.

I still can't believe I did it. I watched our house and everything inside, even our old pictures of Mom, vanish before my eyes. A haunting memory that will stay with me forever.

Dad's confidence, already shattered when Mom left, broke into tiny pieces. Since then he's been jumpy and scared, afraid of losing us and of losing money for our future.

It's surreal that I have a car. We live modestly: no iThings for the Hunters. Just your basic computer and cell, more out of necessity than luxury.

He's a computer engineer, whatever that means. Mona and I guess he's not very good. He works really long hours, including a murderous commute from Seattle to Renton, but the pay, albeit good, is not great. With the two of us all grown up, he spends less and less time with us.

My encounter with the falling tree didn't help things. My father, Mr. Worried-In-Chief, didn't take it well. His knee-jerk reaction was to trade his reliable four-year-old Camry for a slightly less reliable seven-year-old Corolla for him and an—I'm not kidding—old brown Volvo wagon for me. According to him, it's the safest car we can afford, but I can't stop mocking myself in my head.

Even though I'm laughing inside, I'm grateful; I had zero cars before. Now, the guilt of almost killing my sister and destroying our finances is compounded by the guilt of putting myself in danger *again*, and scoring my first ride in the process. It almost makes me side with Mona on this one. Almost.

"Mona, I'll be your driver, what do you say? I can take you to Rain's house and—"

"Her name is Pain, you moron!"

"To Pain's, to the piercing parlor, to the crack den, to that human sacrifice place—"

"Da-ad!"

"That's enough, Drake," Dad says. "He's got a point, though, Mona. You're having some strange company. You remember…"

"We have to police ourselves. I know," Mona repeats *Dad's* mantra. Since he's not around much, he tries to instill responsibility on us via overused catchphrases. Kind of futile after I almost got killed in the woods, but I get him.

"Good," Dad says, as if his job is done. "Now, I have to go to work. Oh, Drake, I got you a new cell phone too."

"Arrrrrgghhh!" Mona yells. She pulls on her hair theatrically and slams the door on her way out.

I know I shouldn't, but I get a kick out of it. I'm shameless.

***

I skip school since the doctor said I should rest, but I show up on Stone Avenue a few minutes after the bell rings. As I expected, I find Skye coming back from school. Naturally, she avoided the trail, even though it's the shortest route and the weather's nice today. For Seattle, I mean.

I pull over and open my window. At least I don't have to *roll* it down.

"Hey," I say, trying to sound nonchalant.

She turns, unfazed, as if expecting me. "Hey, you." She examines the embarrassing piece of Swedish engineering surrounding me. "Nice ride," she says. Then she bursts out in a laugh that would make Sean proud.

"Want one? Apparently, all you need is a brush with death, and they give you one of these beauties." I slide my finger across the dashboard.

"I could go for a coffee," Skye says out of thin air. Before I have time to answer, she walks behind the car. I'm still stunned when she opens the passenger door and climbs inside.

Uh-oh. Is this a date? I really should start planning these things better.

33

Chapter 8: Skye

He takes me to this charming, run-down coffee house on Broadway. We sit outside, watching the people traffic and listening to the city noise. Cars with rainbow flags, a hot dog vendor joking with his customers, a couple of girls with pink hair, a bunch of college students with full backpacks and white earphones. Whenever a homeless guy asks for change, Drake happily obliges.

I sip my espresso, the third today, and ask about the car. He tells me his father wants him to be safe.

"Speaking of safe, he also warned me about you. He said you're a bad influence," Drake says.

I laugh. "He did not!"

"He should have," he says with a straight face. "I mean, can you blame him? He doesn't know anything about you, and it seems you and I will be hanging out a lot."

I raise my eyebrows. "Will we?"

Drake makes a defensive gesture. "That's what he says. If only he knew you better. Come on, tell me about yourself."

He doesn't know it, but he's a charmer. I have to ask Priscilla about Drake's past. I stand up and announce, "I'm going to get a scone. Do you want anything?"

"Are you trying to buy time?" He nails it.

"No, I'm trying to buy a scone," I say, cheekily, and go inside the coffeehouse. While waiting for my treat, I think about what I can volunteer. Hiding too much will only attract attention. I feel like I owe him the truth, or, at least, a slice of the truth. For what we went through together in the woods.

While I'm at the counter waiting for my scone, I sense another Sister. It's a faint signature, but my instincts make me look around the coffeehouse. I peek outside, through the windows. The source is not moving. I close my eyes for an instant, trying to shut out my other senses. I feel it. It's coming from way down the road.

I return with my scone, but stop by the door, still inside. I stare in the direction the signature comes from, but it's impossible to recognize a face from this distance. However, I see something else: a bright red bike, about two blocks from us. Jane.

She probably thinks she's at a safe distance to spy on us. And why not? In her mind, if she doesn't sense me, it means I can't sense her either. However, she doesn't know about my long-ranging True Sight Charm.

I wonder why she would follow us. I chalk it up to curiosity about another Sister coming into her territory. If she's as anti-social as Connor says, it makes sense.

Drake still awaits me. And an answer as well. I almost forgot about him.

Partially hidden by the door, I peek at him. He seems to be watching something amusing on the street, because an easy smile sprouts from his lips. When he smiles, his whole face lights up: his eyes sparkle, his eyebrows arch, his angular chin becomes more prominent. The olive skin and the hazel eyes are a good match. Yep, he's cute.

I'd better not keep him waiting. I go outside to our table, sit down, and say, "I'm from London. I mean, I've been living in America on and off for a few years now." I bite into the scone; it's pure blueberry yumminess.

"Where?"

"New York, mostly. And Vancouver. And other places. My mother travels a lot," I say, my mouth full.

"No father?" When I nod, he continues. "Sorry, it's none of my business, but I have a single parent too. My mom left us when I was little."

I know; his father was candid when we were at the hospital. It seemed as if Mr. Hunter felt compelled to justify Drake's mother's absence. But I just say, "My father died before I was born. Mum never married him. Or anyone else." It's true. She had lots of boyfriends, though.

What I don't say is that my mother is Katherine Lexington-Ellis, a British theater legend who's been working in Hollywood and in indie movies since she won her Oscar nine years ago. I also omit that she's a witch. She named me Skye, after the Scottish island where my parents met. Mum told me he was a charming, powerful male witch, but just a fling.

Drake awakens me from my reverie. "Are you here with her? Do you have plans to move soon?"

"No, I'm staying with a friend of hers, my Aunt Gemma."

"So, you're not an exchange student, after all," he says, sounding pleased.

"No, I'm here to stay," I lie. Actually, I'm here until we find the Singularity.

He seems satisfied, so I finish my scone in silence, absorbing the vibe of this place. I've lived in so many cities, so many hotel rooms, with so many tutors. Mum was always on set, or in another room with her male lead. Now she's onstage in London, and the Mothers sent me here. Alone.

I don't want to think about it and I steer the conversation toward more mundane things. "Who are your friends? The ones with you on my first day?"

"The short one with a buzz cut is Sean. The one that looks like the Terminator is Boulder."

"Sean shouldn't wear sideburns *and* a soul patch."

He chuckles. "I know. And you met Sean after he trimmed them. You should have seen him before."

The conversation dies a little after that.

Drake sips his coffee slowly, watching the city come alive, but glances at me from time to time. We don't feel like we have to say something. It's a nice feeling.

I don't sense Jane's energy anymore. She's gone. Good.

The sights draw my attention again. Three-story red brick buildings surround us. On the street, an old car stands out. On its baby-blue sides someone painted an underwater scene, complete with starfish, dolphins, several types of fish, and seahorses.

My eyes follow the strange car passing on the road. Only because of the car I notice the statue of a kneeling Jimi Hendrix on the next block. What an odd city.

When I turn back to Drake, I catch him looking at me. He keeps staring while I chase after the scone crumbs on the table and stuff them in my mouth.

"What?" I mumble, my mouth full.

Drake smiles and says, "Have you seen the troll yet?"

Chapter 9: Drake

We're headed to Aurora Avenue, but she receives a call. She has to go home. I turn around. I'll show her the Fremont Troll later.

While I'm driving her back, she says, "So, Priscilla tells me you're a good kisser."

Huh? "I've never kissed her," I say. I'd like to, but I haven't.

"She says that's the word around school. So, what's up with that? Did you kiss all the other girls in school?"

Oh, I know. "No, I kissed just one. Brianna. But she gossips a lot."

Skye chuckles. I hope it's from my joke, not from my lack of experience. But I see an opening and take a chance.

"What about you?" I ask. "Do you have a boyfriend?" I make an effort to avoid being hypnotized by her unreal blue eyes.

"No." I was hoping for more, but I see her tensing a little bit.

Since she's new to the city, I take the longest route I can. I think of something to break the tension. "Girlfriend?" I ask. She chuckles again. "Husband?" She snorts.

"No, I'm free as a bird, as they say. But I'm not looking for somebody."

"Oh," I say. "Well, maybe somebody is looking for you."

She shakes her head, and then she stares at me. "If you know what to say at all times, how come you don't have a girlfriend?"

I shrug, my eyes on the road. "I guess I'm very selective."

She looks away, to the houses passing by out her window. I hope she's not into my trick to stretch our time together.

"You have a sister, right? Mona?" she asks, still not facing me.

That's an unexpected segue. "Yeah."

"I wish I had a sister," she says, dreamily. "A real sister. Someone always by your side, you know? Someone you love. Someone you can talk to."

It's my turn to chuckle, and she turns to face me. "What?" she asks.

"Mona and I are not like that. At all. I mean, I like her—"

"You mean, you love her," Skye corrects me.

"Okay, okay, love her," I say, the L-word leaving a strange taste in my mouth. "But from a distance. Especially now that she's in a freakish phase. We don't chat, and we certainly don't, you know, *talk.*"

She stares at me as if I had just strangled a kitten or something.

We reach a light, and I stare back at her. The green light appears, and I lose the staring contest. I snort, but I feel compelled to add, "Guys don't talk."

"*You* do," she says—not asking.

"I don't."

"You would," she replies with authority.

I keep my mouth shut. Yes, I would. Who's this girl, this stranger who knows so much about me? Damn, Skye, stop it. No need to make me want you more.

We mercifully arrive at her house. I want to be with her, but I know the way she can see through me might do me harm. She should come with a warning: enjoy Skye with moderation.

***

I drop by Boulder's after I recover from hurricane Skye. Of course, Sean is hanging out with him. They're taking turns updating their status on Boulder's computer. Hip-hop plays quietly—which strikes me as pointless, but I say nothing.

The futon is free, and I let my body plunge there. It's cool that I can just be there while I try to organize my thoughts. No need to force conversation. Sean browses through an Xbox magazine, sitting close to the desk where Boulder mans the laptop. Sometimes Boulder says, "Check this out," and the two of them stare at the screen, laughing. "That's so messed up," Sean says, shaking his head. Watching them is maddening; they could be talking about *anything*.

Sean finally leaves Boulder's side. He drops on the futon next to me and slaps my leg.

"So, how's the head?" he asks.

"Do I know you?" I deadpan. "Where am I? What is this place?"

Sean's chuckle is familiar and comforting. "We were worried, man," he says.

"Yeah," Boulder booms from the computer desk, still glued to the screen. "When we heard you were alone with a girl."

I can't help but join Sean's laugh.

Boulder continues, "Yeah, you're alone with the new hot chick, you convince her to follow you to the woods, and what do you do? You faint!"

Sean and I guffaw. I see Boulder joining us, his shoulders going up and down.

After our laughter fades, Boulder asks, "Are you going to school tomorrow?"

"Nah," I say. "I'll milk this injury as much as I can. I've got a note from the doctor keeping me from school for a week."

Sean nods in approval. "Nice move. What about the girl?"

"I know where she lives," I say, shrugging. "I can drop by and talk to her away from a crowd."

After a pause, Sean says, "I still can't believe that you took her to the hospital for your first date!" He chuckles again.

"It's worse. *She* took me to the hospital—" I have an epiphany. "A date! I forgot to ask her out."

"Classic Drake," Boulder says from the desk, shaking his head.

Chapter 10: Skye

Drake drops me off just as the phone is ringing. It's my mother, calling from London. I do the time zone conversion: it's 2 a.m. there, 6 p.m. here. Her performance is over and she's checking on me. No way I'm telling her—or anyone else—about the ritual in the woods. I'm not supposed to have performed it. It's way beyond my training.

"How are you?" Her familiar, stage-trained voice greets me. "Found the Singularity yet?"

"Mum!" I say, admonishing her. "Someone might be listening."

"Rubbish! This is paranoia talking. Or are you assuming the spy role? I've always told you, darling, you'd make a fine thespian." Mum sometimes speaks as if her life is a play, which is not far from the truth. "But tell me, any progress?"

"I've just arrived. I'm still meeting people," I say evasively.

"Use your True Sight, find the Sister, and come back to me. I miss you."

No, Mum, you think you do. If I came back, I'd get a week of attention, but soon you'd be back to your fellow actors, parties, interviews. And when you're in a play, you sleep until 3 p.m., leaving me alone and vulnerable to all kinds of dangers. Like Connor.

As if reading my mind (a Charm I'm sure she doesn't possess), she asks me, "So, any good-looking boys on your side of the pond?"

"Mum, please."

"It's only natural that I ask," she says, defensively. Natural to her, maybe. "After Connor left, you never went out."

"I did," I say, but I know what she means.

"With a group, yes, but not with a boy. That's not healthy. Have you seen him yet?"

"Yes, Mum. I saw Connor yesterday."

"And?"

"And he sends his love and says he misses you," I lie, hoping to appease her.

"Oh," she says, delighted. "He's always been a gentleman."

No, he hasn't!

She continues, "Oh, look at the time. I'm meeting friends for drinks later, and I need to get ready. Bye, darling. Kisses. I love you."

Out for drinks at two in the morning? Typical.

"Love you too," I say. Because I do, nonetheless.

***

The next day we have the dreadful PE class. I've always hated sports. If only I had an Athletics Charm… But then I'd be on the other extreme, with world-class skills. Most people think of steroids every time they see a great athlete performing beyond her age, or way above her peers. If she tests negative for performance-enhancing drugs, I'd bet good money she's a witch with an Athletics Charm. It would be fun watching the Olympics onsite some day; with my True Sight I could spot all Sisters from the stands.

We Sisters don't necessarily hide. If everybody knew about magic, it would be easy to identify who's a witch. Some of us possess Charms to grow old slowly, the reason some movie stars never seem

43

to age. It amazes me how people never look into how some actors can change appearances from role to role. The Shifting Charm is handy.

Many Charms enhance a Sister's athletic abilities, but less obvious ones also exist. My True Sight is related to improved magical ability, and Judi, a friend of Mum's and my main tutor in the Craft, has the ability to perform powerful rituals. Mum has the Charisma Charm, while other actors clearly have the Lust one. Intellect-related Charms owners can have great business acumen, visual arts skills, or scientific inclination.

However, some Sisters just waste their Charms. I can't blame them. I could have used my Allure to become an actress or a model. But that would lead to a life too similar to my mother's. A fun life, granted, but that's just not my thing. Also, I'd have to be a foot taller.

"Come on, girls, look alive!" the PE teacher yells from the locker room's door. Running is terrible, but it's better than organized sports: I have no strength, and my timing is always off. I think I cannot hit, strike, or kick even a stationary ball. I leave in a hurry.

We are supposed to circle the school three times. It involves going around the school building, the football field, the yard with outside cafeteria tables, the giant parking lot, and crossing the street to circle the pool building. So, we run. Or rather, the other girls run. I just walk fast, a kind of step-walk. I see a girl who outweighs me two to one passing by me. I have no excuse. This girl with a determined look and rosy cheeks is leaving me behind in last place. I'm a wuss. Being the spoiled daughter of a movie star (okay, an often-sought after character actor) will do that to you.

I drag myself to the gym. With only my pride hurt, I get back much later than the others; our PE teacher is not even around anymore. Almost everybody has already left when I enter the shower. I rush through it, skipping the conditioner, fearful of missing my next class. Still wrapped in my towel, I open my locker, and I notice it's unlocked. I may have forgotten to lock it when I left in a hurry. I am getting late, so I quickly apply my moisturizer. Seattle's weather forces me to take hot showers, and they're wreaking havoc with my skin, making my face dry and flaky. My Allure Charm should take care of it in time, but I want to speed up the process.

After I'm done, I reach for my clothes. Suddenly my face gets hot and prickly, and my eyes start to water. I blink a few times, but my vision blurs, and the burning sensation spreads to my eyes. I rub them with my shirt. With my vision going away, I feel my way to the sink, open the faucet, and splash cold water over my face.

I hear someone's footsteps. "I can't see!" I say. "Can you help me?" My voice is high, panicky. Everything is dark now.

"What happened?" I can't place the feminine, young voice.

"I don't know. The cream. I can't see." The burning is unbearable.

"What do I do?" The voice's owner is nervous too.

"Nurse! Take me to the nurse," I say. I force my eyes shut as if I'm trying to keep the pain outside.

A warm hand lands on mine, and another on my elbow, guiding me. My other hand is still rubbing my eyes. I feel like scratching them out to make the sting go away.

The girl who owns the voice leads me gently but quickly across the room. I feel the chilly air against my warm skin when we leave the locker room: we're outside. I'm still wearing only a towel, but the thought gets lost in my mind; I just want to get rid of this excruciating pain. We walk a few steps more. I can hear other people in the distance.

The hands leave my arm, and I stumble: the towel that wraps my body is yanked off, and I almost fall to the ground, exposed.

Someone yells from a distance, "Naked chick!"

I'm in hell, my eyes torturing me, and I don't know if I should cover my nakedness or just keep rubbing my eyes. I turn and try to walk inside, anywhere, but my shoulder hits something hard, an open door maybe. I stagger and take a step back.

Around me, I can hear shouts and catcalls, whistles and taunts, but I don't care. I just want to leave. Hunched, I try to feel my way, but I trip on something and fall sideways, cold mud hitting my butt, my back, my sides.

I don't get up, caring nothing for my privacy anymore, just begging for the pain to go away. While I press my hands against my eyes, curled up in the mud, someone shouts, "Skye!" It's Priscilla's voice, close to me.

Warmness envelops me, maybe a coat covering me, but that's no comfort.

"My eyes!" I shout. "I can't see!"

I hear other people close now, more voices, words like "nurse" and "water" bandied about, but I can't think anymore.

I'm a puppet, a doll with no will, shaking and screaming, while many hands carry me away.

Chapter 11: Drake

It's always unsettling when the whole school sees your prospective girlfriend naked. Especially when it's before you do.

"What a day to miss school, man!" is Sean's opening salvo. He tells me Boulder and he were going to class when somebody yelled, and they saw Skye naked, flailing about, screaming, bumping on doors, completely bonkers. She fell down, and Priscilla rushed to cover her with a jacket, followed by Ms. Capshaw and the nurse. They created a human wall and carried her away, Boulder tells me, disappointed. I ask the guys many questions, but they're even more clueless than usual and give me only speculation. And anatomic details. They praise my taste.

"She's got a hip tat, you know?" Sean says.

"A what?"

Boulder explains. "A tattoo on her hip. Fancy one, too. Never seen a silver tat before."

I can get nothing useful out of them.

That's why I'm at her Aunt Gemma's, waiting for Skye. The house is one of the oldest lots of our neighborhood, and it shows. Aunt Gemma looks young for her age, but her knick-knacks and furniture surely don't. Add to that the dated wallpaper, the brown-framed single-paneled windows, and the dusty smell, and you've got the typical Grandma's house.

Aunt Gemma comes down the stars, saying, "She asked you to come up." Her frown is so intense it feels like an extra presence in the room. I stand up, and she looks me in the eye as if I'm a criminal, but says nothing. Okay, message received.

I walk up the stairs. All the doors are closed but one, and I glimpse a queen-size bed with flowery bed sheets in that room. I knock on the open door.

"Hey," comes the hoarse voice from the inside. "Come on in."

I push the door wide open and see Skye on a tattered love seat, wearing a robe. Her face is puffy, pink with red spots, and her eyes are swollen. She looks like a wreck, but still attractive. How is that possible?

I'm shocked, but I smile to reassure her. She gives me a faint nod.

Her bedroom is bare, except for her dresser. On top of it, I see a small wooden bowl and a few unmarked glass vials, like small perfume containers.

Otherwise, it looks like a guest room, showing no signs of a personal touch. I wonder if it means she has no plans of staying long.

"Hey, you," I say back. "How are you feeling?"

"I'm better now. The swelling and the redness will go away in a couple of days." She waves weakly to a few plastic orange containers on the side table next to her. I'm guessing they're anti-histamines.

"Good," I say. "But I mean, how do you feel?" I mean the shame, and she knows it, judging by the way she looks at me.

She straightens up on the love seat, a weary look on her face. She makes a helpless gesture. "Well, I guess I'm not the *mysterious* new girl anymore," she says without smiling.

"What they did to you was horrible," I say. I know it's obvious, but I want to say it, and I want her to hear it. "I'm sorry."

"Thanks." She pauses for a while. "You'd tell me if you knew who did it, right?"

It upsets me, but it's her right to ask. She's known me for, what, a few days? "Of course." A second passes, then I add, "When I heard about it, I immediately thought it was Jane, but Sean told me he saw her in the crowd. There's no way it she did it."

She shakes her head. "A girl led me out and took away my towel. I didn't know her voice." She sounds like she could kill someone. I don't blame her.

"What now?" I ask, shrugging. Since she didn't ask me to sit down, I'm guessing it's going to be a short visit.

Her shoulders sag. "I go back to school. What can I do? It's not like I've got much more to hide."

"I notice you and I are using all kinds of excuses to miss school," I say.

"And get attention." She looks at me.

"Especially medical attention."

She smiles. I did it! Mission accomplished.

I point to the door. "I'll let you rest."

She nods. "Thanks for coming."

I just smile all the way home.

Chapter 12: Skye

I ring a bell to ward off any evil. Then I light my candle. I select one of the incense sticks from my stash and light it up too. A bowl already contains my offering: small chrysanthemums, recently picked from Aunt Gemma's backyard.

I begin my cleansing, the gestures and words unique to my ritual. Each Sister is supposed to come up with her own ritual. The energy flow, the prayers, the meaning, they are all personal.

Today I pray to make a speedy recovery and to be protected from any other attacks.

I miss Judi's estate outside London. Our dear Judi would host Mum and me every summer. There I could go outdoors at night and dance, alone, unafraid, familiar with the forest. That's my place. My home. I used to do it a lot when I was younger, but in the last two years I've been traveling with Mum more often, and my connection to the place has weakened.

These thoughts interrupt my meditation. My desire is to be outside. My personal rituals are much stronger when in I'm in touch with nature. Gemma told me Seattle has many parks, but I didn't have time to check them out yet.

It's okay. I don't need a paradisiacal meadow a hundred miles from civilization; any patch of nature with some privacy would do.

Maybe a trail. Maybe the trail where Drake had his unfortunate encounter with the falling tree—I don't remember anyone interrupting us when I was saving his life.

But for now I push these thoughts aside and try to connect with the Goddess.

***

The principal issued a blanket warning and assured me that if any cell phone pictures showed up online, he'd call the FBI guys and sic them on the students. A few angry parents complained, but most of them understood my predicament, and the protests died down. Still, the pics are probably being passed from cell to cell for private viewing right now.

Kids at school don't know me. Why should they care about my feelings? Besides Drake, only Priscilla has been nice, helping me at school, calling to check on me, visiting briefly after Drake left.

I can't imagine who did this. It can't be Jane; Priscilla had told me she too saw Jane in the crowd. Besides, even blind, I'd feel Jane's magical energy close to me. Nobody can turn it off.

Nobody but the Singularity, that is. Maybe. But why would the Singularity do it? It would only attract attention and accomplish nothing, besides scaring me. And if she knows I'm a Sister, she knows Jane's one too. The Singularity would feel threatened by Jane as well.

Bottom line is: somebody tampered with my face cream. It wasn't a coincidence; it was planned. I ended up naked, blind, defenseless, and humiliated.

And nobody besides Jane has been openly hostile to me.

Today I go back. I can't apply make-up to hide the redness because it'll irritate my skin. I don't care; I'm not so vain that a puffy face will ruin my day.

Skincare has never been a concern for me. All my life the Allure took care of zits, small cuts, unwanted facial hair, and other small imperfections. Even the moisturizer cream wasn't really needed; I was just trying to accelerate the healing. Not that I'm using it again: the dermatologist didn't detect any allergies and told me to stop applying anything to my face.

Sometimes I wonder how I'd look like without Allure. I once asked Mum about it, and she looked at me as if I was crazy. "What are you talking about?" she said. "You are who you are. You and your magical energy are one, inseparable. It only leaves you when you die."

I wish I had more days to hide, but I need to help find the Singularity. I have no choice; I've been practically brainwashed to do it. For two years now, all covens have been reminded of the danger of letting the Singularity go unchecked.

At the age of fifteen, a witch has a quantum leap in magical energy: it's our Daybreak. From a very early age, we emit a faint magical signature. When we're that young, only people in close contact to us can feel it. Mothers, being so close to their babies, are generally the first ones to sense our magic. When we reach fifteen years old, give or take a couple of months, we're the source of an outburst of magical energy. Usually other witches in the same neighborhood can feel it. Two years ago, right after I had *my* Daybreak, the Singularity arrived with a bang.

Her Daybreak was felt over the entire West Coast.

All witches have roughly the same power. But this girl, whoever she is, is thousands of times more powerful than any of us. She has the potential of doing things we can't even imagine.

She also may signal the dawn of a new era, an age of great witches. That's why she's called a Singularity—nothing will ever be the same after her arrival.

But we can't find her. After her Daybreak, a Sister emanates energy continuously. Any witch could easily pick up the Singularity's huge signature from miles away. However, since her Daybreak, no one reported such an anomaly. She must have risen magical shields that mask her signature, something none of us can do, not even for a small amount of time.

We are simultaneously terrified of and fascinated with the Singularity. The effects of her magic could be so potent that she'd break the Veil, and people would not be able to reconcile reality and magic.

The Sisters assembled a few scientists with Intellect Charm to create a model to predict what that would mean to us—and to the rest of humanity—if the Veil were broken.

Eighty-two percent of the result scenarios pointed to persecution of some kind. The most common short-term scenario included mandatory testing and registration, vague accusations of terrorism, confinement justified by national security claims. The long-term ones spoke of special prisons or "designated areas" (an euphemism for ghettoization), criminalizing magic use, and the formation of private- and government-sponsored militias to capture or kill magic users.

In other words, a new era of witch hunting.

So, we need to find her and rescue her from herself, for her sake and ours. No coven has her, or so they claim. We believe each other, up to a point. That's another side effect of the Singularity's arrival: it created distrust and animosity between covens, something unthinkable just a couple of years ago.

Also, we all fear she could join a Night coven and become a Night magic user. In this case, all bets are off.

If she's here, in Seattle, close to Greenwood High, I have to find her. My Sisterhood gave me so much, and I've never given back. I've never accomplished anything or done anything, in part because I don't know *what* to do. With no interests, no talent, no hobbies, what *can* I do? My True Sight is the only thing that distinguishes me. I have this golden chance to use it, but I can only help if the Singularity is around here.

I hate the situation, and I hate the Singularity. I just wish I could be a normal girl with normal-girl problems. Oh, and that I didn't have to go to school after being humiliated in public.

Well, since I'm wishing, I'd prefer not to have suffered the humiliation in the first place.

I called my mother, but she simply didn't understand. She saw it as a typical American high school prank. Sometimes I think she does live in the movies and plays. Also, she has no problem with nudity (which always made her a big hit with directors and audiences), and said it was no big deal. I hung up on her after she said that.

Mad at everybody, I march down the stairs, dreading the glares and whispers at school—and that's the best case scenario. Each step is deliberate and hesitant, as if I'm going to my own execution. I'm waiting for a reprieve; I'm looking for good news anywhere. And I think I get them when I reach the last step and my cell rings, the name "Connor" flashing on the display.

"Hi, Connor," I greet him, anxious. I can barely conceal my excitement.

"Skye, your mother called me. She said somebody pulled a prank on you in school?"

"Yeah, I—"

He interrupts me, "Was it Jane?"

What? "No, it wasn't her," I say.

"Good. I was afraid she was trying to sabotage us," he says, sounding relieved. "Listen, I've got to ask you something; it's important."

"Okay," I say, waiting. And maybe hoping.

"Did it have anything to do with the search?"

I say nothing. *What about me, Connor?*

He misinterprets my silence. "If it does, we need to know, Skye. We might be close."

I take a deep breath. "No, Connor. It has nothing to do with it."

"Okay. When are you back to school?"

"Today," I say. I bite my lower lip.

"Excellent. Good job, Skye. Keep me posted." He hangs up.

He hangs up. I stare at the cell for a few seconds, reading "call ended" over and over again. I sit down on the stairs, trying to make sense of it.

He didn't ask how I felt; he didn't ask about what happened. He just didn't care.

What did I expect? That he would show up at my door, all concerned, bringing flowers, sweeping me off my feet? That he would vow to kill the bastards who did this to me?

I expected... I don't know what, but certainly not that. Not a perfunctory, cold business call. Couldn't he stop by? The University District is ten minutes from here. He didn't ask how I was doing. Even as a courtesy to our story together.

Even as a courtesy, period.

Maybe he's keeping his distance, respecting me. He may not want to get involved, even a little, afraid that he's going to hurt me.

My cell is still open. "Call ended," it reads. It ended, Skye.

He's not being cavalier. That's how things are now. The past is just the past.

A tear escapes my eye. I didn't expect anything. When I came here, I wasn't *hoping* we would get back together—that both of us, older and a tiny bit more mature, would realize how much we meant to each other, and live happily ever after. But I have to admit: in the back of my mind, I knew this was a possibility, one of the infinite possible outcomes of us meeting again.

Now, with one phone call, it's clear it's over.

I cry. Not for me, not for us, but for the death of this possibility, for the death of the what-if. It's the end. It *ended.* I cry because it's sad seeing a door closing, that's all.

I look one last time at the cell phone and see the time. I'm late for whatever punishment the mean kids will inflict on me today at school. I turn the cell off, angry. Connor made it clear: I have a job to do, no matter what.

Still broken inside, I wipe my tears on my long sleeves. I stand up slowly and move to the front door. I take a deep breath before opening it.

On the other side, I find Drake and his ugly car.

Somehow his sweetness makes me even sadder, and the flow of tears return, now unchecked.

He sees my breakdown, gets out of the car, and hurries in my direction. He stands in front of me, unsure if he should hug me, or hold my hands, or just leave me be. I make the decision for Drake and embrace him.

I squeeze him tight, but he just touches me softly.

We stay on the porch for a few minutes, hushed, motionless. I sob quietly, my tears and runny nose smearing his shirt, my arms squashing him, but he doesn't move. His breathing is steady, relaxed. And relaxing.

I'm so grateful he's been quiet the whole time. Not only does he know what to say at all times, but he knows when to keep silent. I love how he does nothing, says nothing to spoil the moment. He says nothing better than anybody else.

After I finally release my death grip on him, Drake takes me by the hand to his car, and helps me into the passenger seat. He closes my door gently, walks over in front of the car, his eyes never leaving me, and joins me inside. He gets a Kleenex box from the backseat and hands it to me.

He looks straight ahead, his hands on the steering wheel, and I understand he's giving me some privacy. I blow my nose infinite times, dab my eyes and cheeks. The mirror tells me I don't look good. No amount of Allure can erase severe allergy aftereffects compounded with a massive crying session.

Drake's still respecting my right to be a wreck. I grab another Kleenex and wipe the mess I made on his shirt. It startles him, and he turns. He looks at me, inside me, through me, beyond the Allure, the puffy face, maybe beyond the Veil.

I lean in and our lips touch. It takes him a while to respond, but when he does, it's magic.

Drake lives up to his reputation.

Chapter 13: Drake

When I decided to stalk her a little bit this morning, I never expected it would end like this.

She pulls away from our brief kiss.

It feels as if days have passed. It's a weird sensation, like I'm disconnected from reality, floating in space. The car, the houses outside, even Skye, they all seem unreal.

She still has her hand on my shoulder, the Kleenex squeezed against my shirt. She looks at it, tries to pull the tissue back, but it's stuck. "Oh," she says.

And just like that, the spell is broken. She grabs a handful of new tissues from the box and begins to clean my shirt in earnest. I stay still, searching furiously for something smart to say. Actually, forget smart—*anything* will do.

Skye hasn't smiled yet, and that worries me. She looks around quickly inside the car, and then shoves all the sticky tissues into her jeans' pocket.

She stares outside, at nothing in particular. "Let's go someplace," she says.

I guess she means not school. My inner responsible self twitches, but I calm him down by saying that the school will surely cut us, recent accident victims, some slack. I turn the key in the ignition and the Volvo purrs, obliging.

I'm still stunned, but I do a little happy dance inside my head.

***

We drive in silence. She doesn't even ask where we're going. It's not a long way to Green Lake. I expected a deserted lot, especially in this crummy weather, but it takes me a while to find a parking spot. After we leave the car, she reaches for my hand. We avoid the noise coming from the kids' play area and stroll toward the lake.

We stop by the kayak rental kiosk, but it's closed in October. Behind the kiosk, people wearing jeans and winter jackets play tennis on the court. Athletic and not-so-athletic morning joggers follow the trail, focused, lost in their own private worlds. Dogs are almost as prevalent as ducks and people.

In a simultaneous impulse, we both move to follow the trail. I embrace her shoulders, and her arm goes around my waist. It's not only a protection against the chilly wind. It feels natural.

I don't remember being this close to anyone.

We amble like that for a long time. Sometimes we hear the regional "on your left" warning from cyclists coming up behind us. It's unnecessary here, because the paths are separate for bikers and joggers, but Seattle's people are too polite.

Eventually, an abandoned bench beckons. We sit, still embracing, and stare at the lake. The water's color matches the darkening sky. Green Lake should be renamed Gray Lake for today.

After a few minutes, she says, "So, Drake..." Uh-oh. Here it comes: the dreadful *talk*.

"Yes?" My voice is low, afraid.

"I'm glad we did this," she says, still not moving.

"Did what?" I ask.

She takes a while, but turns to me. She puts her hand behind my neck, pulling me to her, and we kiss. Just one long, tender kiss.

"Oh, this," I say. "Wait. Are you flirting with me?"

Still no smile. Wow. I'm out of ammo. Well, I guess I don't *need* to say much. And if that is the talk, it couldn't be less painful.

I'm ready for more making out, but I'm not *expecting* more. Skye seems fine too.

We just watch the people. A jolly trio of seventy-year-old men on their morning walk, their feet making a crushing sound on the gravel path. A kid on a bike with training wheels laughs manically as she accelerates. Two shirtless guys, being either brave or showy, flirt with a girl wearing a sweater and knitted gloves.

Skye tells me she's hungry, and we leave the bench in search of food. I guide her to a taco and burrito street truck on the edge of the park, close to Aurora Avenue. It's opening for lunch. When we order, I learn she's a vegetarian. There's so much I don't know about her.

The road noise so close to us annoys her. After we get our orders, we go back to the park. I find an empty picnic table and we have an impromptu—and completely unhealthy—brunch. The messy meal couldn't be more unromantic, but she's fine with it, not grossed out by my food. Good, because I eat a lot of crap.

We talk about innocuous things: Seattle and London mostly. Nothing about our past and, maybe most important of all, nothing about our future.

I love listening to her voice. Her accent comes and goes. Every time she slips into British, she forces herself back to American. She talks to me, but her mind is somewhere else. Still no smiles.

We resume our walk, but soon we stop at the Bathhouse Theater.

She inspects the old building while I watch her from under a poplar tree. She stares at the announcements with uninterested eyes. Across the trail from me, an elderly couple tend to a small flower garden. Their deliberation is soothing. I can easily see their love for gardening, and for each other.

She catches me watching them, and she finally gives me a hint of a smile, the faintest curving of the lips. She walks toward me, grabs my hand, and drags me back to the trail.

When we reach a bend with easy access to the lake, she tests the water temperature. Even for me, used to unheated pools, it looks insane. The freezing water shocks her at first, which might have been her intention anyway. But whatever it is she is doing, it works. Skye walks barefoot in the shallow part for a few minutes, and she comes back from her personal tiny Antarctica with a relaxed smile.

She puts her sneakers back on, and we get back to the path. Right then, I see someone who might put her mood over the top. I approach a skinny woman sporting short-cropped blond hair and a "Free Hugs For Everyone" t-shirt.

Skye takes advantage of the woman's written offer (in other words, I force her to hug a stranger). But it works. Skye lets go of the embrace with a giggle. A *giggle*!

With Skye temporarily healed, we circle back to the parking lot.

***

After spending a pleasant morning in the park, we stop by an ice-cream parlor. It's great being free on a weekday, no times to meet, no places to go. The city is ours.

I drive her back to her house, dreading the end of our day.

"Do you want to go out sometime?" I blurt out.

"What, like a date?" she asks, in a not-too-promising tone.

61

"I guess," I say, my newfound confidence already gone.

"What did we just do?"

Okay, it might have been a date, technically, but what I want to know is what's next. Either she doesn't understand me, or she's avoiding the issue.

I change tactics. "What about the party tomorrow?"

"You mean, Priscilla's party?" She looks at me. "Do you think it's a good idea for me?"

She's got a point. She'll have to face the school crowd eventually, but the school, where a code of conduct might better protect her from all the taunting I'm sure will take place, seems safer.

"Let's ditch the party then, and go out. Just the two of us," I say. When I don't hear an enthusiastic agreement, I strengthen my case. "It's the perfect night, actually. We won't even risk bumping into another Greenwood student in town. They'll all be at the party."

She considers it for a moment, and then says, "Pick me up at seven."

Yes! I look at the road, but I can't disguise the smug smile on my face.

I don't know what comes after that. I don't have the practice. I'll just go where she leads me.

Chapter 14: Skye

I arrive back home. From the front porch, the house looks different. I left this morning with the weight of the world on my shoulders, a bleak future ahead of me. Now I return, renewed, hopeful. Light.

Waving to Drake as he leaves with the Volvo, I wonder what's ahead. But I'm afraid to think about it and dismiss the thought. Let me, for once, enjoy the moment.

I open the door and see Aunt Gemma straighten up on the sofa, her eyes red, her hair disheveled.

"What happened?" I ask, alarmed.

"Where have you been? I called your cell; I called the school!" She's completely distraught, shaking. She stands up and walks to me.

"What happened?" I repeat, my voice louder. I'm freaked out.

She grabs my hand, squeezing it with such force I think my knuckles might break. "Your mother had a heart attack."

***

The other plane passengers must think I'm afraid of flying, with my hand-wringing and all. Aunt Gemma sits next to me. We're still on the tarmac, but her sleeping pills are already kicking in. She's terrified of flying, but she wouldn't let me go alone. Even though she's going to be passed out the whole flight, I appreciate the gesture.

I rub my hands together. The pre-flight instructions make me antsy. All I can think of is death, death, death.

My last call to London calmed me some. Judi, Goddess bless her, told me Mum was still unconscious but stable.

I also remember the last time I talked to Mum: I hung up on her because she said the prank was no big deal. As it turns out, she's right; compared to this, it's no deal at all.

Mum can't die. She's so full of life, with so many friends. True friends. It always struck me as a sign of her great personality that her past lovers are still good friends with her, even with the passion a distant memory. To her, lovers are just a special subset of friends.

I feel a little warm inside. Mother was never shy of discussing her romances with me—when I asked. For somebody with her partying lifestyle, she did a great job of shielding me from her life. She would be open about it, but she never tried to imply her choices were the right ones. Or the wrong ones, for that matter.

She raised me as best as she could, as best as her career would allow. In certain times, it was good: I had time alone and independence. But there were times when I missed her being a regular mum, a cook-you-dinner and tuck-you-into-bed fantasy mother out of a sitcom. We did go to the movies, but they were mostly premieres.

Now her awards and her honors (she's *Dame* Katherine Lexington-Ellis) are little comfort. She must reach into her other treasure trove—her friends, her Sisterhood—for strength and support.

I pray to the Goddess.

If Mum dies, my world is over. I'd have no relatives. The Mothers would no doubt welcome me as part of each of their families, but what would be the point? I know nobody of my own age, since I was a recluse from the time Connor left me. I have no old school friends, thanks to the globetrotting and the tutors. I'd be a ship without a port, cruising aimlessly, with no feeling and no purpose.

I look at my cell again. Phones were the bearers of bad news today. Seattle was a bad news place. I'm leaving, and I'm not coming back.

The elation of this morning is a distant dream now. Poor Drake. He never had a chance.

There's one more bit of unpleasantness to go through tonight. Before takeoff, my phone must carry one last mission.

I text Drake, ending our stillborn romance.

Chapter 15: Drake

Skye's gone for good. I can't believe her text.

It's over before it started. Didn't our day out mean anything to her?

I know, I know; I should be worried about her mother. As far as I know her mother is the only family Skye has. I feel for her, obviously.

Which makes losing her even more painful.

Only one thing I know for sure I won't regret doing or saying: I text her, saying I hope her mother gets better.

It's all my fault. What was I thinking? A girl like her and a guy like me? Not in a million years. At least, not something that would last.

The emotions are overwhelming. Simultaneously, I feel anger, pain, longing, regret, disappointment, compassion. How should I feel? All, some, or none of those?

We've never even discussed the weird thing she did in the woods, her with all the chanting and blood, me with the sizzling sensation. Maybe she's into one of those New Age things and thought it might help. I'll never know. I was so caught up in trying to get close to her that I never stepped back to look at what that day meant.

Talking to her is pointless now. And I won't acknowledge her dumping me. Maybe it will make things easier for her when she takes it back.

Right.

***

"Hey, Drake," Priscilla calls me.

She rarely talks to me. We're from different planets. She makes her way through the throng of students. We have some time until the bell rings.

"Hey, Priscilla." Nobody calls her The Predator to her face, but she knows of the nickname.

"Did Skye text you?" she asks. When I hang my head, she nods and adds, "Bummer, huh? She told me you guys skipped school together yesterday."

"Did you talk to her?" I ask, full of hope. I'm not even shocked Skye chose Priscilla, of all people, to be her confidante.

"Before she left," she says, and the hope leaves me. Priscilla anticipates my question. "She's not coming back. Sorry."

"Did she…?"

The Predator looks at me, her eyes suddenly and unexpectedly understanding. "Do you want to hear it? Are you sure?"

"I need to know," I say.

She pulls me by the arm, to a corner away from the crowd.

"Okay, she didn't talk much. Most of time she was crying because of her mother, and packing things in a hurry," she says. "I got bits and pieces. I think she had a boyfriend she's not over yet."

Priscilla looks at me to confirm she should go on. I nod.

She says, "She told me the day you went out she had just received a call from him, and it didn't go well."

The truth dawns on me. "She was rebounding."

"That's my guess too. Are you all right?" It's really odd, this display of concern from The Predator.

67

So I was just at the right place at the right time. In other words, I was the first guy she saw after the boyfriend said whatever to her. "Hell, no," I whisper.

Priscilla moves to touch my face, but she catches herself and withdraws her hand. "It'll pass," she says, steely. "Go have fun. Are you coming to my party tomorrow?"

I shake my head. "Sorry. That's the last thing I want to do."

***

Later, Boulder and Sean see my hangdog face.

"Why so serious, D-Man?" Sean asks.

"Skye's gone," I say, simply. "Back to London."

Surprised, Boulder says, "Jesus, Drake, what's wrong with you? At least you didn't scare the girls away before."

Sean giggles. I'm not in the mood for laughs. I try to explain. "She had to go home. Her mother had a heart attack."

That stops Sean cold. "For how long?" he asks, respectfully.

"Forever," I say, being overly dramatic. "According to her text."

"You got dumped by text?" Sean says, snickering—back to his normal self.

"She didn't dump me. We're not together, remember?" I regret the lie, but I realize I might not be lying after all.

"You're taking this pretty hard, man," Boulder says. "You knew her for, what, a week?"

They don't know about my romantic day, and I want to keep it that way. I don't brag about girls, maybe because I've had few opportunities to do so. In any case, I want to keep that day to myself, even if Skye sees it as an accident, a mistake. Mentioning it to the guys will cheapen it even more. But I have to justify my visible pain to them, or I won't hear the end of it.

"She helped me, you know, when I hit my head and all," I say, lamely. They buy it, though, nodding their heads.

"I get it," Sean says. "But come on, D-man, we've got a party tomorrow!"

"Hunting trip!" Boulder yells and high-fives Sean.

"I'm not going," I say. Their enthusiasm bothers me.

Boulder stops and looks at me. "No, no. What you're saying is you don't *want* to go. But you *are* going." When I open my mouth to protest, he pokes me in the chest. "You are," he says.

Chapter 16: Skye

I hate hospitals. However, in one week, I've been to two hospitals in two different continents. Mum is in her bed, looking surprisingly good for someone who had a heart attack the day before. Maybe her Allure is working overtime.

Aunt Gemma and Judi are in a corner of the room, silent.

I'm relieved Mum's doing so well, considering. Maybe *joie de vivre* isn't just an abstract concept; maybe hers helped her turn this around. The concern remains, but most of the grim thoughts are in the back of my mind now.

"You didn't need to come back, darling," Mum says, her voice betraying some weakness. Her hand clutches mine.

"Of course I needed to be here, Mum," I protest.

"I'm glad you did, though." She taps my arm with her other hand. Age is catching up to her. Slowly, because of her Allure, but nobody can stop time. Not even us. Her eyes still shine with youth, though, even after the scare. She takes a deep breath. "But your mission is important; you must go back."

"What?" What's going on? I voice the same concerns I had before going to Seattle. "Why? We've been searching for almost two years now, and I'm just one of the Sisters planted in high schools over there. How can *I* make a difference?"

The answer I received the first time was: we all need to do our part. Mum looks at Judi, who's been by Mum's side since she came to the hospital.

Judi says, "We're running out of time, dear."

"But I—"

"But *you*, Skye," Judi interrupts me, "are a great asset. True Sight is rare, and yours is powerful. We put you in one of the most likely places—where you can get a whiff of energy to put us on the right path."

"But now is not the time," I say, pointing to my mother.

"Don't you worry about me," Mum says. "I have the best medical support money can buy. Also, I have the best alternative medicine available." She winks.

"Our coven is having a circle of prayer tonight for your mother. And I won't leave her side," Judi assures me.

It's hard to think clearly when the magical signatures Judi and Mum release are so intense. In closed quarters, the combined energy of the two Sisters is overwhelming.

I shake my head. "Mum, I want to be here. You just had a big scare; you're weak and alone. You need me."

"Alone? I have my Sisters and a house full of servants. I'm back home tomorrow," she says.

"I can't leave. You just had a heart attack, and you're asking me to leave? It's not normal."

Mum shakes her head, a weak smile on her face. "And when did we have a normal life, darling?"

***

I'm exhausted. Unlike Aunt Gemma, who slept through the whole nine-hour nonstop flight, I never closed my eyes. We went from Heathrow to the hospital, and now the sleeplessness is catching up to me.

A cab takes Aunt Gemma and me to my mother's house. I mumble hellos to the servants, who all express their concern about my mother. My old room awaits me. It feels familiar and strange at the same time. Mum and I were always on the road, in hotel rooms, in trailers. We rarely came back to the house. When she had time between projects, we went on vacations. To more hotel rooms. Nice ones, some close to beaches, some close to ski slopes, but soulless hotel rooms anyway. We always had this house, but we never had a true home.

I see the flowers people sent her. It must be nice being beloved: friends, actors, directors, agents, studio executives, crew unions(!), and, of course, fans sent all kinds of mementos. Get-well cards, stuffed animals, pictures. Even the not so thoughtful ones—a recent heart attack victim certainly doesn't need boxes of chocolates or bottles of scotch—have a certain sweetness to them. The flower arrangement Connor sent towers above all of them.

Is it wrong that I resent it? That Connor cared much more for my mother than he did for me? I shake my head, feeling selfish and small.

I go to my room, lie down, and close my eyes.

Chapter 17: Drake

Night comes, and of course my previous resolution is shot down. Boulder and Sean drop by to drag me to the party at Priscilla's. It's early, and we just hang out for a while. They tell me to follow them; no way they will climb aboard the Volvo.

"Tell you what: you can drive us back. You'll be our designated driver," Sean says, sitting on the hood of my ride.

"But then you'll probably be passed out," I point out.

"Of course, Drake. No one would ride in this consciously," Boulder says, tapping my car's hood. He circles my car to have a better look. "What is that?" he asks, pointing to its lower side.

"This is called faux-wood," I say.

He slides his finger on the side of the car, as if making sure the wood is really *faux*. He reaches the cargo area door and peeks inside. "A wagon, D-Man? It looks like a hearse."

"Well, when you're passed out, you can lie down in the back," I say.

Boulder says, "It's brown... Or caramel? I don't even know what this color is called—with wood paneling or whatever? Does your father hate you?"

My oversized friend arrives at the front again and sits beside Sean on the hood. The Volvo's front drops half a foot.

"Dad wanted me to have a safe car," I say. "It does have airbags and ABS, you know?"

Sean says, "It's not about safety, it's about style, D-Man. And a car this old can't be safe. How long have these airbags been sitting there? If they deploy, you'll probably die of mold poisoning anyway."

I try to defend my wheeled friend. "This baby goes from zero to sixty in nine seconds."

Sean giggles. "Sure. On free fall."

"Even if it made it in nine, that's not impressive at all, Drake," Boulder says, shaking his head. I have no idea; it's just a stat I read online.

We kill some more time, and then drive in a convoy to Priscilla's. I follow Boulder's slick yellow Mustang. Night is falling.

Priscilla's house is bigger than I thought. I wonder why she doesn't go to a private school. We ring, and Priscilla answers. "You're early," she tells us.

"We wanted a head start," Boulder says while going inside.

"I thought you weren't coming," Priscilla says to me. Boulder and Sean ignore us. They make themselves comfortable, opening the fridge and checking the food and the beverages.

"I thought so, too," I say, nodding in Boulder's direction.

"You have good friends," she says. "Kind of pigs, but good friends."

I shrug, my hands in my pants' pockets.

She says, "How are you holding up?"

"Haven't thought of her until you brought it up," I say.

"Right," she says, seeing through my lie. "Remember what I told you: have fun." She gives me an odd look. We hear a crashing sound coming from the kitchen and she leaves me to attend to it. She yells,

"Can't you guys wait until the party starts to trash my house?"

Priscilla is acting weird, and for a moment I wonder if she's hitting on me. Having had no previous experience, I'm unsure. Maybe she has a collection thing going on, and I'm one of the few, if not *the* only, Greenwood guy missing from her list.

I thought Skye and Priscilla were friends. On the other hand, nobody earns The Predator title for no reason.

No, I'm probably just imagining things.

***

Soon the party begins for real. A swarm of guys and girls pumped up by energy drinks arrive, and not only Greenwood students. Even a few college guys show up, including Priscilla's latest fling, which puts to rest any suspicions of mine that she might be interested in me.

Some of the newcomers sneak beer into the house. I don't care; I don't drink. After you set fire to your house because of a cigarette, you get a Pavlovian response to alcohol, tobacco, drugs, gambling…

Boulder, unburdened by such concerns, already did Boulder things. He drank, barfed in the pool, forgot about it, and then cannonballed into the water. In a testament to his intimidating nature, nobody said a peep. He just sauntered into the house's master bathroom, took a shower, brushed his teeth, and got back to chatting the girls up. It's telling that he carries a change of clothes in the trunk of his Mustang.

Boulder makes swaggering an art form. He saunters as if he owns the place and has a gamble credit and/or a secret file with indiscretions from everybody in the room. He nods to strangers, and they feel compelled to nod back. The day he got his temporary license, he strolled into an Audi dealership—wearing flip-flops—and test-drove the hell out of an A5.

Things that would embarrass, shame, or ridicule the most composed monk simply don't affect him. It's neither charm, because he has none, nor the linebacker's body, because he only uses it to intimidate other freaks of his approximate size. He just exudes this unshakeable confidence... I guess he's so certain of his entitlement that others must feel stupid doubting it.

I envy him like hell.

Since nobody is talking to me, I look for Sean. But he's already sucking face with some girl I don't know.

Like Boulder, Sean always gets girls. He was a kind of groupie wrangler for Boulder, the football star. Which meant Sean got second choice too. His reputation only increased.

I need to stop comparing myself to them. It's reeeally bad for me. However, I don't feel like a loser. I'm very practical. I can't have self-esteem issues if I don't have self-esteem in the first place.

In the opposite mood of everybody else at the party, and bummed that I'm not Boulder, I go outside, ambling toward the dark street. The house is huge—an estate, really—and no neighbors are close enough to complain about the noise. I weave between the badly parked cars on the road, on my way to the Volvo. I parked it away from the house, already thinking about an early escape. The chilly air makes my breath visible under the distant light of street lamps. I'm almost back to my car when I see an unmistakable red bike.

Sitting on it, Jane sips a beer, and smokes a cigarette as only someone who's had years of practice would. The cold night air doesn't bother her: she wears a camouflage tank top. She nods to me and says, "Got lost, Drake?"

"H-Hey, Jane," I stammer. She has never talked to me before. "My car," I point to the Volvo a little down the road, behind her, but she doesn't turn her head.

I'm not going to lie: she terrifies me. First, I truly believe she'd beat me up in a fight, even though I'll never admit it to another human being. Secondly, I wouldn't put it past her having a butterfly knife or something, and being skilled with it. And thirdly, I think of her as a woman. I mean, to me, she's not a girl, but a woman. For some reason, that intimidates me.

"Skye left you, huh?" she says and takes another sip. When she sees my quizzical expression, she adds, "Word travels."

"She left the school," I say.

"Come on, talk to me," she taps the space next to her on the seat of the bike. I obey, mostly because I believe I have no alternative.

"Beer?" she asks. She has a cooler bag hanging from the side of the bike. I just shake my head. Jane shrugs and takes another sip from hers. "Are you okay?"

"Why do you hate each other?" The question bursts out of me. Great, another holiday for my brain.

"Skye? Didn't she tell you?" Jane raises her eyebrows. "I hooked up with her ex. British dude. Goes to U-Dub." She sees my surprised face and asks, "She never told you?"

I shake my head. She reaches into the cooler and produces a bottle.

"I don't think this is the time for drinking," I say.

"Drake, this is the *perfect* time for drinking." She pops the cap with her keychain bottle opener. She puts the beer in my hand. "Come on, have one. It's good stuff. Imported."

I stare at the label. It's in German, I guess. I'm angry at Skye—she wasn't truthful. I'm angry at Boulder—I'm not him. I'm angry at myself. I take a sip.

I've tasted beer before, but I don't remember it being this bitter. "It's strong," I say, not caring that I sound like a wimp.

"I told you. It's good stuff." She raises her bottle toward mine, and we clink them in an unspoken toast. She downs hers and fishes another one out of the cooler.

The terror is gone, and now I'm kind of feeling cool, being friendly with the most badass girl in school. Actually, she's not as scary as I thought.

"Are you still together?" I ask. "I mean, you and the guy?"

"Connor? Sometimes."

I feel small. Boulder and Jane, these larger-than-life people, live in another world, a fuller world, more exciting, more grown-up, more... everything. I felt I'd have a chance to experience it when Skye spent the day with me, but here I am, back to my ordinary existence. I take another sip of my beer, which doesn't taste as bitter now. Jane watches me.

"You look so young," she says.

"What are you talking about? We're in the same grade," I say.

"Yeah, but I'm twenty."

"Really?" I take another sip. "Why are you still in high school?"

She looks at her crimson fingernails. "I got left behind," she says. Her voice has just the slightest quiver.

I cock my head involuntarily. "You look good for your age."

Jane turns to me, a hint of a smile on her full lips. "Oh, you're so cute I could eat you up," she says in a baby voice, while she pinches my cheek. She stares at me for a second, and then her natural voice comes back. "Actually, maybe I will."

I've never seen her so close. She's got these unique features. I mean, I knew she was hot: her tight leather pants leave nothing to the imagination. But now, sitting next to her, I notice Jane as I never did before. Her short black hair actually brings attention to her angular face. Her sunken cheeks are balanced by light gray eyes, thin eyebrows, long eyelashes. And her strong nose, full of personality, matches her serious mouth.

She holds my gaze, and I feel embarrassed for staring. I look away and take a long swig of my beer. From the corner of my eyes I see her finishing her cigarette, flicking it to the ground, and staring into the night.

Under the moonlight, a silver tattoo on her shoulder blade seems to glow. A heart pierced by a dagger.

I'm a little buzzed now, but I don't panic. The chill, the darkness around us, the presence of this strange woman by my side: they all reinforce the impression I'm in this different place. I feel simultaneously empowered and intimidated. I want to explore this new world; I want to know its secrets.

As if reading my mind, Jane turns to me. She throws her bottle to the side of the road. In the otherwise silent night, the sharp noise of shattered glass sounds foreboding.

She reaches for mine and does the same with my bottle. Her hands go behind my neck. She gently pulls my head toward hers, until our lips touch.

I surrender. I don't know where she's taking me, but I don't care.

Jane's kiss is very Jane-y. Her tongue aggressively searches for mine, her breath smelling of beer, nicotine, and cherry—I've never imagined it as a tantalizing combination.

After a while, things become more intense. She bites my lips, my neck; her hands search inside my shirt. Her body scent is minty, earthy. She's a force of nature.

We move away from her bike, going at each other, wrestling, pulling and pushing, angry. It feels wrong and right at the same time. I'm buzzed, suspended from reality. Somehow I open my Volvo and we stumble inside, a mass of two bodies, thirsty, wanting, longing.

That's the last thing I remember.

Chapter 18: Skye

London at night is mysterious and cozy at the same time. Even inside the house, I can imagine the city flowing around me: workers coming home, dinners getting ready, friends calling friends, happy people filling the pubs after a long day. The city is a creature: it breathes, it lives, it has its triumphs and regrets. It's around me, pulsing, making me part of its existence.

It just feels right.

I'm not at the epicenter of ancient magic, but I'm close enough. I feel more attuned with magical energy here. In a sense, it makes me feel like I truly belong with my Sisters.

I leave my room and stop in the hallway. Uneasiness takes over me, as if my own old house is a stranger. Our house is elegant, pristine, and lifeless. Everything is so put together it resembles a movie set. Doors and walls are white, but the doors have details in gold: tiny suns and moons in *bas-relief*. I look down to the floor below to the foyer, a solemn chamber, with its chandelier adorned with several crystals and the light carpeting next to the door. By the lateral walls, tables with intricate carvings are crowned by porcelain vases inhabited by fresh flowers, picked just this morning from the back garden. Tasteful pictures by insufferable artists (friends of Mum's) hang all over the ground floor walls. My gaze follows the staircase—

white and gold, of course—before resting on the door of Mum's room.

Since I lived with Mum, I had my True Sight tingling permanently on. I could sense her comings and goings, and yes, that includes her sneaking lovers into the house or adjacent hotel rooms late at night.

I shake my head and knock on Mum's door. She tells me to come in.

She's in bed. The reading glasses she wouldn't be caught dead wearing in public sit on the bridge of her nose. Cards litter her bed. Mum gestures to them, explaining, "Well-wishers. Friends and fans." With a hint of pride in her voice, she adds, "Not to mention the postings on my web site, the tweets, and Spacebook messages."

I giggle, but I don't correct her. "Since when do you tweet?"

"Of course I don't. It's all Mimi, Goddess bless her soul." Mimi is Mum's publicist. In the last few days I learned that Mum's illness triggered a frenetic time for her publicist and agent, and even for her personal trainer and stylist. I have no idea how she pays this whole staff, but once Mum told me it was "the cost of doing business." They all came to visit her, but the conversations usually moved quickly from "How are you?" to "What's the message?" Apparently, releasing news about her is a balancing act: she must appear sick enough to get sympathies, but not so sick that producers would be concerned and insurance would skyrocket.

"It's a science," Mimi told me. With a straight face.

Mum swipes all the cards to one side of the bed and taps the opened area of the mattress, inviting me to sit next to her. I do, and she hugs me affectionately. "So, how is Seattle?" she asks, after she lets go of me.

I think about it. "It's not London," I say.

She chuckles, but quickly becomes serious. "Trouble?" She puts her index finger on my nose, a gesture from my childhood.

I take a deep breath and explain in detail what happened in the locker room, making it very clear it wasn't only a practical joke.

Her eyes widen, and she says, "Oh, darling! I had no idea." She hugs me again, saying, "I'm sorry. I was so callous on the phone."

She gets it. That's all I wanted to hear. All my hard feelings are gone for good now.

"Do you still want to go back there?" she asks.

I break our embrace and say, "Well, the Mothers made it clear I must. And it's not all bad. I've made friends, actually."

It gets her attention. I never had many friends. "*Boy* friends?"

It's my turn to chuckle. "One boy and one girl. She's a bit kooky but very cool. She's been texting me asking how you are, and she doesn't even know you're… you." I say that because I guess it'll make Priscilla a great friend in Mum's eyes. When Mum nods her approval, I know I'm right. Besides, Priscilla and Mum both love to date. They could compare notes.

"And the boy?"

I shrug and look away. "He's sweet. He came to visit me when I had the locker room… incident."

She cocks her head, examining me. "You two are together." It's not a question.

"No," I say, but she sees right through my protest. I feel the pressure and confess, "Well, we kissed."

She nods, absorbing the information. "What about Connor?"

"Golden boy Connor didn't care I was humiliated," I say. Goddess, I hate how whiny it makes me sound.

"Maybe he made the same mistake I did, Skye," she says, brushing the hair off my face.

Mum, like the other Sisters, thinks Connor can do no wrong. They all would love him as a son-in-law. Of course, they can't understand how I had him and let him slip away, as Judi put it.

They don't know the whole story.

The silence makes Mum uncomfortable, and she says, "What are you going to do with the boy you kissed?"

"Drake?" I tell her about the tree falling on him, and taking him to the hospital, but I don't mention the ritual I performed to save him. I'm not supposed to have done it; I'm not experienced enough, and it could have backfired. But I tell her parts of our day together.

"It seems you shared more than a kiss," she says.

I throw my arms in the air. "But when I left, I ended things with him. Not that there was actually a thing to end."

"But if you're coming back…" Her voice trails off.

"I haven't thought about it much. I need to know where Connor and I stand before I do anything."

Mum looks at me in a strange way.

"What?" I ask.

"Sometimes you have more sense than I do," she says, shaking her head.

Chapter 19: Drake

After hooking up with Jane, I have to reevaluate some things. First one: *that* is what being hit by a truck feels like.

I wake up the next day in my freezing Volvo, alone. The road is deserted but for my car and a minefield of empty cans littering the stretch until Priscilla's house. Oh, yeah, the party.

I groan, and the sound is amplified inside my skull. As a result, I groan again, and it hurts my head even more, until I have the good sense of staying quiet to starve the cycle of torture. I've never had a hangover, but I recognize the signs.

A few sips of beer can do that? I had half a bottle before, and my tongue didn't taste like papier-mâché the next day, nor were all muscles of my body stiff. The world didn't spin around me, either.

My cell is on the floor, showing 11:30 a.m. If I'm not mistaken, I blacked out for twelve hours. Jane was wrong. That beer is not "the good stuff."

Jane! Where is she? My fingers instinctively touch my mouth. I recall the kissing. My lips are even a bit swollen. Some grinding, too. Was there more? I lower my eyes. My pants are on. I search for my wallet and find my condoms just like they've been for the last couple of years: untouched. In a way, I'm glad: I'd like to be, you know, conscious for my first time.

I sit on the passenger side. The door is ajar and my feet are outside. I, very slowly, put my head between my hands, pressing slightly and trying to make the migraine go away.

But Jane! Why did she make out with me? We had never talked before. Maybe she was bored. What did she say? That she and Skye's boyfriend were together. She might be trying to retrace Skye's footsteps, romantic-wise. Or is Jane trying to get back at Skye?

No, that doesn't make sense. She doesn't know about Skye and me. And Skye's gone.

What about Jane? Even with her tough-girl attitude, she was so... feminine last night. So vulnerable, so likable. I have no idea what's going on.

I call Boulder. No answer. I call Sean. After a few rings, he picks up.

"Drake!" he says, but not in a friendly or concerned way. "You bolted, man! You were supposed to take us home. Not cool!" The call ends.

Well, I guess they got home okay—somehow. Wait: why am I worried about them? They left me here, passed out. Okay, maybe they didn't know. Other people must have seen me in my car, but nobody cared, apparently. It doesn't surprise me.

Which brings me back to Jane once again. Did she leave me? What happened?

I raise my head and see Priscilla's house. I walk there. I don't even care the road is spinning.

I ring the doorbell. After a few minutes, Priscilla answers the door. She sports puffy eyes and a murderous look.

"Drake?" She somehow becomes more pissed off after she recognizes me. "Did you forget something?"

"Twelve hours," I say, leaning against the door frame.

She cocks her head, studying my sorry face. Then she yells, "ARE YOU HUNG OVER?"

I slide down the floor in a heap, my hands pressing my ears, my head exploding. "Why did you do that?" I whisper.

Priscilla says, "Come in. We've got to talk." She goes inside, leaving the door open.

***

She makes us coffee without a word. I lean against the kitchen counter, trying to stay awake, failing epically in tuning the kitchen sounds out. She waits until I drink the whole cup of hot goodness.

"I saw you and Jane," she says.

Okay. At least it wasn't a dream. I was thinking I might have hallucinated the whole thing. "Oh," I say.

"You guys went inside that ugly car," she continues.

Maybe she knows what happened. I try to get more information from her. "And?"

"Oh, it's not my business; is that what you're saying? It's all good for you, right?"

It takes me a while to realize what she's thinking. "No, that's not what I mean. Going into the Volvo is the last thing I remember. I thought you could tell me what happened *after* that."

She doesn't answer promptly. "I came back to the party," she says simply. "You don't really remember? Were you drunk?"

I shrug.

"What were you thinking?" she says, shaking her head.

"I wasn't!" It's true.

"What about Skye? I thought you had a crush on her."

"I did. I do." But that's pointless now, I want to add.

"Then what are you doing making out with Jane of all people?"

It's like the Twilight Zone. The Predator is lecturing me about restraint. Priscilla alone is responsible for a spike in contraceptive sales in our city. "Priscilla, seriously? *You* are questioning my choices? You?"

"You're not me, Drake."

I shake my head, but I quickly stop, because it hurts. Incredibly, it's worse than the concussion. It's not a good sign that I suddenly became an expert in headaches.

Priscilla looks fine, though. "Aren't you hung over?" I ask.

"I don't drink, stupid. It impairs your judgment—as you proved last night."

"I don't either. I just had a few swigs. I guess I'm really weak with alcohol." I don't know why, but I feel I have to justify my behavior.

"What now? Are you guys going to date?"

I look at Priscilla. Is she serious? "We just made out. Even *I* know that means nothing. Why are you so concerned, anyway?"

She shrugs. "Skye's my friend."

"Well, guess what? Your friend abandoned you too, Priscilla. Welcome to the club." I stand up, painfully. "Thanks for the coffee."

I drive home. Carefully.

***

I sleep through Sunday. Monday morning I see both Boulder and Sean have texted me, but I ignore them. I drive to school, making a pathetic detour to pass in front of Skye's dead house.

As soon as I park in the school's lot, I notice Jane arriving, the roar of her motorcycle distinctive and deafening.

I wait for a moment when the lot is not too crowded and approach her.

"Hey, Jane," I say.

She turns to face me with menace in her eyes. But when she sees it's just me, they turn back to her usually steely gaze.

"Hey, Drake. Feeling better?" The words are cordial, but her tone isn't.

"I passed out, huh?" It doesn't clarify much.

"During the best part," she says in a hushed voice. "Hey, can I trust you to keep it quiet?"

I don't ask why. I don't want to hear it. "Sure," I say. What else can I tell her? 'No can do, Jane, I want to shout from the rooftops I made out with the hot crazy chick everybody's afraid of'? I just had those amazing experiences with two girls who usually wouldn't even look at me, and I can't share them with anyone. Damn, Drake, you're such a boy scout.

"Thanks. I had fun. Who knows? Maybe someday we can have fun again. I'll let you know." She leaves before I can answer her.

All this conversation went down without a single smile from her. She *is* weird.

And she doesn't want me approaching her again, especially in school. I'm back to my usual status.

So, just like it was with Skye, as soon as it began, it was over. I have very interesting relationships, but they don't last long.

Chapter 20: Skye

One Week Later

Spending a week with Mum is my condition to get back to Seattle for my hopeless mission. I make sure she's comfortable and well cared for in our house. Judi moves into a guest bedroom, indefinitely.

It's been just us girls: Aunt Gemma, Judi, Mum, and me. Mimi, the publicist, drops by now and then. We talk a lot, gossip a lot, watch black-and-white movies. I've never felt so connected to them.

When I have to say goodbye, it's painful. Not so much because of Mum, who's almost fully recovered now, but because of this family life I never had, and I'll miss so much.

***

Even I, used to long and frequent flights due to my mother's nomadic career choice, am bored by the London-Seattle ordeal. If only I could chat a little bit, but my companion is drugged out the whole time.

I didn't tell anyone I'd be back. I thought I should surprise Priscilla. She sent me sweet emails and texts every day, and I answered some of them with news of Mum's health, but I didn't mention I'd be coming back. I was holding out until the last moment, waiting for the Mothers to change their mind and let me stay.

Priscilla turned out to be a real friend, staying in touch even though she believed I'd never be back. I must be more open with her. I could tell her my mother is a movie actress, for starters.

Drake is another issue altogether. I have no idea what his reaction will be. We had no contact since the heartfelt text he sent wishing my mother well. I know he saw more in our day together than I did, and I don't know what to do.

This week gave me a lot of time to think. I can't waste my life waiting for Connor to acknowledge me again. My plan is to have an open talk with him, to make it clear where we stand.

I can't deny the history between Connor and me, and I need to know if there's a chance to salvage our relationship. When he left me, we had a fight, but we never had closure. It's harsh to think of Drake as my failsafe, but that's how things are.

Drake. Sweet, cute, there-for-me Drake. No matter how amazing he is, he can't help but be second-best to an already existing relationship.

I'm almost hoping that Connor doesn't feel anything for me anymore, so I can see where things go with Drake. Am I being unfair?

Maybe I'm over-thinking this. I hate long flights.

***

Aunt Gemma and I are back home. We already called the school from London and explained my long absence. It's a Sunday, so tomorrow I'm coming back. The naked incident happened almost two weeks ago; maybe it's forgotten by now.

I had a good night's sleep and feel ready to go on with my mission and my life. I only need to search for the Singularity until the end of the school year; after that, all bets are off. The Singularity will probably be gone by then. Even the most determined Mother would have given up after two years of a fruitless hunt. "Witch hunt," I say out loud in my bedroom. I let out a dry laugh.

I wait until noon before calling Priscilla. My guess is she wakes up late on Sundays.

A sleepy voice answers, "Yeah?"

"Hey, Pri," I say.

A moment passes, and I guess she must be checking the caller ID, because her voice becomes lively. "Skye? Where are you?"

"I'm back!" I say.

"That's awesome! Come over! I have so much to tell you. I just need to take a shower and wake up."

***

I show up at Priscilla's huge house. I must ask her about last week's party.

She's having a 1 p.m. breakfast in the kitchen, and I join her. My clock is still messed up. She tells me her parents are away: they always go on weekend getaways, leaving her alone. When I ask if she feels lonely, she looks at me as if I'm nuts.

"Nice glasses," she says.

"Oh, these? They're new. I had lost mine." I got the spare pair I had at home. They've been crafted especially for my True Sight. That's how I can see Priscilla's pink aura. But she has a ring of gray around her head.

After she wolfs down half a pancake, she asks without glancing at me, "Have you talked to Drake yet?"

"No, not yet." I wait a bit. "Did you talk to him while I was gone?"

She glances at me, but eats the other half of the pancake before answering. "I gave him your message the day after you left."

"How did he take it?"

"Badly, of course." She takes a long time sipping her coffee. "You could have let him down easily." Her tone is less friendly now.

I feel defensive. "I really thought I wasn't coming back. I didn't even want to," I say, before catching my mistake. I try to fix it. "I mean, I wanted to stay with Mum."

Priscilla shakes her head. "Drake's not like the other guys."

Whoa. Does Priscilla have feelings for Drake? What is going on? She rests her mug on the kitchen counter and grabs my hand. Uh-oh, here it comes.

"Listen," she says. "I'm not a good judge of boys. I've chosen a few bad ones. Okay, many bad ones. But you can see Drake is one of the good guys. I mean, even *I* could see it."

I say nothing. I want to see where this is going.

"You're new here, Skye, so you don't know about my reputation. I've been around. I like boys. I went out with them. Almost all of them."

She went out with Drake. Is that it? That's how she knows he's a good kisser. Is that why she approached me after he came to talk to me in that first day? But he told me he hadn't kissed her. I'm confused.

"I didn't know there was something between you two," I say. She looks at me strangely. "I mean, neither of you ever told me—"

"What? No, that's not what I mean," she says, interrupting me. "I'm trying to tell you I never hooked up with him *because* he's one of the good guys."

"What do you mean?"

She lets go of my hand and grabs a fabric napkin. While fiddling with it, she says, "I did some bad things. Broke some hearts, used

93

some boys. Some of them did not recover, and I don't say it as a badge of honor—I regret it now. That's why I moved on to college guys. They are less complicated and more... resilient."

I wait. She gives me this exasperated look. "Skye, I spared Drake. Of course he's cute, and we would've ended up getting together sooner or later. But I thought I'd do him some irreversible damage, you know? I thought maybe I'd break his heart forever."

That's a side of Priscilla I've never seen before. Her aura suddenly turns all gray. I try to say something, but she cuts me off, as if she can't hold it inside anymore.

"I spared him, but you didn't, Skye."

Oh.

It's as if a film has been lifted from my field of vision, and now I see the world clearly. I had never realized it... Of course I did! I just never took responsibility. I should have—

"You didn't spare him," she repeats. "And neither did Jane."

Chapter 21: Drake

I glare at the buzzing alarm clock as if it is the reason I have to face school once again. Another Monday means another whole week of suckness ahead.

At least the week after the party passed without any more surreal moments.

Apparently, The Predator was the only one who saw Jane and me together. Nobody is talking about it in school. It would be embarrassing, but I also wonder how the free publicity could improve my social life.

I learn it's easier not to be the kiss-and-tell guy when you actually never kiss any girls. Now that I have made out with two mega-hotties, it's hard to keep it bottled up.

You'd think this ego boost would make me more confident with girls, but I feel gloomy and conflicted. It seems my romantic life has already peaked, and it's all downhill from here.

The guilt about Skye crushes me. She's gone forever, but after the make-out session with Jane I feel like I have betrayed Skye. No, not her. I betrayed my feelings for her.

Boulder would tell me to think like a man.

Mona bangs on the door. "Wake up, driver!" she yells.

***

My sister always takes the bus, but today she gets in her head that I should drive her to school. Since it was part of the bargain with Dad, I have no option.

She settles in the passenger side and fiddles with the radio.

"Hey," I say, "never touch a man's radio."

Mona shoots me an angry look. "It's not a man's radio. It's yours."

Everybody I know is a smart ass.

"Drop me off at Pain's," she mumbles.

"What?" That's why she didn't want to take the bus. "Are you skipping school?"

She lets out a deep sigh. "Drake, don't give me the 'tude. It doesn't suit you."

Who is this devil possessing my little sister? Am I supposed to believe that two-year-old ball of cuddliness turned into this girl?

"So, we're going to the House of Pain?" I ask.

She snorts. "You really believe you're the first one to make that joke, right?"

Well, I thought it was a good one. "Do me a favor, will you? Don't come back home with a face tattoo, okay? Or knocked up or something."

She looks at me as if I'm made out of snot. "You don't need to be a jerk about it." Her voice, for the first time in years, betrays a little frailty.

Remembering what Skye said to me, sitting in the same place, I wonder: why don't we *talk* more? What is the big deal, anyway?

"Are you still mad about the car?" I try to break the ice.

"No. Not after I've seen the car," she replies.

The conversation dies. This is going to be harder than I thought.

"So," I say, excising any contempt from my tone. "What's the deal with Pain?"

"What now, Drake?"

"Does she go to school with you?"

"You've known her since forever. She's being going to school with me since kindergarten! Becca? Hello?"

"Becca? Not pigtails Becca? Not princess dress-up Becca?" I remember their play dates.

"You're such a moron!" Mona says, searching for something in her purse.

I still can't get over it. "Little pigtails Becca calls herself 'Pain' now?" I say, sounding like an eighty-year-old. "Why?"

"Why do you care, Drake? Eew."

What? "No, no." Double-eew myself. "I didn't even know who we were talking about. I'm not into little girls."

"Why the interrogation, then?" She gets a purple lipstick out of her purse, swings down the sun visor, and applies the Halloween-ish make-up while looking at herself in the tiny mirror.

I don't answer at first. I wait until a red light, then turn to her and say, "I thought we could, you know, talk."

She stares back at me, confused. "About what?"

I hesitate. "About us? Our lives?"

She cocks her head and narrows her eyes. "Are you coming out?"

"W-What?!?"

"You're coming out to your little sister! That's so cute." And there it is, the first smile I see on her face in weeks.

I raise my hands in desperation. "I'm not coming out!"

"Aren't you ready?"

"I'm straight! Where did you get this idea?"

Her smile fades a bit. "Don't get all worked up. It sounds homophobic, you know?"

"Why do I have to be homosexual or homophobic? Can't I be neither?"

"But your reaction—"

I bang my fist on the dashboard. "It's because it's already hard enough to get a girl. I don't need these rumors."

A horn honks behind us. I look in the back mirror and see a four-car line waiting for me. My hands go back to the wheel, and we move. Sneaking a peek at her, I see the lipstick is gone and she's rummaging through her purse again. Her smile is gone. She doesn't look at me.

"Come on, Drake. What did you expect? I never see you with a girl, you don't play sports—"

"I swim!"

"Swimming is exercise, it's not a sport. Besides, the speedo—"

"I don't wear a speedo! I wear tight swimming trunks! Manly trunks."

"That's not the point. There's this sensitive side of yours, your soft voice, and you just said you're not into girls—"

"I said *little* girls. Like diaper-wearing Becca."

"And you are always hanging out with those two studs. I mean, you follow them like a puppy."

Oh, God, my little sister thinks that Boulder and Sean are studs. Will this nightmare ever end? I look at her, and I'm stunned further when I see a lighter in her left hand, her other hand still inside the purse. I forget all about my supposed gayness.

"Mona! Are you smoking?"

She looks at me, startled. "No," she says with a guilty voice. "This is for, like, incense and stuff."

"Come on, Mona!" I say aloud. Then, my voice turns soft, just like she pointed out seconds ago. "Smoking of all things?" I don't know what comes over me. My eyes are suddenly humid. I keep staring at the road. I can feel she's looking at me, but I don't know what to say.

After a while, she breaks the silence. "Seriously, Drake. It's not for smoking, or pot, or anything. It's just a lighter. For candles—"

"—and incense. Right." My eyes are still on the traffic ahead.

I hear a deep sigh. We don't say a word until we're at Pain's. Or pigtails Becca's. Or whoever's. Mona doesn't ask me to not rat on her to Dad. She leaves the car and closes the door, and then leans on the open window.

"I'm sorry," she says.

I turn to her, at last. "It's okay. It's just the lighter—"

"No," she interrupts me. "I'm sorry you're not gay. We could go clubbing together, looking for guys." She blows me a kiss with her purple lips and laughs her way to the front porch of Pain's house.

I take off. I smile a little bit, but it's bittersweet. I realize that while I was living my life, my little sister became, you know, a person.

Chapter 22: Skye

I've been dreading school, but so far it hasn't been so bad. I guess the news about my mother's heart attack might have softened their luscious desire for mocking me. Maybe it got me a reprieve. Or maybe they weren't so mean in the first place.

Five minutes after I arrive, I spot Drake. Here we go.

When Drake sees me, he freezes up. He stands by his car, a couple of books in his left hand, his car keys crushed in his right fist. I wave to him, looking pathetic even to myself.

He just stands there. He's not making a statement: he is lost.

Well, welcome to the club.

Those two friends of his are walking in his direction. The bulky one glances at me. His eyes bulge. He halts and puts a hand on Sean's chest, stopping him too. They mumble something to each other and walk away. I turn to Drake. He's still paralyzed, oblivious to his friends' double-take.

I'd better make a move. When I start toward Drake, he comes out of his haze. After a few tentative steps, he meets me in the middle, at the lot curbside.

"Hey," I say, using our old greeting.

He doesn't answer with our trademark "Hey, you." Instead, he says, "Are you back?"

I nod.

"Why?" He winces. "I mean, how's your mother? Is she with you?"

So many things to ask, and he is concerned with Mum? Is he sweet or what?

"She's much better. It was just a scare."

His expression shows doubt.

"Her sister is with her," I add, reassuring him. It's just a half-lie.

"Good. And why are you here?"

Oh, Goddess. Maybe he thinks I came back for him! His face is inscrutable. I can't let him down, but I can't tell him the truth. He's right. To most people, my return won't make a sliver of sense, unless you know I'm a Sister on a mission. I need a way out.

The muffler sound hits me even before I sense her magical energy. One does not need True Sight to realize Jane is arriving.

I turn to the parking lot entrance and see her red machine slashing through the traffic, safety be damned. Drake follows my gaze.

After Jane parks, her head jerks up, and she stares straight at us. She doesn't look pleased. Like, at all.

And Drake is visibly upset.

It gives me an idea for a way out. It's not pretty, but it's the best I can do right now. Please don't hate me, Drake.

"Why do you care?" I say, borrowing some acting talent from Mum. "And why are you so worried, Drake?"

His voice is unsure. "Nothing. Just some crap I have to deal with."

I nod in Jane's direction. "Is she the crap you have to deal with?"

He looks at me startled. His expression is a mash-up of surprise and regret. I so wish I could read his aura. Why can't I?

I'm sorry, Drake. I'm sorry.

"Priscilla," he mumbles.

"Yeah," I say, my faked bitchy-ness reaching record heights. Maybe I *am* mad he made out with Jane. "Priscilla is a good friend."

"Yeah, she's *your* good friend," he says. His tone is so… dark. Oh, what have I done?

He walks past me, not saying another word.

It's like a punch to the gut. I want to say I'm sorry again. I want to scream it's just an act. But I don't. I just let him go.

I look at him and see his fake-proud march toward the school. I broke his heart. Twice.

While I think on how mean I've become, I don't realize someone's approaching. The high school Hulk. Appropriately, his aura is green. What's his name again? Oh, yeah. Boulder.

He stands by, staring at me.

I try to preempt an awkward moment. "Dude, it's not a good time to ask me out." I'm still in diva-mode. And I shouldn't use the word 'dude' anymore.

"I'm not here to ask you out." He pauses, then admits, "Don't get me wrong, I would, but my bro beat me to it." He shouldn't use the word 'bro' anymore. "Here's the deal. Don't hurt him. You let him down nicely, or there's going to be some Boulder reckoning."

Way to charm a girl. "You don't think much of him, do you? Are you his babysitter?"

He cocks his head, maybe thinking whether he should snap my neck.

"More of a big brother. Hence the 'bro.' I'm looking out for him. And don't mention it to him, or—"

"A reckoning. Got it." I try to sound blasé, but I'm impressed Drake can command that kind of loyalty. "You're something else, Boulder, you know?"

"Of course I do." He turns and struts to school.

Oh, Drake. Maybe I made a bigger mistake than I thought.

Chapter 23: Drake

Today I want to follow Mona's lead and ditch school.

Skye leaves without a word, dumps me by text, and then calls me out on a drunken mistake? What happened? This is so not her.

Stop making excuses for her, Drake. You did everything right. Well, except for the part where you made out with her... rival?

Not for the first time, I wonder why Jane and Skye hate each other. Maybe it's because Jane hooked up with Skye's ex. The two girls seemed to know each other on Skye's first day.

So, it's not about me. All this is about Skye's ex-boyfriend. I'm just a pawn in their fight for Mr. Darcy.

I know Skye saved me in the woods. But I'm bitter. What else could she do? Let me die? She did that weird New Age thing, though. Now I don't know if it means she cared so much she would try anything, or that she cared so little she thought she had time to joke around.

***

I want to be alone. Besides my daydreaming during classes, I hide in the library during the breaks. Sean and Boulder would never venture there. I wait until most of the students leave to make my way to the parking lot. Just a few vehicles there, including my sorry Volvo and Jane's bike.

Today is a good day for swimming. If being alone is my goal, I can't think of a better activity. Nobody is there after school. My gym bag is in the car's trunk, but before I take a step, I see Jane slithering from behind the cafeteria building. She walks deliberately *past* her bike.

It's like seeing a cowboy without his horse. Jane never leaves her bike behind.

Something compels me to see what she's up to. Since we locked lips, she isn't as scary as she once was. And if I'm being manipulated by those two hotties, I need to know what's going on. So I, as suspiciously as Jane did, slither too.

I'm not the stalking type, and it takes me a while to even understand what I'm supposed to do. Jane helps me by not looking back, not even once.

She crosses the street and looks around. I hide behind the bushes near the parking lot entrance. From the back of the pool building, Skye shows up and greets her.

What?

They stand a few feet from each other. I can't hear them, but I see Jane making a rounding gesture with her pointer finger up. Skye points to the pool building, and Jane nods. The two of them walk inside the red brick building.

What's going on? I thought they were enemies. Maybe they're the Let's-Screw-With-Drake's-Head Club. I imagine them having a glass of wine by the pool, having a laugh about me, comparing notes: "I kissed him and left the country;" "Well, I made out with him and left him asleep alone in the car;" "Can you believe he actually thought he had a chance with us?"

I shake my head. Man, I am paranoid.

Well, girls have this irrational compulsion to talk about stuff. Maybe Skye and Jane are talking about Mr. Darcy. Skye said she didn't have a boyfriend. She may just let Jane know it's okay. Except… girls are territorial, right? They could be fighting about him. Hell, they could be fighting about me.

Right.

I don't know how long I spend running these bizarre scenarios in my head. But it's enough time for my thoughts to swing from them mocking me to them fighting for me.

Fighting. Jane punches guys who ask her out. What would Jane do if she got a rival alone?

I forget my stealth attempts and jump from behind the bushes. I cross the street, running, and reach the side door of the pool building. The tiny lobby is empty, as always. I have an idea. I enter the men's locker room (no way they're in there). The walls in the cheap building are thin enough that I can hear them if they are in the women's locker room. And each locker room has a direct passage to the pool area, so I can sneak a peek if they're meeting by the stands or the pool.

I pass the closed lockers and empty benches. The stench of years of sweat and bleach makes me wrinkle my nose. No sound comes from the women's side. They must be poolside. I approach the door, open it slowly, and look across the narrow gap.

From where I hide, I can see the pool, but not all the stands that go up about ten steps to my left. I hear a low humming. They're somewhere around. I dare to open the door wider. Then I notice it. A ripple on the water. Like someone jumped in.

And bubbles.

Briefly looking up, I see Jane on the top of the stands, sitting cross-legged. Her hands are resting on her knees, *dripping blood*. She is humming something, her eyes closed.

Without thinking, I run from the door and dive in the direction of the bubbles. Cold water envelops me. While I try to reorient myself underwater, I kick my sneakers out. I see a figure slowly drifting to the bottom, leaving a faint red stream behind.

Skye. She's not struggling. I reach for her and catch her lifeless arm.

My summer lifeguard stint comes back to me. I wrap my arm around her. I swim up quickly, and we reach the surface. After a deep breath, I swim to the side, dragging her inert body with me. I get out and pull her out of the water. As if by instinct, my eyes look up.

Jane is climbing down the stairs in a hurry, a knife of some kind in one of her bloody hands, rage in her eyes. She hesitates after she reaches the last step, then she darts to the door.

With Jane out of the equation, I turn to Skye, still in my arms. I lay her down on the ceramic floor with care. When I shake her slowly to get a reaction, a wound to her temple catches my eye. She's bleeding. She's not responding. And her chest is not moving.

The CPR training kicks in. First, call 911. I reach for my cell. It's drenched in water and dead. I search for hers, and I find it tucked in a back pocket. Also wet and useless.

I put my face next to hers. No sound, no breath. She's not breathing.

Oh, God. Oh, God.

I force her mouth open and see nothing blocks her throat. I unzip her jacket. I hesitate for a nanosecond before ripping her t-shirt off. After finding the center spot of her chest, I begin applying pressure.

Pump, pump, pump. Thirty pumps. No response.

I tilt her head back a little bit and glance worriedly at the blood pouring from her temple. One step at a time. I pinch her nose, cover her mouth with mine, and blow twice. Nothing.

Back to pumping. Pump, pump—

A gurgling sound! Water comes out of her mouth, the gagging reflex making her whole body spasm. She takes a deep breath, a long gasp, as if she had just come into this world.

Her eyes are wide open. She's coughing, reaching for me, and trying to look around us. I've never seen someone so terrified.

"She's gone," I say.

Her chest heaves as she sucks air with desperation. She looks into my eyes, into my soul, for a moment. Then she grabs me, and we embrace.

Slowly, I push her away. She looks at me in bewilderment.

"You're bleeding," I say, motioning to her right temple.

Her hand follows mine, and it dawns on her.

"Jane hit me," she says, still breathing hard.

Her voice is hoarse, throaty, but I'm glad she's conscious, talking, and remembering.

"She hit me with the butt of the knife," she adds. Then she has a brief coughing fit.

I say, "Stay here. I need to call an ambulance."

She grabs my arm. "No!"

"No? Can you walk then? There's a phone in the lobby."

She squeezes my arm. "No. Don't call anyone."

"What about the police? She attacked you!"

"No," she pleads.

She's confused. I try to reassure her. "It's okay. We have to."

"Don't do it." Her penetrating look convinces me.

***

At Skye's request, I search for her glasses. I find them by the side of the pool, smashed. Someone stepped on them. Jane, probably. I collect the pieces and the twisted frame, and hand them to Skye.

She sighs. "Another pair gone."

"We'll get you another," I say. I'm more worried about her head.

"No, we can't. They're special prescription. Made in London. It'll take weeks."

We reach an agreement: I won't call 911, but I'll drive her to the ER. I tell her she needs to have x-rays, and she agrees with reluctance (after all, I'm experienced in head injuries).

"How are you feeling?" I ask.

She coughs more before answering. "Half-dead."

"Will you tell me what happened?" My eyes are on the road. I go as fast as the law allows. No sense crashing the car on our way to the hospital.

She says in a low voice, "I was so stupid. I actually believed Jane wanted to talk. But she asked me—as a Sister."

"Sister?"

"Later," she says, her voice tired and raspy.

She uses her ripped t-shirt to stop the bleeding. She's wearing my spare shirt I keep in the gym bag. I sneak a peek and smile.

"What?" she asks.

"Not many girls can pull off wearing a 'Yes, I'm handsome' t-shirt," I say.

She looks down at her chest and sees the wet circles of her bra. She deliberately wraps her arms around herself.

"You didn't waste any time undressing me," she says.

I smile, not because of the joke, but because she seems to be doing well. I say, "I'm a trained lifeguard. It was all very professional."

"Did you sneak a peek?"

"No comment," I say, grinning.

"You saved me," she says. "Thanks."

"I guess we're even now."

Chapter 24: Skye

Drake fills out the ER paperwork for me. He's a little surprised when he learns I want to pay for it and not use insurance, but he doesn't ask any questions.

They insist on calling Aunt Gemma. I'm only seventeen, after all.

A young doctor arrives and says, "Hey, it's you guys again."

I recognize her. She attended to Drake when he had a concussion. When we tell her I hit my head and almost drowned, her eyebrows go up.

"How did that happen?" she asks, sounding skeptical.

Drake opens his mouth, but I cut him off.

"Drake was in the locker room, and I was by the pool. I was monkeying around while I waited for him. I slipped on the wet floor, hit my head, and fell into the water."

"Uh-huh," she says, not entirely convinced. "Let me take a look." She examines me for a while and adds, "You bumped your head on what, exactly?"

"I... I'm not sure," I say.

Drake says, "I guess it was on the ladder's handrail. She was close to the steps when I found her."

I shoot him a thankful look. The doctor glares at him.

"How long did it take to resuscitate her?"

111

Drake narrows his eyes. "From the time I heard the splash to the time she was breathing again... about two minutes?"

She nods. "I'm ordering a CAT scan." She asks Drake, "Would you mind going to the nurse's station and asking one of the nurses to come here, please?"

Drake is eager to comply. After he leaves, she turns to me, "Are you sure that's what happened?"

She's onto my lie. Oh, Goddess. I stall. "What do you mean?" I ask, trembling a bit.

"Did he hit you?"

I exhale. I smile to her. "Drake? Are you kidding? He's the sweetest guy I know."

"Are you sure?" She is looking into my eyes.

"Yeah!"

"And he saved you? Performed CPR and everything?"

I nod. She doesn't say anything for a while. We're having a staring contest. Finally, she leans forward.

"In that case," she whispers, "you hold on to this guy." She winks.

I'm stunned. Before I can say anything, Drake is back.

"The nurse will be right here," he says.

The doctor checks my injury again. She asks to see Drake's scar, and he shows it to her.

Shaking her head, she says, "Now you have matching scars. Almost in the same spot. You could have just sprung for matching tattoos instead."

***

Aunt Gemma is freaking out when she arrives. I told her to not call my mother, but she is taking none of it.

112

"And what is that boy doing here?" Gemma whispers to me.

I'm glad Drake is at the cafeteria getting coffee. It's his turn to walk around the hospital in drenched clothes. And it's my turn to spend the night in the building.

"He saved me and brought me here. I guess he earned the right to stay."

"Did you slip and hit your head?" she asks, as suspicious as the young doctor.

I recite the same story I told the doctor. Gemma swallows it, but gets back to Drake.

"What about this boy? Connor should be here. I'll call him," she says, reaching for her purse.

"No!" No way I want to see Connor, especially in this situation. He would meet Drake, and I'm not ready to handle this right now. Yes, it's not as important as the search, but it's still a big deal. To me.

Gemma eyes me. I say, "Connor has nothing to do with it." She has the phone in her hand now. I add, "Besides, he must be busy with the search. No need to distract him with a trivial matter."

This placates her. "What about Katherine?" she asks.

"If she knew, she'd call me back to London." I lower my voice and whisper, "And you know the Mothers need me here."

Gemma nods, deep in thought, and leaves the phone alone. Thank Goddess the Knowings are so gullible.

Drake comes back. After a few awkward moments between Gemma and him, I tell him he can go home. I shoot a look to Gemma, who huffs and puffs, but leaves us alone for a moment. I beckon to Drake.

He approaches my bed. I think about kissing him. But it would only confuse him further.

113

Instead, I whisper in his ear, "Thank you. I'll tell you what happened. I promise."

He nods, but leaves without smiling.

Oh, Goddess.

Chapter 25: Drake

Skye called my house this morning. She wants to meet and talk. I'm glad she's keeping her promise. I pick her up. Yep, I'm skipping school again.

We need to get new phones (Mona is going to be mad). I choose a mall on the Eastside. We cross the 520 bridge on our way over, the waves splashing on the sides of the floating structure. I want to put an ocean between us and Jane, but I guess Lake Washington will have to do. Besides, I don't want to run into anybody I know while we have our little chat.

At the store, I ask for waterproof phones. The sales clerk gives us horrible service, but Skye can't stop laughing.

I know of this big, beautiful park south of the mall, nestled between tall office buildings. We buy ice cream and amble over there. We pick a bench apart from everybody else and watch the joggers circle the half-mile ring around the park. On the lawn, away from us, a dog fetches a Frisbee. To our right, water cascades into a mirror pool. I don't like being so close to water after our recent experience, but Skye doesn't mind.

We finish our ice creams and take our time.

"So…" I say.

"So…"

"Ladies first." I bow theatrically.

She sighs and looks down. Then a burst of words comes out of her.

"Jane approached me when school was over. She wanted to talk, away from other people. I still can't believe I fell for that."

I put my hand on hers. "You're just too trusting."

She shakes her head. "I should have learned not to be by now."

"What do you mean?" I hope she's not talking about me.

Skye glances at me, but soon lowers her eyes again. "I thought the pool building would be empty, and we went there. We talked a little bit, and when I got distracted, she pulled out a knife and hit me with its butt. That's the last thing I remember."

She looks at me with expectant eyes. Maybe she realizes I know she's lying. Well, no reason to leave her hanging.

"What did you talk about? Me? Mr. Darcy?"

She turns to me and says, "Who?"

"Your boyfriend? Or is he Jane's now?"

Her hand grabs the bench. "Jane's?"

I'm angry, but I can't leave her in the dark. "Jane told me she hooked up with your ex. British dude. What is he doing here?"

Her other hand covers her mouth. A light shines in her eyes. "He knows her! Wait. *That's* how he knows her?"

She bites her fist softly, staring into the distance. It's like I'm not here.

"Snap out of it, Skye. Do you think that's why she attacked you?"

Skye turns to me, her eyes wide. "It might be." She sounds detached.

I try to forget what her shocked reaction spells for me. She has

116

feelings, huge feelings for this guy. I'll go into that later. Now I need to know something else.

Slowly, I reach for her hand, the one still covering her mouth, and ask, "What did you talk about then? Why did you act like you knew each other on your first day?"

She looks past me. She's making something up.

Even now, she won't tell me the truth.

I give her another chance. "Before you answer, there's something you must know. When I arrived at the pool, Jane was in a trance of sorts, chanting or praying or whatever, with blood on her hands, totally spazzed out."

Skye's body jerks back. She tries to pull her hand away, but I hold it firmly in mine.

I hate myself, but I have to go on. "Just like you were when the tree hit me."

She stares at me. For a long time, she doesn't move a muscle. I slowly let go of her hand.

I have to close the deal. "So, you are in a cult. And you're messed up enough to try to kill each other."

She bites her lower lip. All that, and she *still* won't talk to me. I reach for my ultimate weapon. I say, "I'm cool with that, as long as you invite me to your naked dances in the woods."

Not even a smile. Tough crowd.

Chapter 26: Skye

Jane performed a ritual. And Drake saw me performing mine in the woods.

Oh, Goddess. I broke the Veil.

I try to think of a story. Anything will do. He mentioned a cult. That's a good one. Go with it, Skye.

But I draw a blank. My thoughts keep coming back to Connor. To Connor with Jane. To Jane. Why didn't she finish me off? Why would she perform a ritual while I drowned? I list the rituals I know and the ones I've only heard of, but nothing fits.

And Drake knows. He just knows. That's why he's overwhelming me with all this. He looks at me in a way he never did before. He's not exactly angry, or sad. But all his sweetness is gone.

As if on cue, he says, "Won't you tell me the truth?"

I can't bear it. "What do you want me to say? That I'm a witch? That's ridiculous!"

He shakes his head. "Skye, in the woods, a tree hit me. My dad was right. I should have been gone. I *was* gone. You brought me back."

I'm trembling. "I was gone, and *you* brought me back," I argue.

"Through CPR, not some weird voodoo!" his voice rises. "Level with me, Skye."

I look down. "I just can't."

He sighs and says, "Explain it to me, or I'll go to the police. Give me a good reason why Jane shouldn't be in juvie right now."

Drake isn't kidding. I look at him. "You wouldn't understand."

His voice is cold, and it breaks my heart. "I've been nothing but understanding since I've met you. Come on, Skye. You owe me that much."

Forgive me, Goddess. I just can't go on.

"I'm a witch. And Jane is a witch. And Connor, too. A male witch." I can't believe I'm saying this out loud.

And I hope he can't either.

"So, is that a cult, a religion, a New Age thing?" No sarcasm in his voice.

I'll just lay it on him. "It's none of those. Well, it *is* a religion. But it's the real deal. And we can do magic."

"Do it, then." His expression is inscrutable.

"What?"

"Do you have to hide? Is that it?"

Something's wrong. "I don't understand," I say. "Do you believe me or not?"

He sighs. "I believe you believe it, or you wouldn't waste time doing a ritual while I was dying. And I believe Jane believes it, or she wouldn't let you drown while she did her thing. So," he says, leaning back, "unless you are *both* psychos playing with other people's lives, I imagine you have a good reason to say you can do magic."

I look around. We're still alone. "We can do it. It's just a part of our philosophy, but we can do it. Through rituals, enchantments, potions, Charms."

"You have no idea how silly this sounds," he says.

"Of course I do."

"Okay…" he says. "So, there's no wand? No turning into a toad? Or, what else? Oh, I know. What about controlling the elements, shooting fire from your fingertips? No?"

It's disheartening watching Drake turn into this cynical, cruel guy.

"That's not fair," I mumble.

"Yeah. To me," he says.

"Put yourself in my shoes, Drake. What do you want from me? *You* asked me about it."

He shakes his head. "Okay, okay. Just assume I'm stupid, and tell me how this works."

"Do you believe me?"

"Let's not get into that right now. Just convince me."

This is ridiculous. I don't want to convince him, quite the opposite. But he'll go to the police and create a real mess. I prefer trying to explain it to him than to anyone else. I imagine a detective telling me, *So, you're saying that when the victim, Drake Hunter, was lying unconscious on the ground, you, instead of calling for help, decided to perform an ancient, ahem, ritual. And you're the daughter of Katherine Lexington-Ellis… Not the British actress, I presume?*

They would involve Aunt Gemma. And Drake's family. The school too, since Jane attacked me on the school grounds and we're both students. They would bring Jane for questioning: who knows what that psychopath would do then? News sites would carry the log line, "Movie star's daughter caught in intrigue of murder and witchcraft," or something cheesy like that. Oh, Goddess, imagine the tabloids back home! The Mothers would go insane.

That would be a huge breach of the Veil, in addition to totally compromising the search for the Singularity.

Forgive me, but I'm going to break the Veil a little bit, to just one person, because the alternative could be catastrophic.

And I still have a little hope he won't believe me.

Chapter 27: Drake

Skye pauses again, calculating. I don't care. We have the whole day.

"If I tell you, do you promise you won't go to the police?"

"I can't promise that," I say. "She did try to kill you, after all. But I'll tell you what: if you give me a good reason, I promise I'll consider your request."

She nods. This must be hard for her. She looks at the trees, as if begging their forgiveness. Or maybe I'm getting crazy too.

"The ritual I did was an old one. It was supposed to stabilize your body, or to affect your blood flow. I don't know how it works, actually. Mum never explained it to me."

"Your mother? Is she a witch too?" Now I'm wondering whether Skye was brainwashed as a child.

She bites her lower lip before saying, "Y-yes. We can go into that later. What I don't know is why Jane didn't stab me."

"I have no idea," I say. "Maybe to make it look like an accident?"

"I don't think so. Maybe it's related to the ritual that she was performing. I bet she wasn't trying to save me. I really don't know."

"You don't know much, do you?" I'm amused.

"It's all very complicated. It takes us years—a lifetime—to learn. I doubt there's even a single person that knows all the rituals and everything that's behind them. Jane and I, we're so young; we know just the basics. And not the same things, obviously."

I kind of settle into the wackiness of the conversation. We might as well be talking about music, or the weather. I lean back on the bench, asking casually, "What about the other things? Enchantments and whatnots?"

My posture relaxes her a little bit, or maybe she's just that into the subject, because her mood improves. No more hand-wringing now. She says, "These are incantations we say out loud, usually protection and shield rituals. Some of us do them every morning."

"Like prayers?"

"Kind of, but they are more effective."

I nod. What can I say? I have no religion. I am a non-practicing, no-thinking-about-it generic Christian, and I go to church exactly once in never. But I respect other people's beliefs, and I try not to mock them. You know, just in case they got the right answer, and I'm somehow angering their god. Or gods.

But I give her the same look I give Scientologists.

She must be expecting it, because she doesn't miss a beat. "The potions can be beverages or oils or creams or—"

"Like the one you used on your face," I interrupt her. "You know, when you went blind?" I say without thinking. Boy, I didn't even notice I was getting carried away.

She stares at me. Then she slaps my leg. "Of course!" she says. "That was Jane! But that doesn't explain how I didn't feel her presence—"

"Wait!" I say, raising my hand. "You can feel each other's presence? Like the Force?"

"Like what?" She narrows her eyes.

"The Jedi thing?"

"Oh," she says. "Well, when you say it like that…"

"Sounds crazy, I know." I say, nodding.

She slaps my leg again, this time trying to hurt me. "Stop it! You wanted to know."

"Doesn't mean I can't have fun too," I say, rubbing my thigh.

She ignores my comment. "We all can feel each other when we're close. But I have this special Charm that lets me feel other…" She pauses, casting a furtive glance over her shoulder. "…others of my kind from much farther away."

"A Charm?"

"Yes, it's like an innate power. We can't turn it off. We all have two." I look at her inquisitively, and she goes on, "My other is Allure. This sounds embarrassing saying aloud but… I just look good."

"I agree," I say. Come on. That was too easy.

"And it's not just that. My skin recovers fast. Minor imperfections go away. I never had an acne problem. I bet my scar"—she points to her right temple—"is going to heal much faster than yours. You'll see."

She pauses, probably catching her breath. Or wondering if I'll run away from the crazy girl. This gives me time to think. A new batch of questions pops into my head.

"So, what do you call yourselves?" I ask.

"Sisters," she whispers. "Or Mothers, if you're an elder. And, okay, sometimes, witches."

"No, I mean, the name of your church or whatever. What do you call yourselves, I don't know, in the online forums or in the Facebook groups?"

She looks at me as if I'm the delusional one. "We don't have this type of public discussion. It's not something that we announce to the world."

"I can imagine why," I say. Sometimes I wish I'd shut up.

Her hoarse voice takes an authoritative tone. "Drake, it's not a fad. It's the real thing. We don't sell our teachings for ten bucks. There's no downloadable PDFs, no webinars, no speaking gigs, no selling spells on eBay, no workshops. The knowledge is truly secret, passed verbally or via handwritten books, from generation to generation. And only to the true Sisters, the ones who possess magical energy. The ones who had a Daybreak."

Skye probably sees a big question mark where my face should be. She sighs. "The day our magical energy activates is called a Daybreak," she says. "It happens when we're fifteen or so. Have you ever heard of debutante balls or quinceañeras? Those are remnants of ancient celebrations of girls' Daybreaks. The true meaning is lost nowadays, of course."

Something comes to my mind. As much as it pains me to talk about it, I need to know. "But what about your ex? I mean, he's a dude, right?"

"Very much so," she says, and then she looks at me in alarm. "I mean, it's rare, but sometimes a man can be a witch."

So, the boyfriend is a rare bird. Like a straight male ballet dancer. Which means all the straight female ballet dancers will fall for him, eventually.

Stop being an ass, Drake, you have more important things to consider.

"It's too much," I say. I lean forward, resting my elbows on my knees, my hands pressing my forehead.

"Hey, you wanted the crash course."

Staying still, I ask, "Is there any way you can prove it? To make things easier on me?"

I wait for a response, but I don't have to wait long. "We can't create fireballs or ice storms, nothing like that. The effects of a spell are subtle, sometimes over a long time."

"Can't you brew me a strength potion, or something?" I say from my hunched position. "Do you have this? Like love potions?"

"I know how to brew a Fancy Me potion. It's very basic, but it lasts just a couple of hours. It's huge with recent Daybreakers. It makes the boy dizzy and open to suggestion."

A spark ignites a memory inside my head. I straighten up out of reflex.

"Seriously?" I ask. "How does it taste?"

"What?" She cocks her head. "Why—"

"Just tell me," I plead.

"You want to see if I'm making this up, right? Like, if I can't come up with ingredients, you'll know it's a lie."

"Humor me," I say with a hint of impatience.

"Okay. I won't give you the specifics, not that you could brew it. Even if you could, you have no personal magic. But it's still a secret. It takes wild berries, silica powder, honey—"

"Anything citrus?" I ask, interrupting her. "Like orange?"

Her jaw drops. "Yes, orange, or grapefruit. How—"

"And an earthy flavor?" I can barely contain myself.

"Yeah. A mushroom. Why?"

"Because," I say, "I think that if you mixed it with beer, it can be a powerful date-rape drug."

Skye's eyes bulge. "How can you possibly know that?"

126

Jane drugged me and took advantage of me. I have mixed feelings about that.

Also, I'm concerned it's going to sound like the lamest excuse in the history of excuses.

Chapter 28: Skye

Drake tells me what he's been thinking. His theory is not as far-fetched as he thinks. Based on Jane's actions, it's totally possible—probable, actually—that she would drug Drake to get some information about me. Or was it just to get Drake to go along with her seduction?

This is the part where I'm surprised at my own reaction. I recognize the sensation I had many times while (and sometimes, after) dating Connor.

It's like this tiny, forgotten part of me is having an anxiety attack. You are well, but this small piece of you keeps nagging you, nibbling your brain, tugging at your heart, making you uneasy for no apparent reason. Yep: jealousy.

So, I do have feelings for Drake. Huh. For a moment I wonder if it's just a territorial thing; a sense of entitlement maybe. I feel childish: how dare Jane try to win over *my* man? Never mind I abandoned him forever and dumped him by text: I called dibs on him!

I smile in my mind, but my smile somehow spills over my face, and Drake sees it.

"What?" he asks, half-smiling himself.

I assume a serious expression. "Nothing," I reply. "I think you may be right. Drugging you sounds like something Jane would do."

"I know, right?" He seems overly satisfied with my acceptance.

"What now?" I ask.

He shrugs. "Is there any way I can go to the police to accuse Jane? Can you think of an explanation that doesn't involve witchcraft?"

"We could think of something, but I'm afraid that Jane, if cornered, could bring up the subject. Maybe just to murk things up, maybe to damage our culture. The police wouldn't believe her, but word would be out and damage would be done."

He shakes his head. "How have you managed to keep this secret for so long?"

"We're a tight-knit community. We have rules and safeguards." I don't mention a few well-positioned friends in government and media. "The Veil is essential to us."

"What are you doing here in Seattle? Did you come after your ex?" he asks nonchalantly, but his eyes betray his concern.

I can't make him trust me by telling half-truths. I spend the next half hour telling him about the Singularity.

He lets out an exaggerated sigh. "That's more like the kind of witch I've heard about."

I need to show him the Veil's importance across one more time. "Do you see how she's a big liability to people who want to remain hidden? That's not all. If somebody discovers the existence of the Singularity, there will be a witch hunt. They'll come for me and everyone I know."

"What? How do you know that?"

I shrug. "I just know."

"How sure are you?"

"Eighty-two percent?" I say, reciting the number the scholars told us.

He chuckles and asks, "Where does Jane fit into this?"

"Jane is a free agent. Doesn't seem to belong to a coven. Nobody controls her."

"I'll say," he mumbles, shaking his head. "But aren't you worried about Jane? What if she attacks you again? What's your mother going to say?"

There we go. Okay, no more secrets.

I tell him about my mother, her career. He blushes. "What?" I ask.

"Nothing…"

"Tell me!"

He rubs the back of his head. "It's just that… I saw your mother naked in a movie once."

He and half of the world. Yep, that's Mum.

Drake is mortified, but I have other concerns. He listens while I tell him about the publicity it would attract if Katherine Lexington-Ellis's daughter walked into a police station.

"Couldn't the cops keep it quiet? Or the press?" he offers.

"You don't know your own country very well, do you? And you certainly don't know England. I don't want my face on the TMZ website or on The Sun's front page."

He shrinks a little. No doubt he's realizing the implications of dating the daughter of a celebrity.

Did I just use the word "dating"?

"What's next, then?" It's his turn to ask.

"We go to school as if nothing happened," I say.

"Skye, she tried to kill you!" He stands up. "There's blood all over the pool building!"

"Nobody saw us. The school doesn't know about it, or your dad's phone would be ringing," I argue.

"That's not what I meant. A person you see every day wants you dead." He opens his arms wide. "If we don't do something, tell someone, she'll try again. Aren't you worried at all?"

I tug on his shirt, pulling him to sit down on the bench again. A couple of joggers were looking at us. "Of course I'm worried," I whisper. "But you'll protect me, won't you?" I can't suppress a giggle.

"Come on, Skye…"

"Okay, okay. You and I are going to be more careful. I'll perform the strongest rituals I know to protect us every morning. We can also drink potions to ward off any spells against us," I say, pretending I don't see his eyes rolling.

"Are they FDA-approved?"

"And we'll do something about it," I say. "Are you with me?" I add, staring at him suggestively.

Skye, you flirty little devil.

"You have to ask?" he says.

Is it wrong that I'm finding this so much fun?

Chapter 29: Drake

She's a cipher. Well, getting mixed signals from a woman puts me in the company of three and half billion men. It's a small solace.

Of all we discussed today, including witchcraft and Hollywood, what strikes me the most is what we didn't mention: our... situation.

I expected that, with all the things going on right now, dating would be the last thing on my mind. I was dead wrong.

My head is spinning at the prospect of having her back. Well, not having her *back*, because I never had her in the first place.

Still, as we leave the downtown park, I glance at her, and she seems different. Even with the gathering of gray clouds above us, she looks sunny. A sunny witch.

I don't care if she's delusional, or if she's maybe dragging me into her madness. Right now, I don't need to make a decision about believing her or not. I can just go with it. I have plenty of evidence (the potions, the rituals, Jane and Skye's behavior) that she's telling the truth. On the other hand, there's also evidence (everything else in the world) that she's a lunatic.

It doesn't worry me. Even if this is madness, I want to be part of it.

Chapter 30: Skye

I know I'm probably not behaving like an attempted-murder victim should. But Jane's attack awakened something inside me.

And the conversation with Drake made everything clear.

I had no purpose in life. I was a spoiled princess. Beautiful, rich, witch. Have I ever actually done something useful? Helped someone? Volunteered somewhere? Goddess, I don't even do things for *me*.

Besides the Craft, I have no hobbies, no interests, no passion. I spend time reading or fiddling with my playlists. But now I know what to do. I'll find the Singularity and hit back at Jane.

***

I don't want to, but I have to face Connor. I need the information.

I'm finally living up to the motto I chose when I moved to Seattle: I won't feel sorry for myself.

Drake doesn't say anything when I ask him to drop me off at UW, I mean, U-Dub on the way home. I told him Connor attends the university.

When we're close to the parking lot, Drake says he'll wait for me in the car. Since I want separation between him and Connor, I tell him no. But he won't budge.

"What if Jane is waiting for you there? She knows him," he

argues.

"I can sense her, remember?"

He shakes his head. "Well, can't she do something from a distance? Like shoot you?"

I'm just too tired to argue. He tells me he'll be reading a book in the car. He takes my brand new cell phone from my hands, the one we got this morning at the store, and adds *his* new number to my speed dial.

"Don't let it get wet," he tells me.

A light drizzle falls. I march down Memorial Way again. The first time I did it, I was so scared. Now I feed off the energy of the trees, the powerful buildings, the people.

The familiar tingling starts. It's a good sensation. I like to follow it, feel it diminishing, backtracking, and picking up its trail again. The True Sight leads me to the Suzzallo Library building. I walk up the imposing staircase. On the second floor, I sense it. Stronger.

Navigating the aisles, I feel like the books embrace me. I crisscross the rows until I zero in on him.

He's being smothered by a redhead in jeans and high heels. It's a long, slobbery, kiss. They're very much into it, their hands reaching places. That's probably why Connor hasn't sensed my presence yet.

As I'm about to clear my throat and help them avoid a public indecency charge, an idea comes to me. There are more entertaining ways of doing it.

"Connor!" I yell. My cry shatters the library's stillness.

They disentangle, startled.

"How could you?" I continue, still loud. Someone on another aisle tries to shush me. "You leave me and the twins at home to suck face with this skank?"

The shushes die. The redhead looks at him. A couple of students stare.

"Skye, I—"

I don't let him speak. "That's why I slave every night, waitressing? Paying your tuition? And you're here, still using that fake British accent to pick up girls!"

He shakes his head. The girl is now mad at him, not even caring about me calling her a name. More people gather around us.

"The twins don't have shoes! And you know there's one more on the way," I say, touching my belly, adding a slight hint of quivering to my voice.

The girl slaps him. Hard. And struts away. She stops by my side to say something to me, but I close my eyes and raise my hand to silence her. She just leaves.

Mum has an Oscar, you know.

Connor pleads, whispering, "Can we take this somewhere else?"

My hands cover my eyes (because I don't know how to cry on cue), but I nod. The crowd disperses.

After we leave the library, I start to laugh. Connor puts his hands on both sides of his head and looks at me as if he's seeing me for the first time. I can't stop laughing. Maybe it's a release from all the tension of the last couple of days.

He takes my arm and leads me away from people.

When I calm down, we stop. The rain is picking up, but we don't care. He asks me, "Was that really necessary?"

I take a deep breath and stare into his eyes. No more fun and games.

"I died yesterday," I say. "Jane killed me."

"What?"

"She tried to drown me, but I was resuscitated," I say, my voice icy.

"How?" he asks. "Why?"

"I'm okay, by the way. Except for the scar." I lift my hair so he can see the wound, but he barely glances at it.

"What's going on?" he asks me.

"You tell me. I know about you and Jane."

He takes a step back. Not a good day to be Connor, I have to admit.

"Is that what this is all about?"

"No, you bastard! She tried to kill me! Are you deaf?"

He opens his arms in an apologetic gesture. "She can be quite dodgy, but violent? I just don't understand," he says. What a leader the Mothers picked. I guess looks aren't everything.

I sigh. "Just tell me what went down between you two."

He does that lame duck routine, standing on one foot and scratching his head. He points somewhere to my left and says, "Shall we get a—"

"Yeah, yeah, go get your coffee," I interrupt him, making a dismissive gesture.

After a moment, I follow him and order tea and milk. Connor and I walk around the campus, until we find a seat outside in a covered area. The tea is a nice defense against the chilly wind. Sometimes a student passes by, but we're not so concerned about the Veil today.

"I'm going to give you the short version, okay?" He shoots me an expectant look. When I say nothing, he looks away, and goes on, "When I arrived I had to organize the operation, visit all schools, assign a Sister to each high school, and train them. In a few of the schools, I felt the presence of Sisters; one of them was Jane."

He sips his venti-whatever-whatever-mocha. "All the other Sisters here belong to covens. Our coven in London contacted them, and we all agreed to collaborate. But Jane is a free-lancer. The local covens didn't have information on her. So I got close and asked if she'd join us. She agreed at first, but she was always asking questions. We ended up getting involved." He glances at me while taking another sip. "You know her."

"I know *you*," I say.

"*Touché*," he says. "Sorry to say that, but she is very persuasive. And she's into strange things."

Is he serious? "I really don't need the details," I say.

"No, I mean, her Craft. She's into weird stuff. She's much more willing to sacrifice animals for divination, for instance. And her morning rituals are creepy. Once she—"

I raise an eyebrow. "*Morning* rituals?"

He just looks away again. "Goddess, Skye. I don't know what you want from me. Either we're adults, and I'm telling what you asked me, or we're in this jealousy game."

"Screw you, Connor! You're always twisting things so I look guilty. I want to know what happened, but I'm a person too, you know? You can tell me things *and* be considerate."

"All right, then. After I told her some things about the Singularity, we broke up. She said she'd keep an eye on things, but she was always vague, noncommittal. That's when I asked the London Mothers to send someone else to cover Greenwood High."

"What else are you not telling me?"

He sighs. "Okay, you need to know that too. I just put the pieces together. I mean, if she really attacked you. It all makes sense. Jane's weird Craft, her habits, her... demeanor." He stares at me. "Now I

137

think she may be a Night witch."

Uh-oh. My contempt for him is gone, replaced by concern. "She does Night magic?"

"Very likely. Not only that, but you can't master Night magic alone. She must know other Night Sisters, maybe even a Night coven."

This changes things. Night magic is rare. I knew it existed; I just have never faced it. Connor's parents are Craft scholars, though. He knows what he's talking about.

Connor continues, "You know how we always say the Singularity's Daybreak happened on the West Coast? Well, some Oxford Sisters put their minds together and triangulated the reports, based on the intensity and distance, and figured out the most probable area—"

"Seattle. Green Lake neighborhood. I suspected that."

"Yes," he says, his voice uncharacteristically weak.

"And Jane knows it."

Connor looks down and nods.

"The most probable location, Skye," he says, "Think about it. That's why the Mothers sent you here. Your True Sight Charm is rarer than you think. If they are right about the location, *you* are supposed to find her. You."

I hunch without realizing it. It's as if I can feel the crushing responsibility on me. Shaking my head, I say, "I can't. I've been walking the school, the streets. I don't sense anything besides Jane. Are you sure it's not her?"

Connor stares at me. "She isn't. Trust me." he says, his tone full of authority now. "We feel her energy. The Singularity's energy is probably off the charts, remember? Besides, if Jane had all that power, she wouldn't be in school, especially not with me and you snooping around."

"But then," I say, "why would she try to kill me if she's not the Singularity? Couldn't she be trying to protect herself?"

"Think, Skye," Connor whispers. "Yes, she probably went after you because you're searching in her turf. But it doesn't mean she's it. It just means she wants to find the Singularity before we do. Imagine if she can turn the Singularity into a Night Sister. We have got to find the Singularity before Jane."

Chapter 31: Drake

She comes back from the meeting with her ex. She's soaking wet, but neither of us bothers with the damage to the Volvo's upholstering. I hand her one of my towels from the gym bag. She takes her time.

"Jane wants to find the Singularity before we do," she finally volunteers. I don't know if the "we" means me and her, or her ex and her. Maybe it means all of us.

"That's not all. Jane's a Night witch," she adds.

"I'm assuming this is bad," I say.

Skye uses a knowledgeable tone to describe, well, the idea I used to have about witches. "Night magic deals with the horrible stuff: sacrifices, destructive spells, blood magic. It's banned by the established covens. Their potions and spells are more powerful too. If Night witches get hold of the Singularity... If they get hold of all her power, they'll be tempted to use it against other Sisters," she says. "And non-magical folks. They might not even care about the Veil anymore, and that would harm all of us."

I'm somewhat glad she's all business. All the catastrophic scenarios I ran in my head when she was alone with Mr. Darcy are washed away. She came back. To me.

God, she looks gorgeous. The cold makes her tremble a bit,

spreading goose bumps over her arms and neck. She wipes her face with the towel; while she can't see me, I can't help but notice how her wet clothes cling to her body.

I move her hand and the towel away from her face. She looks at me, but says nothing. My hand slides up her arm until it stops on her shoulder. I lean over slightly; her eyes flicker to my mouth.

Our lips touch, hers cold and tempting. My hands will themselves to cradle her neck gently, my fingers entangled in her wet hair. I love the chilly, soft texture of her skin, her faint jasmine scent. My passion grows, and she responds. We search for each other in an intense kiss.

Her arms embrace me, and we twist as a single entity, our upper bodies connected. I feel her wet clothes against mine, her breasts heaving slightly with her respiration. We meld. Our mouths search for each other and our minds travel to another dimension.

***

We move away from each other simultaneously in a slow, unwilling withdrawal. It's a bittersweet moment, coming back to reality.

However, these few seconds afterward, when we stare into each other's eyes and acknowledge our desire, are the sexiest of my life. By far.

She breaks the silence, and the magic is gone. "Your body is so warm," she says, the hoarse quality of her voice taunting me.

"Are you trying to say I'm hot?"

She giggles. It's not a girly giggle, not with her voice. Somehow, that's even more enticing.

"You know, you could catch pneumonia. I don't want to go to the hospital again. We probably should get you out of these wet clothes," I say, grinning.

141

She raises an eyebrow, also grinning. "I'm glad you're concerned about my health."

"Well, you know me: always thoughtful."

She touches her lips absent-mindedly. She's killing me. As if that's not enough, she says, "You're right, I need to get rid of these clothes."

A long pause. "You can drop me off at home," she adds, smiling coyly.

I shake my head, faking disappointment. I don't need to fake much, actually. "You tease," I say.

She smiles a new smile. It lights up her face. Her eyes play with me.

She's definitely changed.

No more Miss Nice Skye.

Chapter 32: Skye

After I enter the house, I realize I can't stop grinning. I lean on the closed door and sigh. Goddess, I'm swooning! What's wrong with me?

Noises come from the kitchen, and I find Gemma there, putting a lasagna in the oven. She looks at me inquisitively—I'm still drenched. I announce I'm going to take a shower.

I catch myself skipping all the way to the stairs. Skye, seriously?

The dresser's mirror doesn't lie. The smile on my face is plastered; my brain can't dismiss it. I can't help but check my reflection, seeing me as Drake saw me: my hair messed up and chunky, my face devoid of make-up, my slightly purple lips. How this wreck of a person had that effect on him, I'll never know. Thank Goddess for the Allure.

I undress regretfully, throwing my clothes, my partners in crime, into the hamper. Something makes me hesitate before I go into the hot shower. I realize it's the idea of having Drake's scent washed from my body. I sigh, but enter the world of warmth anyway.

It's a long shower, where daydreaming is the main activity.

***

My actions after Jane's attack are surprising even me. From my control of the situation at the hospital to my teasing Drake, I am a different person. I hope it's not a temporary thing. I like the new me.

I even confronted Connor. Granted, I haven't called him out yet on our most important issue, but the old Skye would never corner him, curse him, make him feel small. Serves him right.

While I brush my hair in front of the old mirror, a plan comes to mind. In order to find the Singularity, I must be more active. I can't just wait for her magical energy to find me.

Even if she has some kind of magical shield, she can't entirely suppress her energy. I wonder if she uses it for rituals or spells; maybe the places where she used it carry some traces of energy. Even things belonging to her might carry her energy, as they carry her scent. I never knew magic worked this way, but old rules don't seem to apply to the Singularity. I mean, hiding your magical signature? That's unheard of.

Or, maybe if I get really close to people, I can sense it. Maybe if I touch her. Yes, I could try that. I could be like Priscilla, who's unable to carry on a conversation without patting, hugging, poking, leaning over, or touching whoever is chatting with her. Especially men.

That's a good excuse to touch people indiscriminately. I could be like that. Skye, the Personal Space Invader.

One thing is certain: I have to get Jane off my back. Especially if she's indeed a Night witch. Now that she knows she can attack me and I won't go to the police, she is free to try whatever her twisted mind can imagine. I have to show her I'm not afraid, and that I can be dangerous too.

Chapter 33: Drake

The rain doesn't let up. When I'm almost home, I see Mona walking alone. She looks more drenched than Skye.

I approach her slowly, not giving the car any gas. When I get very close, I honk the horn. I was hoping to startle her, but the effect is bigger than that. She lets out a horrific scream and jumps to the side, hitting a fence with her hip. Her hands clutch her chest, and she has a terrified look on her face. She searches for the source of the noise; when she finds me, she begins to cry.

I leave the car, motor running and everything, and rush to her. "Sorry!" I plead. "Sorry, Mona!" She can't control her crying. "Are you okay?"

She manages to answer me between sobs. "No, I'm not okay! I'm very un-okay!" she yells.

"It was just a joke, Mona. I'm sorry. For real," I say. I really don't know what to do. Physical affection is not huge in the Hunter family. I just stand by her, shifting my weight from one leg to another, trying to figure out how I should behave.

Finally we have some contact. She punches me in the guts. I don't even register it, but it pains me in other ways. "Why are you so mean to me?" she asks. "What have I done to you?" She balls up her fists and throws a barrage of weak punches on my chest.

I do what I haven't done in years. I do the unthinkable. I hug my little sister.

She nests herself on my chest, sobbing quietly. I'm her shelter against the heavy rain.

"What's going on?" I ask softly. "Are you in trouble?"

She doesn't answer, but I sense her tensing up a bit.

"Can I help?" I say. She shakes her head, still buried on my chest.

The frustration bubbles up. I hate myself for not being able to help Mona. Out of nowhere, these words escape me: "I wish Mom were here."

Mona immediately stops sobbing and pulls away from me. "Why? She's never done anything. She left us!"

"I don't know. Maybe she could help. She's a mother; that's her job. Right?"

"I don't even remember her, Drake." Mona sounds tired.

"You're lucky," I reply.

"Because she was horrible?"

"No," I say. "Because she was great."

***

I don't remember much about our mother. The pictures that helped me puzzle together my few memories were lost to the fire. In my mind, I have glimpses of her. A short and strong woman of extraordinary beauty. Hiding my face in her curly light brown hair. Being carried away and cared for when I broke my toy car. And songs before we went to sleep.

I could never remember the words though.

She left us absolutely. Besides the pictures lost to the fire, there was nothing else of hers. No clothes, no jewelry, no mementos. Those pictures—and Mona and I—were the only evidence my mother had ever existed.

Dad never told us exactly what happened. In his oblique way, he let us know she didn't love him anymore. He never elaborated on that and deflected our probing questions. With time, we got frustrated and stopped asking.

I was five; Mona was two. Total calls, letters, postcards, emails since then: zero.

Dad rarely speaks of her. We're a happy family, but not a complete one.

After I drive Mona home, I wait in the living room until she changes her clothes. She comes back with her spunkiness restored.

"Playing the big brother role scares you to death, doesn't it?" she asks.

"You have no idea," I say.

"It's sweet of you, but you don't need to worry." She sits on the couch, and I see she brought some purple nail polish with her. She starts to work on her toes.

"Come on, Mona. What's going on?"

She shakes her head, but she doesn't look up. "It's nothing, Drake. Let it go."

"Is it boy stuff?"

She snorts, her eyes still down.

I wish she were more comfortable talking to people. Mona saw a therapist a while ago, but left after two sessions—and nobody can make her return.

"I'm not into boys," she finally says. "Yet," she adds when she sees my expression. She paints one of her toenails deliberately, and I wait. At last, she says, "I'm trying to figure some stuff out. Nothing serious."

"But the reaction you had—"

"I was feeling down, and you scared the hell out of me. Everything came crashing," she says, shrugging. "Don't worry, it's not sex, drugs, or money problems. I won't turn into a Lifetime movie, okay?"

What can I do? I have to trust her. "You know you can count on me, right?"

She finally raises her eyes. She smirks at me and cocks her head.

I feel stupid. "Okay, I don't have any answers, but at least I can listen, right?" I say, my arms wide open in an apologetic gesture.

She doesn't answer. I stand up, write my new cell phone number on a piece of paper, put it by her side on the couch, and leave. My clothes are still wet, and I need to shower.

When I'm almost at the stairs, Mona says, "Hey, Drake. The lighter. I threw it away, okay?"

I don't turn. I just keep walking, smiling.

***

I drop by Boulder's. Of course Sean is there too. I find them in the garage. They're raiding the fridge. Sean has a Mountain Dew, but Boulder got a beer. The Mustang's radio is on, the announcer trying to sound hip and ten years younger.

"Hey, D-Man! Want a cold one?" Sean asks.

"No, my body is a temple," I say.

Boulder snorts. "Yeah, yeah, but the congregants are Doritos," he says, conveniently forgetting he usually asks for two meals at McD's. "Where have you been? You missed school again."

"Drake's got a dark side," Sean says, faking an ominous voice.

"Doesn't your dad get calls from the school?" Boulder asks.

"He does, but I tell him I'm not feeling well." I tap my scar.

Boulder and Sean nod admiringly. I've earned their respect.

"I should have thought of that when I got mine," Boulder says.

We all feel awkward, thinking the same thing. Boulder's concussion reminds us of football. Boulder is sitting out his last season. It'll cost him a college scholarship, probably. In the first game of the season, he took exception to a tackle at his knees, and pushed and shoved the entire o-line of the opposite team (our hated rivals, the Eagles). He got suspended, but he didn't stop there: he stole an Eagles' offensive lineman's girlfriend. In his return game, a rematch, he tried to take on the entire team, earning him a ban for the season and a civil lawsuit for breaking the Eagles' tight-end's collarbone.

He also ended our shot at Regionals. Our own team shunned him. Now he hangs out with us full time.

And talking about it is taboo.

Sean breaks the stalemate. "You still driving the grandma car?" he asks, pointing his soda can in my Volvo's direction.

I shrug. I remember the front seats are still damp from all the wet people who sat on them today: Skye, Mona, me.

More uncomfortable seconds pass. Our minds are still on Boulder's deceased season.

Boulder himself rescues us. "Hey, I didn't see your girl at school today either." He squints. "What's going on, D-Man?"

I look away. Sean laughs. "Is he blushing?" he asks.

The best answer is not answering. But Sean won't let it go. "Nah, it's probably nothing. You're not interested, right, Drake? We only saw you with one girl."

I take the bait. "That's because I'm discreet." No, it's not. Maybe I'm just a… a what? A late bloomer?

Boulder says, "Well, D-Man, if you're not interested, please—

please—let me know. I'd like to tap that."

This gets me going. I put my finger on Boulder's chest, which looks ridiculous, because he's like a foot taller and another foot wider than me. "Hey! Hands off. She's mine," I say.

Boulder and Sean look at each other for about two seconds, and then they laugh at the same time. Radioactive-green soda comes out of Sean's nose. Now I'm really blushing. I step back.

"Who knew there was a caveman inside Drake?" Boulder says. Sean high-fives him.

I look outside, to the rain falling on the street. Images of the make-out session at U-Dub's parking lot come to my mind.

"No, I don't mean it that way. I just like her. I think we might be soul mates," I add. My brain betrays me again.

Sean stares at me. He's too stunned to even laugh.

Boulder puts his free hand on his forehead. "You sooo need to get laid," he says.

Chapter 34: Skye

Drake was supposed to come to Gemma's for our morning ritual, but I called him last night and canceled. Today I'll do a proper ceremony, something that I've been putting off since I arrived. I need more protection. Those improvisations I do every morning help, but aren't powerful enough. The ideal spot would be the wilderness, away from the city vibe. But one of Seattle's many green areas will have to do for now.

I leave the house before dawn and go west to a bus stop on Aurora Avenue. The early morning walk is invigorating. The streets aren't busy: the businesses are closed, except for the coffee shops, and only a little traffic disturbs the chilly city. The bus leaves me a few blocks away from Ravenna Park.

With my hands tucked in my jeans' pockets the whole way, I arrive at the park. I don't see anyone around and just keep walking. Bird calls saturate the air. The early fog brings a primal quality that can only be helpful to my purposes—the mist beckons to me.

At a creek, I discreetly fill a vial for my ritual.

A perfect spot is hard to find, but I settle for a small clearing behind the yellow-leafed trees. It's far from the pathways. I need some privacy, even though I haven't seen other people in the park yet.

Kneeling on the dirt behind a thick hedge, I line up my props on the ground. I do my breathing exercises, and when I feel relaxed enough, I begin the placement. The only moment I lose focus is when I ring my ceremonial bell: someone might hear it, even from a distance.

In the dirt, I draw a circle, then a pentagram inside it with my ceremonial knife—my athame. It has a white handle with my family crest embossed in gold. The preparation is part of the ritual, helping the Sisters transition into a heightened state of consciousness.

Before touching each of my items, I rub a little bit of the lake water from the vial on my hands. It doesn't matter the water is not clean, just that it's from a natural source.

I put a single candle in the middle of my arrangement and light it. I add my selected herbs to the cast iron mortar: wormwood and hyssop. Then it's time for my special gesture, unique to my ritual: I touch my chest, mouth, and forehead slowly with my left hand. A long time ago, I realized this combination brings me peace and comfort, so I incorporated it into my rituals.

After grinding the herbs with my iron pestle, I light the mixture. The flames liberate its fumes, which I inhale.

I pray to the Goddess for protection. I ask for special shields for me and Drake. I beg for Mum's health (even though I know London's Mothers are performing much more powerful circles of prayers with the same intent).

My own magical energy meshes with the world's magic and returns to me. The sensation, an elation unlike any other I've ever experienced, overtakes me.

Judi, my teacher before my Daybreak, once described it to me as "sensual," which at the time didn't help my understanding of it at all. After she saw my twelve-year-old, clueless face, she settled on, "it's like a hot shower after a long walk in cold rain."

It's much more than that. It's a high, not a drug high, but a universal, ancient energy flow that, for those brief moments, invades your body and permeates you, bringing clarity to the mind, peace to the heart, confidence to the gut, and happiness to the soul.

I reach an enlightenment that I can't explain or understand. Only it doesn't last. I don't care.

It's the instant you're one with the Goddess. It's what I live for.

***

"Are you all right?" Priscilla says. "You missed school yesterday."

"I'm fine," I lie, hoping my hair still hides my scar. I thought about wearing a hat, but decided against it. It would call attention to the area, not divert it. Besides, the Allure Charm should take care of it soon.

I open my locker and stare at my books as if they're strangers.

Priscilla smiles. "Oh, good. I thought your mother... How is she?" She starts to rummage in her locker too.

I smile back at her. Who would have guessed Priscilla would be so thoughtful? "She's doing great. I mean, she likes to be pampered." I call Mum every morning now, which is the middle of the afternoon in London, and she tells me about her day. So strange how I'm feeling more connected to her now, half a world away.

I still feel a little guilty about not telling Priscilla the truth about my mother. It's not that I don't trust her; I just need more time. I've always been reserved. It's hard to change overnight.

My True Sight makes me tingle. Not for the first time, I wished I could turn it off. Jane is probably parking, and I can sense her all the

153

way from there. Since the sensation intensifies the closer the subject gets to me, I can trace Jane's steps all around school. I have a personal Jane radar. Sure, it's useful, but it's also a constant reminder of the danger she represents to me.

And to the Singularity.

"Hel-lo?" Priscilla says in a singsongy voice. "You've been staring into your locker like a zombie."

"I… uh… forgot to do my assignment. Again," I say. Actually, this is true. "Can I copy yours? Or your notes?"

Priscilla snorts, but tastefully. "You're clearly confusing me with someone else," she says. "Schoolwork is not my thing."

I smirk and get my books.

Priscilla closes her locker and nudges me with her elbow, whispering, "Soooo, I noticed Drake disappeared yesterday too. Anything you want to share?"

Okay. I can't hide everything. During lunchtime, I tell her about my day with him. Omitting all the supernatural parts, of course.

"That sounds like one über-hot day!" she says. "What did you do after that?" Her yogurt spoon is halfway to her mouth, and not moving.

"He drove me home."

Her eyebrows rise. A mischievous smile sprouts on her lips. "And?" she says, her spoon trembling a bit.

"He went home," I say.

She stares at me for a while, and then finally eats her spoonful of yogurt.

"It was just kissing," I lie.

"It may be. But making out is a gateway drug to sex, you know?" In between spoon licks, she asks me, matter-of-factly, "Aren't you

154

guys doing it?"

I giggle—what's wrong with me? "I just got back," I say, trying to deflect her question. "We're not even dating."

Priscilla leans over and whispers, "You have done it, right?"

I don't answer. She senses something is wrong. She lays her spoon down on the table and turns to face me. I know my expression has darkened.

"I've done it," I say, with a cold voice that isn't mine.

Priscilla's response is to scan the cafeteria for prying eyes. Then she stands up, pulling me by the arm. I don't move. She tries again, now with surprising strength for a girl her size. I let myself be hoisted up. She holds my hand and commands, "Follow me."

She takes me outside, to this lonely picnic table behind the school. I didn't even know this part of the school existed. No windows face us; not even the cafeteria noises can reach us.

"Good place to make out," she says, as an explanation, while we sit side-by-side. "Sorry," she adds, realizing her faux-pas. "What happened?" she asks. Her voice is soft.

I've never talked about this.

Don't feel sorry for yourself, Skye.

Cleansed by my morning ritual, I feel safe. Free. Unafraid.

I take a deep breath and look into her understanding eyes. I say, "I did it. In London with Connor, my ex. He is two years older. We'd been dating, and I knew he had hooked up with other girls, even when we were together. Finally, we did it."

I pause, not for effect, but because I never spoke the next words aloud. "But I didn't want to," I add.

Priscilla's eyebrows go up and the corners of her lips go down in a concerned expression. Her eyes are pools of sorrow. She rests her hand over mine.

"Did he...?" She can't finish the sentence.

I shake my head. "No. No, it wasn't like that. But he did force me in other ways. He knew I was unsure, that I wasn't ready. I thought the only way I could make us exclusive was by going along. He could have stopped; he could have waited. It's like this invisible force, this pressure..." I stop. Putting it into words is harder than I imagined.

She just taps my hand. I'm glad she doesn't feel the need to say something. May the Goddess bless silent friends.

After a while, I'm ready to continue. "It was an ugly, negative, bitter thing. I didn't know... I didn't realize I could have stopped him—us. It was all my fault."

This stirs Priscilla's indignation. "It wasn't your fault at all. He manipulated you. He was older, in a position of power; he knew he had influence over you."

I shake my head. "It was my responsibility too. I should've been strong. But what I can't forget is that when I didn't enjoy it as much as him, he said it was all my fault, that I was empty inside. And after I made it clear I didn't want to do it again, he dumped me."

Priscilla's jaw drops. I know the feeling; I've had it for the last two years.

I can't stop talking. "While I traveled with Mum, he strayed. I was afraid of losing him. How can you share your life with someone for so long, and then it's over?" Empty, yes, but only *after* he left.

"Jerk!" she says, unnecessarily. "Actually, he's beyond jerk level, now he's been officially promoted to douche bag," she says, maybe trying to make me feel better.

Priscilla hugs me. I welcome her embrace. For a long time I believed it was my fault, only mine. Her gesture is an acknowledgment that I'm not insane, that he's indeed a jerk.

During our hug I try to forget that even after he left me, I was stupid enough to pine for him, to fantasize about us together again. Connor used to take me out around London, but after he dumped me I never returned to those places: not only did I worry I would run into him, but to me it was as if the places belonged to him.

I've been afraid for too long.

I'm so grateful to Priscilla. She realized something was wrong with me and made me spill my guts, which was exactly what I needed. To put it into words. To vent. I don't know, to have some closure.

We disengage, and I just nod at her. I feel lighter. She smiles and I realize I have a true friend.

To my credit, I don't cry. This new Skye is already stronger than I expected.

Chapter 35: Drake

After school, I go to the pool building. We didn't report anything to the school, and I want to know what people think about the mess we left.

In a way, it's like returning to a crime scene. Not *my* crime, but still.

Coach Summers is in there, alongside Bill, the janitor. Bill doesn't look happy.

When Coach sees me, he beckons me to join them.

"Hey, Mr. Hunter," Coach says. "Did you do a few laps on Monday?"

"No. Concussion, remember?" I point to my head. I really recommend getting a concussion; it's an excuse for all times. "Why?"

Bill's annoyed voice answers me. "Some funny guy came over and spilled paint into the pool, on the stands, even in the lobby. It's all clean now. Damn tough to get rid of it." He shakes his head, and I get the feeling he'd like nothing more than get those imaginary vandals alone. "We should have locks on the doors."

"As I asked you two years ago," Coach says.

Bill ignores the jab. "Anyway, Summers, I'm done here. See you at the league tonight? A pint later?"

Coach and Bill do an awkward handshake thing. Bill leaves and

Coach turns to me.

"Are you going back to swimming?" he asks.

"Sure thing," I say.

"Any chance the hit on your head made you see things clearly? Do you want to be part of the team?" Coach crosses his arms, his standard posture.

"I'm afraid not," I reply.

"But you're a good swimmer; you wouldn't be embarrassed. You could even be JV, if you prefer. Come on, Drake. It would improve your standing with the girls."

No, it wouldn't. But I say, "That's not a good enough reason, Coach."

"Or the boys," he says, raising his hands. "I don't judge, as long as you keep it away from the locker room."

I need to parade around with a girl soon, so these gay rumors don't leave the joke realm. "I'm unsure if what you just said violates some code of conduct," I say.

"It actually does. Go report me." Coach makes a dismissive gesture.

I shrug. "Nah. Too much trouble."

"As always, a kid's laziness helps me keep my job."

He gives me a little punch on the arm and leaves. I stare at the pool, sighing. The school has no idea what happened. Skye and Jane dodged a bullet.

I go into the locker room, change into my *manly* swimming trunks, and get back to the pool. While I stretch, I wonder if I'll be able to feel Skye's blood in the water.

Without a previous agreement, we avoided each other at school. We're back to that are-we-or-aren't-we place. Weird place to be.

Every time I saw her today, I wished I could do something. Scream to the whole school we're together. Run to her and kiss her. Dance.

"Wow! Why have you been hiding this six pack, Drake?" A voice echoes in the building.

I turn and see Priscilla with her hands on her hips, looking at me admiringly. At her side, Skye suppresses a giggle.

Priscilla turns to Skye and says, "Seriously? Look at him! He should walk around shirtless!"

"I know!" Skye says.

Okay, this is going from flattering to embarrassing real fast. "Don't you girls have Prince Charming to dream about?" I yell.

"Oh, but we do," says Priscilla. After Skye slaps her softly on the arm, Priscilla adds, "Okay, okay. I'll leave." She kisses Skye on both cheeks and walks away.

I approach Skye. Self-conscious, I cross my arms around my midriff. I'm not used to this type of attention. "I think I just saw a live demonstration of what a BFF is," I say when I get close to her.

"Isn't it nice?" Skye asks, then she mutters, "We're going to the mall tomorrow."

I fake a shocked expression. "Don't turn into..." But words fail me.

"Into what?"

"Someone else."

She smirks. "Don't worry."

We stand in front of each other. I don't know how to act, and I bet she doesn't either. Something crosses my mind. "Are you okay? I mean, being back here."

She nods a few times while scanning the pool area, as if reassuring herself. "I guess so. Besides, you're here with me."

All right, even I know I can't pass that up. I lean forward and kiss her. She takes my face into her hands and prolongs our entanglement.

I'm about to embrace her, when I become suddenly aware of my attire. I gently break the lip lock, hating myself for it.

"So, I wasn't sure if I should pick you up this morning," I say, trying to disguise the awkward moment and failing epically. "You told me you'd cast a spell on me."

Her eyes dart around us, but we're alone. She smiles. "I already did that."

"I'll say."

Skye chuckles. "No, I mean, the Protection spell. Even if you're not there, I can do a weak one. But you're right. You should drop by in the morning so I can do a proper one. Would you mind giving me a ride every morning?"

"I'd love to."

She looks at me obliquely for a moment. "Okay. We have to talk."

Uh-oh. "Yeah…"

"Don't worry. It's not *the* talk. But I need to know. Are we a thing?"

"A thing?" I ask.

"Yeah. I mean…" She looks away.

This is hard! "I guess we're a thing. I just don't know *which* thing."

"Okay."

"Is that what you were asking?"

She nods. "Pretty much."

I put on my mischievous face. "You know, being a thing brings some responsibilities."

"Really?" She smirks. "Like what? Do we have to hang out more often?"

I nod. "And for longer. And make out. Making out is essential. Don't forget that."

"Hard to forget. And maybe… flaunt it?"

"What do you mean?"

She does a deliberate cutesy shrug. "Let's not hide anymore."

This is serious. Our thing is now an official thing. I'm all for it.

"I'm all for it," I say, agreeing with myself. I lean forward for another kiss, wardrobe be damned, but she puts a finger on my chest.

"Later," she says. "Now I want to watch you in the water." She nods in the pool's direction.

"Really?" I ask.

She slides her finger down to my abs. "Come on, put on a show for me."

When she wants, she can melt a stone statue. "Sure," I say, turning and starting my strut to the pool. Before I get away from her, though, she slaps my butt. Softly, but still.

I hear her giggle, but I don't turn to face her. She does know how to turn me on. I just walk faster to the pool and dive in, welcoming the cold water.

Chapter 36: Skye

I'm glad my Jane alarm isn't going off. She left right after the bell, but I still asked Priscilla to come with me to the pool. Despite what I said to Drake, coming here does make me uncomfortable. How could it not?

But I don't regret coming. Priscilla is right. Drake should never wear tops! Ever. I have no idea why he doesn't show it off, but his upper body is yummy. He's not buff like those gym rat guys, but lean—skinny and muscular at the same time. He looks a bit stronger and taller with his shirt off. And his abs, Goddess! What is that?

Why do you hide it, Drake? Of all of Greenwood High's secrets, you are the most delicious.

Watching him swimming soothes me. Maybe it's the repetitive movements, the cadence, the metronomic splashing sounds, but it gives me a center. I see his sinuous underwater figure do the same movements over and over, in a leisurely pace, never tiring or slowing down.

It gives me peace. I bet it does the same to him.

The minutes pass without me noticing, and soon he's out of the water. His heaving chest and the water glistening on his body make him look even hotter.

He smiles at me, and I wonder if he's aware of his effect on me.

163

Either he's a gentleman or the most oblivious guy I've ever met.

"An athlete," I say. "Who knew? I had you pegged as the couch-and-video-game type."

"Why can't I be both?" he says, shrugging, his words difficult as he catches his breath. He comes closer and shakes his head a few times, raining water everywhere, including on me.

"Stop it!" I say.

"Come on! You've been drenched yesterday and the day before. A few drops of water won't hurt you." He thinks he's made a bad joke, because he stops smiling and says, "Sorry."

Before I can say anything, he adds, "Do you think you'd be okay going into the pool soon? I just thought it would be nice if we could enjoy the pool together."

"I don't swim," I say.

He stares at me and then bursts out laughing.

"What?"

"A witch who doesn't swim," he says between laughs.

"Witches drown…" I say when I realize what he means.

"I'm sorry," he says, raising his hand apologetically. "I just can't stop."

I chuckle. "That's not the worst thing," I say. "I'm also allergic to cats."

I love laughing with him.

***

Somehow I end up in the men's locker room. Drake wouldn't let me wait alone for him in the lobby or in his car. We agreed I'd be close to the showers, talking to him the whole time so he knew I was around. The jury is still out on whether he's overly concerned or just being naughty.

"It smells worse than the women's locker room," I say, my voice loud so he can hear me over the shower running.

"I bet the women's locker smells like flowers, and honey, and... angel's breath or whatever."

"Not really," I reply.

I've not been a half of a couple for a while. It'll be interesting to see how I mesh with a personality so different from Connor's.

It doesn't frighten me. Being in a relationship, I mean. I thought I'd be scared, but the reality is, I'm tired of being scared.

I'm looking forward to this. And to those abs.

Chapter 37: Drake

This is my first official "dating situation." Of all the ways I imagined this, I've never expected the first thing in the morning would be participating in spell casting.

The one she chooses is a howler. I have to lie down—on her bed, no less—while she does this cleansing thing all over my body. She never lays her hands on me, but knowing her touch is less than an inch above my skin is pleasuring and torturing at the same time.

I try to focus on other things, like the incense burning (sandalwood, she told me) that washes away the slightly moldy odor of the house. Skye's bed sheets are soft and smell like her.

But then I hear and feel her breath close to me, and my heart pounds hard again.

The possibility that she's teasing me crosses my mind.

"You can open your eyes," she says. "We're done." It's both a relief and a disappointment. She takes care of the disappointment part by leaning over me and giving me a gooooood kiss. I want more, but she breaks it up and says, "We're going to be late."

While I leave the bed, Skye snuffs out her incense, and a brief flashback of my house fire comes to me.

"Magic feels awfully normal," I say.

She shrugs while putting her things away. "If you think about it, it's not magic. It's just knowledge that most of the world hasn't gained yet."

"Who discovered it? And how?"

"I'm not giving you a history lesson. But it was noticed by accident a long time ago. A happy accident. Like discovering gunpowder or penicillin. You know what? It's like science."

I chuckle. "Way to remove anything magical from magic."

"No, seriously. Magic is science. Imagine that centuries ago, if you were sick, you'd go to a witch doctor or shaman, who would poke and probe you. He'd give you a mysterious substance, tell you to drink it up at dawn and dusk, and to rest. Is that any different from a visit to the doctor today?"

I ponder her claim while she stuffs her backpack. When she reaches to the top shelf to get a book, her shirt goes up, and I see the tattoo the guys mentioned. It's a bird that resembles an eagle, only it has a crown, and its feathers look different. A phoenix, I guess. The drawing is silver with a black outline. It begins waist-high on her right side and continues down her hip, the rest of the design hidden by her jeans.

"Hey, nice tat," I say.

Skye turns, startled, touching her side instinctively, but she recovers soon. "Oh, that. Haven't you seen this before?"

I'm about to point out I was the only one at school who didn't see it, but I don't want to be indelicate. I didn't even notice it when I was performing CPR on her.

Instead, I move my hands close to her and say, "May I?"

She nods, but her eyes are trained on me. I raise her shirt a bit and caress her tattoo with my fingertips. It gives her goose bumps. "It's silver. Isn't it rare?"

"It's a tradition amongst my kind," she says.

With my index finger, I lower the hem of her jeans just an inch. The bird's tail continues even further down.

"Is it a phoenix?" I ask, prolonging the moment. I won't lie: I enjoy touching her skin.

"Yes," she answers.

"Love the artwork. I'd love to see the whole design," I whisper, half-joking.

She squints playfully and delicately brushes my hand away. "Sure you would. Come on, we have to go."

I let out a deep, theatrical sigh and give the tattoo one last longing stare.

When I open the bedroom door for her, we find out that Aunt Gemma is waiting for us at the end of the stairs. And she doesn't look happy.

"Wait until I tell your mother about you bringing boys to your room," Aunt Gemma says.

It doesn't faze Skye. "I talked to her earlier this morning. I should have mentioned it, actually. Knowing her, she'd be so proud of me."

"Young lady—"

"Aunt Gemma, we're behaving," Skye says, friendly. "Besides, we've only been there for five minutes. If we were doing something, that would have been… a letdown."

Bad Skye.

***

I arrive at school as a conqueror. I have a glimpse of Jane's life, with all eyes on Skye and me. We leave the Volvo, our royal carriage, and make our way to the entrance, cutting through the gossip and the incredulous stares. It's a little sad to realize I'm as shallow as everybody else, but it feels so good to be dating her.

As if to reinforce the image, I put my arm over Skye's shoulders, and she welcomes it. She seems to be enjoying it, but she tenses a little and looks at her right in a sudden motion.

Following her gaze, I see Jane and Brianna talking to each other, away from us. Brianna is the first girl I've ever kissed. The one who created my good-kisser reputation.

It doesn't surprise me that Jane and she were on speaking terms (I mean, if Brianna was capable of kissing me when I was a pariah, she is capable of anything). But I find it weird when Brianna nods, then walks in the direction of the school entrance, her path on a collision course with ours.

Skye and I don't stop, but we keep staring at Brianna. When Brianna is close to us, she whispers, "Blinding potion, bitch."

"Hey! Watch yourself," I warn her.

I release Skye and put myself between the two of them. Brianna turns and starts walking back to Jane.

But Skye takes two quick steps toward Brianna and touches my first make-out partner on the back of her neck. It's a soft touch—not a slap, or a shove. Somehow, that startles Brianna even more. Brianna panics, yelling and rubbing her neck repeatedly where Skye touched her.

Skye retreats to my side, giving Brianna a triumphant look. Which only makes Brianna even more freaked out. She runs to Jane, who holds her, and tells her something. But Brianna won't calm down, and Jane slaps her on the face, in the only way Jane knows it: hard.

Brianna is stunned but stops her crazy act. Jane grabs her by the arm and drags her to the back of the parking lot.

When they leave, everyone's stares turn to Skye and me. Nobody understands what just happened, least of all me.

Skye holds my hand and leads me through the school gates, smiling as if we had never been interrupted. "She's not the Singularity," she whispers to me. "Who is she?"

"My past," I say, as if I have a past.

Skye's eyebrows go up. "The gossip girl you kissed, huh? Interesting."

Instead of leading me through the doors, Skye makes a sharp detour, and we arrive at a picnic table behind the cafeteria. "What did she mean?" I ask, seeing we're alone.

"The cream. It wasn't an allergic reaction. Jane and that girl put a blinding concoction in my moisturizer. And your ex led me outside and yanked off my towel. I recognized her voice."

It's like one of those blurry pictures that suddenly snaps into focus.

"She still likes you," Skye says.

Afraid to say anything, I realize that every girl I have ever kissed is a psycho of some sort.

Maybe magic *is* real: I must have some curse or something.

Chapter 38: Skye

After the incident with Drake's ex, the school has a few more smaller surprises for us. At different times, both Drake and I are summoned to the principal's office to account for our days off. We give our versions (mine: invented Mum's health complications; his: invented returning headaches). The principal is very understanding. Drake and I are becoming expert liars.

When we're at our lockers, Priscilla asks me what happened with Brianna.

"She's jealous," I reply.

"Okay. What about you?" she asks me. When she sees my puzzled expression, she adds, "You went after her! I thought you were going to hit her."

I try to think of a good explanation, but the best I can come up is, "I just wanted to let her know Drake's with me now."

Priscilla chuckles. "You *are* into him!"

I smile slyly, but I don't answer.

The whole day I sense Jane around school. She's like a shark circling me. She never gets close, but the constant reminder takes a toll on my nerves. When the final bell rings, I can't wait to leave the grounds. Drake gives me a ride. We stop at a deli and go eat the subs (mine vegetarian) at the Gas Works Park.

He shivers and says, "It never gets this cold in November. Can't your kind slow down global warming?"

"We already did. This—" I point up "—is us slowing it down!"

He stares at me, hoping to detect a lie, but I keep my poker face. This is fun.

"Seattle is growing on me," I say, gazing over to the boats cruising Lake Union. Even on a cloudy Thursday afternoon, the waters are busy. "Have you lived here all your life?"

"Yep," he says, relaxed.

I reach for his plate and take a carrot stick. "In the same house?"

"Same neighborhood. We had to move after our first house burned down."

The stick stops halfway to my mouth. "Your house burned down? How come you never told me this?"

"Well, it's not something I volunteer on the first few dates. *Hi, I'm Drake. I set fire to my house.*"

"*You* did it?"

"Not intentionally. I'm not an arsonist."

I finally eat the carrot.

But this heavy silence is upon us. Drake probably notices it too. He has more to say. "Okay, I'll tell you. I stole a cigarette from my father and went to the basement to smoke it. I coughed a lot, my first time, you know, and dropped the butt. I went for a glass of water in the kitchen, then outside for some air, and completely forgot about it. Next thing I know, the walls were hot, the curtains on fire, and I..." His voice trails.

"What?"

"I rushed upstairs and found Mona. She was unconscious—the smoke. I almost killed her, Skye."

172

My hand reaches for him. I stroke his hair, his face, and he holds my hand in his, pressing it against his cheek.

"I don't like to talk about it," he mumbles.

"It was an accident, Drake," I say.

He nods, but he looks away toward the lake.

I move behind him, sit on the grass with my legs around him, and embrace him. He leans back on me. I kiss the side of his neck softly, once. We stay quiet for a while, but this time the silence is comfortable.

I touch his messed-up hair. "Are you going to do something about your hair?" I ask.

"Nah. I'm just having a bad hair year," he says softly.

That's the last thing he says for a long time. I just keep running my fingers through his hair.

The cold wind makes us get even closer. The cuddling is so simple but so satisfying. I forgot how nice it's to... be together.

"Where are you going to college?" His voice is distant.

That's an odd question. "I'm not. At least, I don't have plans yet. You?"

"Don't know. Don't have the money. Yet."

"Did you even apply?" I ask him.

"Nah. It's no use. Mona is the future of the family. If only one of us goes to college, it should be her."

Aha! That's the link between college and our previous subject. I guess that's his guilt talking, but I don't ask him about it. Instead, I say, "But what are you going to do?"

"I guess I'll just backpack across Europe."

"Really?" I did it. Kind of. I used taxis, trains, airplanes, and four-star hotels. Since it doesn't count as a backpacking experience, I don't mention it. "Do you like Europe?"

"Not really. It just sounds like something a slacker like me would do." He shrugs.

"You're not a slacker. Priscilla told me you do well in school. That you're even doing Pre-Calc. Can't you get cash for college?"

"I can always sell my body to some rich horny Euro women." His voice is mischievous.

"Like me? Is that what you're saying, you naughty boy?"

"Maybe." He tries to rotate his body to face me, but I don't let him.

"If that's what you want, let me check the goods," I say. Since I'm still embracing him from behind, my hands go under his shirt, caressing his chest, his abs. He doesn't complain. "Yeah, I think we can make a deal."

He chuckles. "Why is it *sell* my body? Shouldn't it be *lease* my body?"

"That's beyond my area of expertise."

Even with my playful excuse gone, I continue to explore his upper body with my hands.

He chuckles softly. "Are you trying to seduce me, Miss Skye?"

I grin, but I don't answer him. It's insane being around him. Every glance, every touch, every thought feels like foreplay.

I think about our future. I think I may be over my bad experiences with Connor. Talking to Priscilla helped me. Apparently, all I needed was some sympathy.

With Drake, I'd be starting over, in a different relationship. A different *kind* of relationship. Drake and I are equals. I trust him. That makes all the difference.

With Connor, I wanted the experience. With Drake, I want

Drake.

I plant a gentle kiss on the nape of his neck. He's dreamy. Delicious.

Without realizing it, I blurt it out. "You're dreamy-licious…"

He doesn't say anything for a few seconds, probably confused by my assertion. "Even my girlfriend is calling me names now…"

To my surprise, I don't flinch after he utters the GF word.

Chapter 39: Drake

Sometimes I feel like Skye does everything she can to drive me crazy. In many, many ways.

Her hands are all over me, making my blood boil—the good kind of boiling.

She coaxed a confession out of me about my past I have never discussed with anyone.

She inspired me to reconnect with my little sister.

Oh, yeah—and the witchcraft stuff.

After I call her my girlfriend, I expect a reaction of some kind. Her body stiffening, her hands leaving me, some sign. But nothing changes.

I have no idea why it's so important to me to label our relationship. Maybe I'm afraid she'll leave me again. I don't know. But at least we don't have to talk about it and try to define what our "thing" is anymore.

We just *are*. And that's good enough for me.

My mind wanders. I come back to this morning.

"Why did you go after Brianna?" I ask.

"After I sensed Jane's presence—"

"As one does…" I cut her off.

"Hey! After I sensed Jane, I had an idea. I had to touch Brianna to make sure she's not the Singularity," she says. "I think that if I touch her I can feel her hidden magical energy."

"But didn't she touch you when she trapped you in the locker room?"

"I was distressed at the time; if she was leaving just traces of energy, it would be hard to sense it. I mean, my face was burning. I'm not sure I'd notice the tingling sensation of another Sister nearby."

I nod, as if it makes perfect sense. I still can't believe that I believe it. "Do some more magic," I say. "Something that I can see. It doesn't need to be anything amazing, just something that will show me neither of us is crazy."

I feel her chest heaving behind me, probably a deep sigh. "Let me think of something," she says.

***

The next day we are at the school lot, and I have a decision to make. We arrive early, after our morning spell/lay-on hands/tease session. The warm mug Skye has just handed me looks suspicious.

"What is that?" I ask.

"You wanted proof that I'm a witch," Skye answers.

"Is this poison?" The concoction is purplish and smelly. "What did you put in there?"

"You don't want to know." But she sees my face, sighs, and adds, "Okay. Among other things, beets, bug juice, some roots I'm not—"

"Wait! 'Bug juice'?" I don't think she's kidding.

She chuckles. "It's just a different kind of smoothie. Just drink the damn thing." She pushes the mug towards my mouth, but I resist.

I take a step back. "You still didn't answer me. What is it?" I unscrew the lid. I want to take small sips. Just in case.

"It's a Truth potion," she says, looking away.

I only raise my eyebrows until she looks at me again.

She extends her hand. "If you don't believe me, let me take a sip and ask me again."

"Ha-ha," I say. "No, seriously, what is it?"

Boulder comes out of nowhere. "Hey, Romeo," he greets me. He nods toward Skye. "Ms. Romeo."

She rolls her eyes.

He turns to me. "Tickets arrived, D-Man. You owe me sixty bucks."

Tickets? "What—"

"Hey, I need some coffee." He takes the mug from my hands.

"No!" Skye and I plead at the same time.

Boulder looks at us suspiciously and grins. "What?" He raises the mug above his head. My girlfriend and I jump like small children trying to reach it.

"Don't drink it," I say.

Boulder wags his finger at us. "It's spiked! Is that it? You little devils." He lowers the mug and takes a deep breath. "It smells nasty! It's not coffee. What is it? Energy drink? Blueberry juice? Açai? I love açai."

I try to wrestle the mug away from him, but Skye lowers my arm. She shakes her head, sporting an impish smile.

He looks at both of us, shrugs, and takes a deep gulp from the potion. "That's the stuff," he says before downing the rest of the contents. We can almost see the flow of liquid inside his massive neck.

"Any time now," Skye murmurs to me.

Boulder wipes his mouth with the back of his hand. "*That's* how we should start the day."

Skye nods. She's so confident, I don't doubt her anymore.

"You two look particularly hot today," Boulder says.

I raise my eyebrows. Skye gives me a furtive look. "Really, Boulder?" she says. "So you think Drake's hot?"

"Sure he is," he says with a tone that implies that Skye is crazy for doubting my hotness.

I cringe.

But Boulder is on a roll. "I try to surround myself with handsome men. Not that I'm into guys, but half the fun of being in the gym is checking out each other's bodies, isn't it? Comparing. And it's nice to be around beautiful people. Like you, Skye. And The Predator. Where is she?" His eyes scan the lot. "Oh, she's not around."

"Do you like Priscilla, Boulder?" I ask.

"I love her, D-Man. She rocked my world. She caught me right after the football ban, and she was there for me." He nods to himself, absorbed in deep thought, and I see his teary eyes. "I don't know what I'm going to do without a scholarship. It keeps me awake at night."

He shakes his head. I'm afraid to say anything.

"I was hoping she would stay with me; that she'd make things easier. I thought my big stick would be enough to keep her around, but she told me she isn't a one-man girl."

Skye mouths to me, "big stick?" I nod. Boulder is anything but modest. She giggles.

Her giggle catches his attention. "And you, sweetheart, don't you dare go breaking D-Man's heart."

"What makes you think I'm going to walk out on him?"

"Historical evidence," Boulder says. He points to her. "Remember—"

"A reckoning, I know," Skye says.

Huh?

Boulder nods and hands me the mug back. "Catch you lovebirds later," he says and walks away slowly, his shoulders hunched. A never-before-seen posture on him.

"Is he going to be okay?" I ask Skye.

"It should wear off in a few minutes. I made it mild." She looks amused.

"So, this potion causes depression or what?"

"Most truths are unpleasant, Drake," she says.

I stare at her. "Is that what you were trying to do to me? What were you going to ask me?"

She grins. "Nothing too personal. But don't be mad. Cheer up. Your best friend thinks you're hot!"

She has a way of making me believe that things can't get any weirder. And of shattering that belief moments later.

"That's beyond disturbing," I say. Now this thought will never leave my mind.

"He's not the only one, you know," she says, resting her hands on my sides and pulling me to her.

I can't stay mad for long.

Chapter 40: Skye

After school, I want to hang out with Drake, but he has some errands to do for his father. One of the drawbacks of owning a car. So I call Priscilla, asking if we can go on our mall excursion.

She gets excited and shows up at my door twenty minutes later. I jump into her watered-green Prius, where blasting angry-chick rock welcomes me.

"Wow, she is pissed," I say, referring to the girl singer.

"What?" Priscilla looks at me bewildered. "Those are empowering songs."

"Sure they are," I reply, but she can't hear me over the squeaky voice and heavy beat from the speakers. I try again, yelling, and now without the sarcasm, "I don't think writing twelve songs about how you're over your ex, and then singing them in front of thousands of people every night for six months is empowering. Or healthy. Actually, it's a clear sign she's definitely *not* over the guy."

"I don't know what you're talking about."

After a while, we naturally raise the volume of our voices so we can talk over the music. Turning it down never crosses Priscilla's mind.

"So, what are we shopping for today?" she asks after we go inside the multi-floor consumerism temple.

My cheeks blush a bit. "I was thinking about a nice new outfit... for a date."

I've never seen such joy in her eyes. It's as if I handed her a mission from the heavens.

"I thought you'd never ask," she says. "How come you're not a New York snob is beyond me. You can't be a hot girl if you're dressed in rags."

"Hey!"

"Sorry," she says, very un-sorry. She grabs my wrist and drags me with her. "Are you thinking about a whole outfit? Do you mean dressy? We should start with shoes and then build the whole thing up. I know just the place."

We go into one of those snotty stores where the salespeople truly believe their knowledge of shoes is some kind of ancient wisdom known only by the chosen ones. Sometimes they go out of their way to be unpleasant. It makes me uncomfortable, but the hostile environment doesn't scare Priscilla. Actually, she relishes it.

After she out-bitches and out-eye-rolls the entire staff, we leave with an obnoxiously priced pair of Jimmy Choo peep toe pumps that have absolutely nothing to do with me. Priscilla assures me that a trained eye will be amazed by them, though.

Withstanding the ordeal earns us a snack break. We stop by a juice place, and I learn that ordering a smoothie in Seattle is as confusing as ordering a coffee. We find a table for ourselves at the food court.

"What?" she asks.

"The shoes are too fancy," I say. "I don't believe Drake would take me to a fancy place."

She nods, absorbed in her thoughts. I think it's a good time to tell

182

her about Mum. I spill everything.

"Get out!" Priscilla squeals while slapping the small table with both hands, her bracelets clacking. She leans forward. "Do you have pictures of her?"

I show her a couple I carry in my purse.

"That's unreal! A movie star!"

I snort. "It's not like that. She's not that young, not that famous…"

"Are you kidding me? I see her in movie posters all the time. She looks good."

"Airbrushing," I say.

Priscilla gives me a weak slap on the arm, her sharp fingernails slightly scratching me. "Stop it. She's got an Oscar and everything."

"It's in London. I'll show you when you visit us."

Her mouth's sides almost tear when she smiles. I think it's about the Oscar, but she says, "I'd love to visit you."

"Aren't you mad I didn't tell you earlier?" I say, hesitant.

She shakes her head. "Don't be silly. I'd do the same. It's cool that you told me." She slurps her smoothie loudly. "So, you are a princess, and Drake is broke. That's why you're concerned with the pricey shoes."

This makes me feel shallow. "I don't mean it in a bad way. It's just I don't know if he's touchy about it."

She nods while drinking more smoothie. It seems fruit helps her think.

"So, here's what we're going to do. We'll go easy on the rest of your clothes. Something breezy, but classy."

"What about the shoes?" I ask.

"Keep them. You still can use them on your date. Men don't

183

notice shoes unless you're stepping on their chests."

I want to ask, but I leave it at that.

***

On our way back, I tell Priscilla about the new me.

"You helped. You listened when I needed it," I say.

She dismisses it as if it's no big deal. Maybe it isn't, to her.

"As you may have noticed, I don't have many friends either," she says. "I mean, I'll never be the prom queen. Of course I'm hated. Every girl in the school is dating an ex of mine. Only transfers like you talk to me."

I had never thought of that. I'm unsure of what to say, but Priscilla moves on quickly.

"Let's celebrate the new you," she says, enthusiastic. "Let's do something crazy."

"Like what?" I'm scared of whatever Priscilla considers 'crazy.'

She taps her fingernails on the steering wheel. "What wouldn't the old Skye do?"

I shrug. "Anything exciting? Actually, anything, period."

"Be more specific," Priscilla says.

"I wouldn't date, but that's taken care of. Going out with friends meant dinners and back home. No sports or…"

"You lived in New York and London and didn't take advantage of nightlife there?" Before I can answer, she snaps. "I know! Girls Night Out! Woo-hoo!" she shouts.

"Woo-hoo," I say quietly—and lamely.

Priscilla tsk-tsks me. "We're going to have to work on your woo-hoos," she says.

***

All the clubs are carding. Priscilla does have a fake ID, but I don't (mine is valid, and from the state of New York). We're shut out of all the Pioneer Square bars. Priscilla chats with two skinny guys wearing beanies and t-shirts two sizes too small. They look like a pair of colorful Q-Tips.

Not that I can mock them. Priscilla picked my outfit: jeans, high heels (killing my feet), a rock band t-shirt (killing my pride), and a leather jacket she let me borrow. I'm afraid to stand alone in the street; somebody might offer me money any time now. I walk up to her.

"Let's go," I say. "It's no use."

"Hi, Tina," Priscilla answers me, her eyes full of meaning. "Evan here—"

"Ethan," Q-Tip number one corrects.

"Ethan here knows the front guy at the Crucible. I explained to him you forgot your ID at the hotel…"

"Stupid Tina," I say, slapping my forehead. I have no shame.

"No problemo," says Ethan. "Shall we?" His hands stay in his pockets, and he points forward with his chin.

I drag Priscilla, so we walk behind the guys. "What is it going to cost us?" I ask. "I am a betrothed woman, remember?"

Priscilla taps my arm, calming me. "Don't worry. Ethan is an old flame—"

"Really?" I can't hold it back.

"That's what he says. I don't really remember him." She grimaces. "Anyway, he just wants a little sugar tonight. You're off the hook. I'm Bridget, by the way."

"Bridget?"

"That's what he called me; what can I do?"

"Nice to meet you, Bridget," I say.

185

Sure enough, Ethan whispers something to the door guy, who takes a long look at me before letting us all in. Ethan's hands never leave his pockets.

When we're inside, Q-Tip number two approaches me.

"I'm Tyrone," he yells over the music.

"I like girls," I yell back. What? I don't want company. And it is a daring thing to say. To me, at least.

Priscilla is already off to the dance floor with Ethan. It's odd seeing my friend in her natural habitat. She seems more confident, as if this is possible. Soon she owns the place, her dance moves making men and women take notice. Lucky Ethan gets a kind of standing-up lap dance.

Priscilla whispers something to Ethan, who leaves exhausted to a corner. She comes to my side. "Want a drink? You should really take the opportunity."

"I don't know…"

"Come on, live a little. I'm driving."

"Aren't you drinking?"

"I don't drink, silly," she says, giving me a one-armed hug.

Since I'm almost of drinking age in England, I give myself a pass. "I'll have a Buck's Fizz."

"A *what?*"

"A mimosa," I say.

From the look she gives me, I might as well have ordered a live chicken. "I'll get you a real drink," she says before vanishing in the mass of sweaty bodies.

I try to be inconspicuous while I wait, but my swinging to the beat betrays my clumsiness. I'm as bad at dancing as I'm at sports. Priscilla comes back to save me.

"Here, down this," she says while handing a glass shot full of a sparkling blue liquid. Now I understand how Drake felt when I handed him the Truth potion. Well, I have to trust my friend. Besides, arguing with her is futile. I take a deep breath and gulp down the poison.

My throat burns, followed by my stomach. It leaves a bitter aftertaste in my mouth.

"What was that?"

Without bothering to answer me, she hands me a tall glass. "Now, go easy on this one."

"Will you tell me the name—"

"Later," she says.

We just stand side-by-side against the wall, dancing to the hip-hop. Seeing me dance, people probably think I'm already drunk. Hey, good excuse.

Still, I'm afraid I'll end up on YouTube.

We left our jackets at the door. Priscilla's breasts are almost popping out of her tank top, and I feel like a prepubescent girl next to her. Somehow she makes her bouncing seem classy.

A carefully unshaved guy, wearing a fedora hat and a scarf, too cool even for Seattle, watches me, but he doesn't make a move. I try not to flirt with anyone.

My new drink is very sweet but it doesn't mask the insane amount of alcohol mixed in. At least it tastes good.

A few minutes later, Priscilla and I are on the dance floor. My glass is empty somewhere.

I dance with her, trying to create an impenetrable two-person circle. Priscilla does all the hard work with her sexy, crazy moves. I'm getting a no-touching version of her earlier lap dance. I just have to follow the rhythm and avoid tripping.

It *is* fun! People notice us, or at least, they notice me next to Priscilla. The lights are trippy, the music not so loud anymore, and the previously stale smell of liquor and sweat now just feels right.

I let it go, shaking my hips and shoulders, and making what I hope look like sexy faces. Some guys try to cut in, but Priscilla pulls them to her and talks to them. Somehow, they leave us alone.

The music drowns my laughs, but my woo-hoos are already improving. There's a familiar tingling sensation that I can't place at first. It increases steadily, but I'm too busy with my new persona to take notice. Only when it's so strong that I can't push it to the back of my mind anymore, I become alarmed.

I grab Priscilla's arm. "Jane!" I yell.

Priscilla looks at me quizzically but only asks if I'm okay. I look around, dazzling lights blinding me, waves of faces popping up in the crowd, but I don't see Jane.

The tingling intensity now indicates close proximity. A girl with short, dark hair, pierced eyebrows, and black make-up is right in front of me, smiling. She is gorgeous.

She gives a weak wave with one hand while discreetly drawing a triangle in the air with her other hand's pinkie. Nobody does that by accident.

"Hey, Sister!" she yells. And *hugs* me.

Priscilla stands back, amused. My arms are alongside my body. But with my head resting briefly on her shoulder, I can see a silver moon tattooed on the back of her neck.

The goth girl lets me go. "I'm at Ballard High. Where are you?"

"Greenwood High," I say in her ear.

"Any luck?"

I shake my head.

She takes a cell from her mini-purse and hands it to me. She cups her hand around my ear. "I'm Greta. Punch your phone number. I'll call you, and you'll have mine." When I look at her trying to decide if I should trust her, she adds, "We've got to stick together. I hate that jerk Connor. Tried to hook up with me. Can you believe that guy?"

That will do it. I type my number—not an easy task when you're drunk and in the middle of a dance floor. I hand her the cell back. She smiles at me, grabs my hand, pulls it to her lips, and kisses the back of my hand. It's an ancient, secret greeting no Sister uses anymore.

"Goddess be with you," she mouths the words to me. Then she leaves in the sea of partying people, her Allure dragging some stares her way.

"She's cute," Priscilla shouts. "Really cute."

"Shut *up!*" I shout back. Uh-oh, I'm shut-upping people now.

***

Next thing I know, Priscilla is driving me home. But she stops close to a huge "Park closes at dusk" sign. I have no idea where we are.

"Let's go," she says coming out of the Prius.

I'm too buzzed to protest. We walk a little and squeeze between the closed gates of the park. She grabs my hand, guiding me in the darkness. When we're on the other side of the lot, she produces a mini-flashlight. She leads me to the edge of a lake. Something, maybe the moonlight, makes it not so dark anymore.

She lays her flashlight down, still turned on, on a boulder near us. "Take off your clothes," she commands. "We're going skinny-dipping."

She takes her jacket off, but stops mid-movement when she sees I'm not mimicking her. "Do you prefer to do it alone?" she asks. "I don't even have to look if you don't want to."

"You already saw me naked at school, remember?" I say. When I hear myself, I realize how silly my inhibitions are. I also understand I *need* to do this. No way I'm letting Jane's trap make me feel a victim. I can't let her dictate my life. *I* am in control.

Taking off my jacket, I say, "Feel free to join me."

She giggles and undresses. I can't help sneaking a peek. Her breasts are indeed perfect. I feel a little jealous. I look away and try to concentrate on unbuttoning my jeans.

Soon I'm out of my clothes too. Only when the chilly night air hits me, I have doubts. "It's cold."

"Let's go!" she says, running toward the cold water. "The head has to go in or it doesn't count." It's not deep enough to dive, so she goes thigh deep and immerses herself for a second.

She's already coming out of the water, trembling, when I muster the courage. The icy lake water hits my feet, but before it can scare me away, I'm up to my knees. No backing off now. I dive.

The dark waters engulf me. My hands feel the muddy bottom of the lake for a second, algae entwining in my fingers. My body becomes numb and weightless. It's a primal thing. The Sisters would approve.

I cleanse myself and all my concerns about nakedness and water abandon me. All the fears Jane tried to instill on me are gone. I feel indeed like a new Skye. The sensory deprivation experience is actually liberating.

But I resurface soon. "It's bloody freezing!" I yell. I start to come out of the water, but I see a still naked Priscilla holding my cell phone in front of her.

"Say cheese," she says. "It's just for you. You've got to remember this."

It actually sounds good to me. I strike a Victoria's Secret pose, taking care to hide my private parts. My silver phoenix tattoo reflects the moonlight and shines. Priscilla snaps a picture, looks at the result, and gives me a thumbs-up.

Soon both of us are getting dressed as fast as we can, our bodies still wet, our feet still muddy. We would be giggling if our teeth weren't chattering. With our shoes in hand, we rush back to the car.

We close the doors, and she turns the heat on. Then we look at each other and start laughing hysterically.

"That was insane!" I scream.

"But also a great cure for drunkenness!" she shouts. "Woo-hoo!"

It's my turn. I belt out the greatest, most satisfying, guilty-free woo-hoo of my life.

Chapter 41: Drake

The temperature is ridiculously low. I thought it would be a good idea bringing Skye to Green Lake again on what promised to be a sunny day, but Seattle's deceptive weather—and deceptive weathermen—tricked me once again. Instead of having a blast, we're huddled together on a bench, trying to survive the morning chilliness.

Despite the cold, the park is busy: mothers push jogging strollers, dogs take their owners for a stroll, a father chases after a runaway kid on a scooter, men fish on the pier.

Two middle-aged women holding hands walk by. To my left, on a nearby bench, a young guy works on his laptop and sips coffee.

We are halfway between the trail and the busy Green Lake Drive behind us. City and lake sounds merge.

Above us, gloomy clouds.

This is Seattle, all right.

"I need a nickname for you," Skye tells me dreamily. She's resting her head on my shoulder.

I'm unsure if I should divulge it. Nevertheless, I say, "The guys call me D-Man."

"I can call you D-Licious."

"Please don't."

I hate this weather. I could be feeling her body against mine, but we're wrapped in heavy coats. We need to go indoors pronto. I look back longingly to the appropriately brown-colored chocolate store on the other side of the street. I'm about to suggest we head there when she says, "Drake?"

"Yep?"

She turns to face me, blushing. "I have a surprise for you…"

"What?"

"Aren't you curious about what Priscilla and I did last night?"

I shudder. "You got nipple piercings? Like, matching piercings?"

"No!" She punches me weakly in the arm. But then she looks down, and I can see she's imagining it. Did I give her an idea?

"Hello?" I say. "Surprise?"

"Yeah, right. You've got to promise me you won't tell anyone."

I raise my eyebrows. "This is getting better and better."

She gives me a glimpse of a picture on her cell. I must be imagining things. I grab her wrist and say, "Let me take a better look."

She pulls her hand back, laughing. "No!" But she slowly loses the tug-of-war—willingly.

The image is little grainy. It shows Skye, completely naked, on the edge of a lake, at night. "Skye!"

"Are you mad?" she asks, still giggling.

"Of course! You should have used the flash!" I want to make a poster of it. "Send it to me." She shakes her head. "Come on…"

"Only if you send me one of you."

"No way!" I protest.

She lets out a hearty laugh.

"Ah, well played," I say.

She makes a little curtsy.

"You are a different girl," I say.

"Bad different?"

"Just different."

She takes the cell from my hands, and it pains me to let it go. "It's thanks to you," she says. "And Priscilla."

"Do you have one of Priscilla?" I ask. She gives me her 'seriously?' expression. "I mean, Boulder would love it."

"Right…" she says, doubting me. "Let me ask you something," she adds with a hesitant tone. "Do they make fun of Priscilla?"

Uh-oh. We're entering confidential territory. This is supposed to be just between us guys. I don't want to go there, but I don't want to lie to her either. It's not cool that she's asking, though. "Of course," I finally reply.

"Why?"

"Come on, Skye…"

"No, I want to know."

I shrug. "It's not a mean thing. At least they don't think it's mean." She looks at me, and I explain, "They make fun of her, all right?" My tone is annoyed. "It became a competition. They like to be creative and top themselves. I mean, *we* do. We all do it, okay?"

"What do you say?"

"I'd rather not go there."

"But I don't understand… Boulder even has a crush on her."

I shrug. "Don't read too much into it. It's just guys being guys. Yeah, it's not cool, but that's how it is. We have a lot of free time. Why are you asking this?" I use an accusatory tone.

Skye looks away. "She doesn't have friends. I mean, at all."

"She has many male friends, believe me," I say, still feeling guilty about betraying my peeps' confidence and confessing to my own shortcomings.

"Don't be insensitive, Drake. All the girls look down on her; they think she's a slut."

I want to say 'There's a reason for that' but keep my mouth shut. Am I bitter today or what?

She continues, "And the boys too. I guess that's why she came to the new girl in school." Skye points to herself.

I had never thought of that. It must be hard for Priscilla. But she must have known she'd get this reputation when she started serial-dating all the guys.

Worst of all, she is a nice girl. I remember my hangover morning after the Jane debacle and how Priscilla, even mad at me, was nice and offered me good advice.

Now I'm feeling doubly guilty. For Priscilla, and for betraying the guys.

I don't like it that Skye pointed that out. I already have trouble dealing with my things; no need for her to make me feel bad for something like that.

"You don't respect her."

"Come on, Skye…"

"No, really. Would it be okay if you made fun of me behind my back? Actually… do you?"

I don't answer. I just look away, disgusted. We are at the same place where we had our first day together, but the mood couldn't be more different.

Skye and I don't speak for a long time.

***

That argument ruins our afternoon. We don't talk about it, but I don't feel like hanging out anymore, and I sense she doesn't either. I drop her off at her house and go see the guys.

Sean is at Boulder's. I think he lives there.

Boulder is rummaging through his garage. He comes up with a couple of snowboards.

"What do you say, D-Man? Website says it snowed in Stevens overnight."

"I don't know," I say.

Boulder stops for a moment. "Come on, I'm paying for your lift, how about that?"

No offense meant, and none taken. I shrug. "All right, then."

Sean sticks his head out from some boxes. "You've got a bad case of the downers, Drake. What's up? Your wife left you hanging?"

"Kinda," I say. I really don't want to talk about it. "Isn't it a little too late to go to the mountains?"

"I just woke up," Boulder replies, his back turned to me while he looks for his boots. "We have to stop by a McD's on our way." He fishes bright yellow boots out of a box, turns, and points beyond me. "Is your ride all-wheel drive?"

***

We make stops at a fast food joint and a 7-Eleven. I'm the designated driver while Boulder takes care of a six pack. Even though he's exposing me to an open container citation, I'm glad to pay back my lift ticket. Sean is just having a soda.

We didn't need a ski rack. The Volvo is a long wagon, and we just put the snowboards in the back. Sean and Boulder didn't even make fun of the car.

Daringly, I double-check that Boulder doesn't remember his potion-induced confessions. "Hey, big man, do you remember what you told me the other day about Priscilla?"

He squints. "When?"

"Yesterday? At the parking lot? Ring any bells?"

"No…"

Sean, who is in the backseat, leans on my seat, pressing me forward. "Speaking of The Predator," he says, "I got a new one for the twins: Priscilla can ride the three-person carpool by herself."

"Ouch!" Boulder says, but he high-fives Sean nonetheless. "I had one, but it was only a variation of 'They have their own zip code.'… Not worth it."

"Do one, D-Man!" Sean slaps my head.

"Hey, driver here!" I yell.

"Come on, Drake," Boulder shoves me lightly, ignoring my protest. When he sees I'm not following for it, he sing-songs, "Her boobs arrive on time, but Priscilla is always a couple of minutes late…"

In spite of myself, I chuckle. I'm so going to hell. I was just a victim of peer pressure, I justify myself.

"He has a soul!" Sean roars. He takes a big gulp of soda and belches.

"He's got a sense of humor," Boulder corrects. "Come on, Drake. We won't tell on you."

I wrestle with my conscience. But it's not that hard of a decision. I just don't feel like it. "I can't think of anything," I say.

Boulder frowns. "Damn, Drake. You did one the other day. A geek one. What was it?"

"I know. 'Her center of gravity is two feet in front of her belly button.'" Sean laughs out loud, slapping my seat.

I was very proud of that one. Today, it doesn't sound so funny.

"Come on. Priscilla is cool."

"Of course, she is! What does that have to do with it?" Boulder asks, puzzled.

I don't answer.

Boulder shakes his head. "D-Man, I'm all for you and the new girl. But don't forget your friends. And don't forget who you are."

Chapter 42: Skye

I just realized that I almost compromised Mum's career. I dodged at least underage drinking, trespassing, and public indecency charges last night, and I might even have done other illegal things I'm not aware of… yet.

I owe Priscilla.

After Drake leaves me at my house, our mood ruined, I feel alone. Aunt Gemma is somewhere bird watching, and the house feels empty.

This itch compels me to call Priscilla. I wonder if she has more adventures for me. She takes her time to answer.

"Hey," I say. "Are you awake?"

"I am *now*." I hear a long yawn on the other side of the line. "What's up?"

"Thanks for taking my picture. Drake loved it."

She chuckles. "Guess he didn't know the girl he is dating."

"Do you have plans for today? Drake kind of ditched me."

"Really?" She sounds fully awake now. I guess she's thinking the same as me: not a good sign when you show your boyfriend your naked picture and he leaves you alone. But she reacts fast. "I was thinking spa."

"Spa?"

"We've got to recover from last night's hard work," she argues.

Once again, when I play my objections in my mind, they sound silly. "What time?" I ask.

***

It's a salon/spa. The salon staff and clients are the nosiest bunch of people I've ever met. Surely, they do pay back—and then some—in the form of over-sharing. The woman to my right, for example, a soon-to-be Master in Chemistry from WSU, just told me she doesn't want kids and imposed only one condition to her fiancée: that he gets a vasectomy before they marry.

I look around and realize I'm the only one cringing. It gets worse. The woman giving her a pedicure comments nonchalantly, "I hope it doesn't give him an excuse to cheat."

The kid-hater doesn't even blink. "I thought of that. I told him if he ever cheats on me, I'll give him a more permanent solution," she says while making a cutting motion with her hand. They all laugh.

I want to stuff my head inside the paraffin bowl. By my other side, Priscilla shows an unconcerned smile.

This is an experience.

Later, Priscilla and I lie on massage tables side-by-side, belly-down. A girl a little older than me is laying warm rocks on my back, while a short middle-aged woman massages Priscilla. The two women are silent, and I guess that's the most privacy we're going to get in this madhouse. The spa side is much less crowded, and much quieter, than the salon side.

I ask Priscilla something I've been meaning to mention since last night. "So, have you hooked up with Boulder?" I know the answer, but I try to keep Boulder's secret... secret.

She turns her head to face me. "I did," she says, a little loud. Then she mouths, "OMG, he's huge."

I raise my eyebrows, feigning surprise. "And?"

"It was fun," she says. She tries to shrug, but the masseuse's hands are stronger than Priscilla's back muscles. "Ouch!"

"That's called a deep-tissue massage," the diminutive woman says, unapologetically.

"Do you like him?" I ask.

"Sure, what's not to like?" Priscilla grins.

"Have you thought of… you know… going steady?"

"With Boulder?" she asks, as if the thought had never occurred to her. "He isn't the boyfriend type. He's always looking for the next girl."

That's not what he told me, and I *know* he was telling the truth. "Really? What if he… changed? What if he wanted to be with you?" I realize it's not fair to Priscilla, because I know she's lying.

She eyes me. "What is this all about?"

It's my turn to shrug, upsetting the rocks on my back. "I don't know. Girl talk. I mean, you can have any guy you want, so why don't you just pick one?"

Priscilla doesn't answer at first. I'm glad I chose this moment: she's actually pinned down and cannot run away. Finally, she says, "If I can have *any* guy I want, I'd like to have *every* guy I want."

"What do you mean?"

She gives me an exasperated look. "I'm only seventeen, Skye. I'm not looking to settle down just yet." She probably misunderstands my shocked expression, because she adds, "I mean, I'm not saying you're wrong or anything, but it's just not me, you know?"

I keep my mouth shut, hoping I didn't say anything inappropriate.

Priscilla goes on, unprompted, "I see my parents. They're like these empty shells. They go to work, all right, but they set some time for fun too, right? They have friends, go on vacations all the time, Dad goes golfing in Scotland, Mom goes to charity events. It's all scheduled fun. Nothing spontaneous. And their passion—it's gone too. I saw their pictures from college; I heard their stories. They were more complete people back then. Do you understand?"

I give a half-nod, because I half-understand. But she wants me to understand it fully.

"They were in love; they did all kind of crazy things. Now they go through life as if it's a to do list: gym three times a week, sex on Tuesdays, friends over on Fridays. I see them. They're not enjoying themselves. While they're throwing a dinner party, they're not *in the moment*; they're already planning the next fun thing they will most certainly not enjoy either."

She turns her head and looks away from me. She seems sad and mad at the same time. After a while, she turns back and says in a low, serious tone I've never heard her use before. "I'm not a spoiled girl…" Her voice is fragile, all pretense of privacy abandoned long ago. "I'm not doing this for attention. I just want to enjoy life. Because if you don't, what's the point?"

I raise my eyes and see the pocket-sized sadistic masseuse, beyond Priscilla's line of sight, nodding along.

Chapter 43: Drake

Sunday morning I still don't want to call Skye. I just drop by Boulder's, back to my old life for a while.

Sean and Boulder are playing an intense one-on-one basketball game.

"Where we at?" Sean asks Boulder.

"Nineteen-six. I know you know the score." Boulder is not amused.

Sean cackles and says. "Just checking. Join us, D-Man."

"I don't play. You know that."

"Maybe when you grow some chest hair," Boulder teases.

Sean is faster, a far better player, but Boulder is Shaq, complete with hard fouls and swagger.

"I've got ball skills, big man," Sean taunts, dribbling the ball between his legs.

Sean proceeds to school Boulder, and Boulder makes things rough. A missed block becomes a hard foul. A drive to the basket has Boulder running over Sean.

But it's not a problem to Sean: he goes down laughing every time. He seems to be on a Zoloft diet. It makes Boulder madder.

When Sean charges the lane, Boulder body slams him. Sean goes careening over a hedge. Boulder sighs deeply and helps Sean up.

Sean is smiling. "Ready for another?"

Boulder shakes his head and laughs. "Nah. Hydration time."

We go inside the garage, and Boulder opens the old fridge. "Gatorade for me," I say.

Boulder gets a Red Bull and hands me a Gatorade. Sean's choice is Mountain Dew. At least they're not drinking beer.

"So… Drake finally got him some girl. Well done," Sean says, raising his can. Boulder and I join him in the toast.

"That's my man!" Sean says, putting his hand on my shoulder. "It's fourth-and-one, Drake."

"Yeah, go for it," Boulder says.

Oh, yeah, the fourth-and-one pledge. We promised one another that we'd always be bold. If faced with a safe decision or a riskier decision with better payoff, always go for it. Never punt on a fourth-and-one situation.

Boulder takes a swig and presses his cold soda can to his forehead. "When is the big night?" he asks.

I'd be lying if I said I hadn't thought about it.

"I hadn't thought about it," I say.

"Right…" Sean snickers.

I feign indignation. "Why do you give me so much grief? Get off my case! You two don't have girlfriends. Actually, you hang out all the time. People talk, you know…"

"Not cool, Drake," Boulder warns me.

I can't let it go. "Yeah, I keep hearing you go to the gym to *spot*," I make the air quotes. "Well, my point is, I have a girlfriend, and you guys don't."

Sean nods. "Yeah, but it's a conscious decision. It's just because one-nighters are actually much less drama than a relationship."

I throw my hands up in the air. "It's impossible to win a discussion with you guys."

"And yet, you still try," Sean says.

***

Soon, it's 9:30 p.m., it's dark, cold, and Boulder and I are standing in front of a tattoo studio that just closed its doors. In our faces.

Boulder talks to the closed door. "Come on, man, ink me. The other shop did it, look!" He shows his Gears of War tat. To a closed door.

"Kid, I already told you. Go away." That's the voice of the woman who just kicked us out.

"Ink me!" Boulder yells.

"You're drunk," a man's voice says from inside the shop. "Don't make me call the cops. That would be very uncool, man."

"Ink meeeeee!"

We're in a loop. "Do NOT ink him!" I yell.

Boulder looks at me, his eyes glazed. "Hey, back me up here."

"I am! Just not in an obvious way."

Boulder pokes me in the chest. "I need this tat, and I need it tonight."

"Believe me, Boulder, you don't need a naked Priscilla permanently on your back," I say, before realizing that probably came out wrong. "Where did you get this sketch anyway?"

"I drew it from memory," he says, sitting down on the curbside.

It's getting late, and this part of Shoreline is somewhat seedy. Some people, a few of them drunker than Boulder, are already coming in our direction.

It's bad enough babysitting a drunk guy who weighs way more than I do, but having to negotiate drunken conversations with strangers is really annoying. I'm tired, and I stopped having fun hours ago.

I try to lift him by the arm. "Dude, I'm taking you home."

He swats me away. "I can drive back! I did it before."

"Yeah, and you parked in your neighbor's garage."

"So?" He cocks his head.

"Without opening the garage door?" That's my closing argument.

Boulder shrugs. "Those houses all look alike."

"Just promise me you'll never, ever drive after a beer, you stupid ogre. Give me a call. I'll get you. Just don't drive."

Boulder's eyes are glazed, but he nods solemnly. "Okay, mommy."

I should be mad at him. I want to. But it's nice for a change to have his back. In my mind, I imagine Boulder and I are best friends.

Why am I thinking this now? Best friend is just a label, Drake. Just another label.

I drag him to my car and drive him home.

***

When I turn the corner on my street, a sight freezes the blood in my veins.

Jane is right in front of my house, sitting sideways on her red bike. She smiles—she actually *smiles*—at me.

Rage is pouring from me. I walk up to her. She straightens up and faces me. When I come closer, she raises her hands, not in a gesture of defiance, but as an offering of peace. Yeah, right.

"Listen, Jane—"

"I need to talk to you," she says, interrupting me. The urgency in her voice gives me pause, but I come to my senses in a second.

"You psycho bitch!" I never use these words, but if someone

deserves them, it's her. I keep my hands alongside my body to suppress my urge to punch her.

"Can we forget that for just a moment? We need to talk." Her voice is firm. My anger means nothing to her.

I don't want to listen. "Are you insane? I have nothing to talk with you. You tried to kill Skye!"

"Your precious witch," she says, staring into my eyes.

"What did you say?" My blood freezes for a moment.

"I know you know, Drake. You told me that night. Ritual in the woods? Ring any bells? Love potions make you trusting. You told me everything I asked. I know she saved you with magic. And you've seen me perform my little ritual at the pool, didn't you?"

I remember how important the Veil is to Skye. "Are you high? What you're saying makes no sense."

Jane squints and mumbles something, while her hand make a conjuring gesture. Before I realize, I flinch and take a step back.

She cackles. "A-ha!" she says triumphant. "Afraid of magic, Drake? Don't worry, you didn't break the Veil. *She* did."

I'm defeated, but I won't admit it. "What do you want, Jane?"

"I'm just messing with you. Nobody can do magic this way. Freezing rays and the like. Didn't she tell you?"

"No, I mean coming here. What do you want?"

She lowers her voice. "I want you. No potions this time."

"I know you're lying," I say.

She comes closer. "It was fun, you know. I felt a spark between us."

Standing still, I say nothing. My face conveys my contempt for her.

Jane shrugs. "Worth a shot," she says, back to her normal, cold

207

voice. "Okay, here's the deal. Make her leave. Or I'll make her leave. Got it?"

"What?" I can't control myself anymore. She sees my fury, and it's her turn to step back. "You get close to Skye again, and I'm going…" A thought crosses my mind: is she expecting my reaction and recording my threat to blackmail me later? That's exactly the type of mind game Jane would play. I don't care. "Just stay away from us, or I'll kill you. I mean it!"

Jane's stony face shows no emotion at first, but then her expression softens. "No, you won't," she murmurs. "But you know I would. And I may not even stop at her."

Then Jane says in a pleading voice, "Drake, *please* tell her to go away. This is much bigger than you can imagine. You're ruining everything." She sounds tired. "Don't make me hurt her." She turns away and climbs on her bike.

Her strategy works. I can't attack someone from behind. Attack? I'm kidding myself. I feel guilty about *threatening* somebody, especially a woman. Even if it's Jane.

The motorcycle roars and she goes away. I'm left at the street, wondering if I just imagined the surreal confrontation.

***

It's hard to be with Skye in this situation. I mean, every nanosecond that I don't tell her the truth, I'm lying. I think.

I spent the whole Sunday staring at my bedroom wall. The everlasting rain helped me stay inside and wrestle my demons.

Jane is bluffing. No question about it. I know it. I'm sure of it. The only thing that keeps me on my toes is: what if she isn't?

She tried to kill Skye before. Why wouldn't she try again? I always thought it was a desperate measure, that Jane saw an opportunity and decided to act on an impulse. She wasn't thinking clearly. The death of a witch would actually bring attention to the school and hinder Jane's search for the Singularity.

But now it is clear she doesn't care for the consequences. She wants revenge on Skye for—what? Skye's ex? Also, I'm not sure what Jane meant when she told me it was a big thing. Did she mean the Singularity?

This is beyond weird.

If I tell Skye, she'll freak out. I know Jane is just trying to mess up with our heads. Maybe I don't tell Skye, but I keep an eye out for Jane. At least for a while.

This is the point where I bury my head in my pillow, as if trying to smother her threats into oblivion.

Chapter 44: Skye

Early Monday morning, Drake shows up.

"Is this the place where they give free Protection spells?" he says after I open the door.

With just my index finger, I ask him to come in. He follows me without a word.

We have coffee in the kitchen. "So, how was your weekend?" I ask at last.

"Uneventful," he says, looking at the cabinets. "What about yours?"

"Eventful," I say. Oh, Goddess, am I playing games now? I don't want to cling to false pride. "I missed you," I say, while resting my mug on the counter. I don't care if I sound needy.

He gives me the perfect reply. "I missed you too." He lays his mug down and leans forward.

Accepting his offer, I walk around the counter and stop in front of him. He kisses me eagerly. He acts his words, pulling me tight as if not wanting to let me go—ever.

His mouth has the flavor of coffee and minty toothpaste. It tastes like a new morning.

***

When he's driving me to school, I say, "I was thinking about

Jane."

He stiffens. Wow, he *is* upset with her. He's so protective of me.

I brush my hand against his cheek while he drives, but he doesn't move. "I thought we should see what she's up to."

"What do you mean?"

He uses a monotone voice that doesn't sound like him. I think talking about her brings the pool incident to his mind.

"Maybe we could track her."

"Why? Why would we do that?" Is that fear in his voice? What's going on? We were back to our dynamic in the kitchen and in my bedroom, during the ritual. Now he's acting all weird.

But I don't want to bring this up so soon after we made up. I just continue as if I haven't noticed anything. "What do we know about her? I have no idea where she lives, where she hangs out, what she does. Most importantly, I need to know how close to the Singularity she is."

He takes a deep breath and comments, "But Jane's not close. If she thought she was, she wouldn't even bother with you... I mean, us." He glances briefly in my direction. "She'd just finish the job, whatever her job is. Right?" Drake speaks so fast he almost mangles the words.

"I can't afford to wait. Would you help me?"

Drakes takes a long look at my face. "Did you drink a hyper potion this morning?"

I slide down the seat, kick out my sneakers, and put my bare foot on the windshield. "I had a massive dose of Priscilla this weekend. That's what happens when you're not around," I say, trying to lighten the mood.

"I'll stay closer to you from now on," he says, but his tone is not flirty at all.

We arrive at the lot. He parks, but before he can get out of the car, I grab his arm. "Did something happen?"

Startled, he glances at me, but soon his eyes stray. "No! Why? We're… going to be late."

"Drake…" A sudden sadness invades me. He's lying.

He puts his hand over mine. "Let's think about it, okay? Jane is not close to the Singularity. We have time to figure this out, what do you say?"

I nod, but I can't hide my disappointment. He's lying about something. I don't even need a Truth potion to see it.

***

I've been frustrated since yesterday. Drake's evasiveness stalled my plans. Maybe I can track Jane by myself. I can do it from a safe distance, so she doesn't detect me. Even if she figures out I'm following her, what's the worst that could happen? I miss my chance, that's all. It's not like she can get madder. I hope.

Priscilla and I are getting our books from the lockers, but as soon as I open mine, I see something different. A photo is taped onto the inside of the locker's door.

I look around. My body is not tingling, so I know Jane's not around. I rip the picture free.

At first glance I think it's an astronomy image: a grainy picture of an unidentified shape. A rectangular shape seems familiar; it looks like a bed. White linen. In the center of all whiteness, a person? To her right a dresser.

I've seen this before. It's… it's… my room. At Aunt Gemma's.

I am the person sleeping on the bed.

A huge gasp comes from behind me. I turn and meet Drake's

bulging eyes staring at the picture.

"We've got to talk," he says.

***

"How? How did this happen?" I ask him. We're in his car, windows closed. The proximity is not what I wanted now, but there's no other place to talk about it.

"She came to my house to threaten you." His voice is not apologetic.

"You knew about this?" I yell at him.

He moves his head side to side, not on a negative, just trying to shake the question off. "It was two days ago. I thought she was bluffing."

"And you didn't tell me," I say. I never knew you could *hear* venom. Especially spewed from my own mouth.

"I was pretty sure she was bluffing just to get this reaction." He points to the both of us. "And she's got exactly what she wanted, it seems."

"Why didn't you tell me? I trusted you, Drake. With my most important secret. A secret that's not even my own. I broke the Veil for you."

He looks at me. "The truth is, I had most of it already figured out—"

"So, that's okay, right? Since you're so smart, it's okay that you know about the Veil? It doesn't matter how it makes me feel? Like I betrayed my Sisters?"

"No, no, that's not what I meant," he says in an alarmed voice. He tries to embrace me, but I wiggle away, refusing contact. He continues, "What I meant is that you shouldn't feel guilty about the Veil, because I had already pretty much figured it out. Besides, if

213

anyone broke the Veil, it was Jane."

I say nothing.

He takes a deep breath. "As much as this scares you, it scares me even more. Way more. Let's think about it, okay? First of all, don't blame me for something she did. Second, I didn't tell you because that's exactly what Jane wanted. Third, it was my problem, not yours."

I interrupt him. "Of course it's my problem too, Drake. It's all because of me."

He looks at me, initially annoyed about yet another interruption, but then his expression softens. "I was trying to shield you from all that," he says. "I thought I could just not play her game, and that it would go away."

"But now we have proof she isn't bluffing," I say, waving the picture. "She broke into my house. Actually, I think it was Brianna. Otherwise, I'd have woken with the tingling of a Sister so close to me. Let's find out more about Jane, that creepy witch. Maybe she is threatening us because she *is* close to the Singularity and she's afraid we'll find her first."

Drake shakes his head, frustrated. "I mean, who knows how her mind works?"

I say, "That's exactly my point: we need to know more about her. I'm done googling her: nothing comes up. But I looked up the school's directory, and her address is listed."

He squints. "Wait a minute. How?"

"I saw they had the admin password taped onto a drawer at the office. It was easy," I explain, ignoring his half-admiring, half-perplexed look. "I knew she had a valid address in the system; she needed one to enroll, right? The point is, we could track her. And, at the same time, make it clear to her that we're not afraid of her tricks."

"Do you really want to follow her?"

"Or Brianna. You could easily get close to Brianna."

He groans. "Skye, don't ask me this."

I slap the dashboard. "Do you have a better idea? Because I don't. And I'm tired of waiting for things to happen to me. I want to *make* things happen! I want to be the one in control of this mess."

Chapter 45: Drake

Skye's in James Bond mode, and she won't let it go. She convinces me to go to Jane's house and try to find out what I can. First, we have to figure out whether Jane's address is really her own: Jane might have faked her school documents.

Skye offers a sensible solution. "We'll wait until the school bell rings and then beat her to the address. If she goes there, we know we got it right."

The uniqueness of my car is a huge problem. Parking it on the street as if I'm in some bad cop movie is ridiculous. My old Volvo calls attention anywhere. Also, I can't figure out how the cops pull that off. It's clear that a stranger sitting in a car for hours will make residents call 911. Even if the Volvo had tinted windows (and I thought my car couldn't look worse than it does), that would be even more suspicious. And I'm not budgeted for a disguised service van with fake plates and the latest in surveillance equipment.

Skye and I are still in a weird place. I don't have the guts to kiss or even touch her since our discussion in the car. We mostly talk about our plan.

I can see many flaws with her plan: chiefly, what if Jane makes a detour? But with Skye's plan at least I wouldn't have to wait hours and hours and be arrested for loitering or worse.

So we follow our best bet. As soon as the bell rings, I join my almost-estranged girlfriend in my car, parked strategically at the lot's exit, and drive to Jane's presumed address.

I stake out Jane's house while Skye waits in the car. We don't want to trigger any witch alarms. Skye is parked a block west, on Dayton Avenue, working like a human radar. We'll be in touch via cell.

We know this might not even be Jane's real address after all. But if it is, I'm willing to break in and find everything I can about her and about her progress in the search for the Singularity. Skye is right: we can't be passive about it anymore.

The house I'm watching is typical North Seattle, except more rundown: a long, narrow fixer-upper squeezed between similar one-story houses, with a raised front yard. Steps lead to the front door, and tall hedges grow unchecked on each side of the small stairs.

The street has no people traffic, which makes me an oddity just by being there. I decide to walk as if I'm just passing by. I expect Jane to show up soon, or I'll have to think of a better plan.

The cloudy skies above me turn a darker shade of gray. I hope it doesn't start raining.

My cell rings.

"She is close," Skye warns me.

Three minutes later I see Jane approaching on her bike. I hide behind the hedge of a house close to the street corner. Jane doesn't notice me. She parks in front of the house we're stalking and goes inside.

I call Skye. "That's it. We got it."

"Did you see anyone else? Brianna?"

"No, and no other cars. I think she lives alone," I say. She's over eighteen; it makes sense if she lives by herself.

"Could she afford rent?" Skye asks.

"I guess. I mean, she's got one expensive motorcycle, right? Wait!" I say.

Jane leaves the house. She climbs on her bike and goes back the way she came.

That was quick. I tell Skye about Jane's departure. "I'll take a look," I say.

"Be careful," Skye says.

"I'll leave my phone on vibrate, just in case someone's there. Let me know if you sense Jane coming back," I add.

I cross the street and approach the house. I try to act natural, but I don't know how. Well, as long as I don't tiptoe around the house, I won't look suspicious. I walk up the stairs and ring the doorbell. I have a story planned, if anyone answers the door.

Nobody does. I see no lights through gaps in the battered curtains. I go around the house, checking the windows, all the way to the kitchen door. I told Skye I would try to break in from the back of the house.

I peek inside. The house is bare. I can see utensils in the kitchen. A half-eaten sandwich on a rectangular table in the nook.

The other side of the house has no windows, so I come back to kitchen's door and try the doorknob. It turns and clicks. I hesitate for a second, but then I remember the fourth-and-one pledge.

Betting this old house has no alarm system, I open the door and walk inside, confident.

Two steps in, I feel a dull pain in my right temple, and everything goes black.

Chapter 46: Skye

Jane's energy fades as she rides her bike away.

I was afraid that she would come in my direction and get close enough for her to sense *my* energy. That's why Drake parked away from the natural route from school to her address. We're lucky she left the house heading west away from me.

So far, so good.

My fingers drum on the steering wheel. I'm glad Drake's car is automatic. I keep glancing at the cell, waiting for his call. I imagine he got inside the house.

I expect her to have a computer, or better, an external hard drive that we can steal. I don't feel bad or guilty about it at all. She may have info on the Singularity, and that's all that matters.

An uneasy sensation bothers me, and I suddenly realize it's my True Sight.

The tingling is back. *Jane* is back.

I immediately speed-dial Drake, almost fumbling the phone. It rings—or vibrates—five times, but he doesn't pick it up.

It means he can't answer. He's with someone. And it's not Jane.

The tingling increases. I have to beat Jane to the house. I turn the key in the ignition, and the Volvo's engine rumbles. I hit the gas and drive up to Jane's. No use being discreet now: I park in front of the hedges.

Still no sign of Jane or her bike, but her signature is increasing. I get four blue glass flasks from my purse before I leave the car. I don't bother closing the Volvo's door.

I climb the stairs, ignore the front door, and head straight to the back, where Drake told me he would try to break in. I open the first of the flasks while rushing alongside the length of the house. I can't see anything through the windows.

Before I turn the corner, I stop and sneak a peek. The kitchen's door is closed. I walk slowly and look through the window.

A heavily tattooed, bare-chested guy has his back to me. Beyond him, I see another guy, about my age, but creepily skinny and pale. In front of him, Drake sits in a chair, his face all bloody.

My heart beats like crazy. Goddess, this is going too far.

The tingling sensation is overwhelming; Jane must have arrived.

No time to think. I put two flasks in my jeans' back pocket, open the other two, and keep one in each hand.

I try the kitchen door, balancing the flasks. The door makes a creaking noise when it opens. As soon as the tattooed guy turns, I throw the flask's liquid in his face.

He's startled by the attack, but he doesn't make a noise. He brushes his fingertips quickly against his face and looks at them. Then he collapses in a heap, unconscious.

My mind registers I used the Sleep potion. Drake and the skinny guy don't move; they both watch me with glazed eyes. Then Drake tries to get up to divert the guy's attention.

I use this moment to throw the contents of the second flask on the guy's gaunt face. I hope it doesn't spill on Drake.

The potion's effect is immediate. The skinny guy starts to flail about. The second potion was Shivers.

I glimpse a silhouette against the front window. Jane. Ignoring Drake, I race to the front door. I reach for another flask from my pocket.

Jane, no doubt already sensing me, opens the door, switchblade in hand, trying to figure out the scene inside. I don't wait. In one motion, I pop up the lid and throw the potion on her.

She ducks.

My potion misses her and goes out through the front door. Jane straightens herself and smiles. Without looking back, she closes the front door behind her.

"What now?" she hisses, challenging me.

Behind me, I hear Drake stumbling. Jane is still three steps away from me. I get my last flask and try to pop up its lid, but Jane closes the distance insanely fast, and closes her fist over my hand, preventing me from opening the flask. Her hand is crushing mine. I'm afraid the flask might break. The potion is going to spill on me.

Her smile is horrific—as if her face is made of pure evil. I cower. I feel weak, defeated, but something inside me compels me to fight. It's not real.

Not real.

I force myself to see her how she really is: I try to pierce through her Intimidation Charm.

The glass flask is about to crack under her death grip on my hand. Turning the bottom of the flask in the direction of her face, I push with all my strength, in a stabbing motion.

She tries to turn away, but the butt of the flask hits her cheekbone and breaks. Tiny pieces of glass get stuck deep into her flesh. Liquid spills over her face and my hand.

I yank my arm from her grasp and look at my hand. There were only two potions left. One is Decay. The other…

Jane puts her hands over her eyes and screams. The same scream I let out in the locker room.

Breathing hard, I manage to whisper, "Blinding potion, bitch."

Broken glass decorates my right hand, and droplets of blood emerge. I look at them, bewildered. Something inside my head reminds me not to get my hand, dripping with a little Blinding potion, next to my eyes.

I barely notice when Jane swings her arm swiftly in my direction. I try to dodge, but I'm too slow. A sharp pain comes from a deep cut on my forearm, just below the elbow.

I gasp and step back, trying to avoid her wild swings. She's got her switchblade in her hand, and even blind, she guesses my position.

A while ago, I took a single self-defense class. I use the only thing I've learned then. Her swooping slashes leave her body hunched forward, her arms wide, and I see an opening.

I kick her in the groin with all my strength.

She whimpers, falling backward. The knife drops to the floor, beyond her reach. She reaches for her aching crotch, gasping in pain.

Drake stumbles in my direction.

"You okay?" Drake asks with a raspy voice. He trips and almost falls down. I support him with my shoulder.

Looking at his bloodied face, I say. "Yeah. Let's go."

I guide him to the front while Jane lays on the floor. Not screaming anymore, just moaning. For some reason, it's scarier.

The street is deserted. I'm guessing screams are a common occurrence around here. I help Drake into the passenger's seat and run to the driver's side, disregarding the trail of blood I leave on the sidewalk.

Jane's bike is parked behind us. Defenseless.

I check the empty street for onlookers, then awkwardly use my left hand to put the Volvo in reverse and smash the side of her precious machine. The bike tumbles to the road.

"Whoa," Drake says.

I twist again to put the shift in drive and hit the gas, leaving all things Jane behind.

Chapter 47: Drake

We don't go to the hospital this time. We're in Skye's bedroom. I suggested going to my house, since Dad's at work and Mona is wherever freakish fourteen-year-old girls hang out, but Skye told me she had healing herbs and potions here. Aunt Gemma is out, bird watching again.

We only need to clean the bloodstains from the hardwood floor, that's all.

After examining the bump on my temple, Skye makes a quick bandage and hands me a huge ice bag.

"They hit you exactly where the tree hit it," she said.

"Guess I can recycle the scar then," I say.

I use tweezers to pick every tiny shard of glass from her hand. Instead of using soap or antiseptic, she brushes a few herbs over her wounds and pours cold water over her hand. I don't even ask. I hope she doesn't get an infection.

Even with the odd circumstances, I feel warm inside, having her hand resting on mine, while I do glass-picking duty.

"How are you going to explain the gash?" I say, nodding to the bandage on her other arm.

"I'll just wear long sleeves."

I find another piece of glass, slowly pull it out, and drop it on her dresser.

"So, great plan, huh?" I say, my eyes fixed on my job.

The answer is slow to come. "It was a car wreck."

I'm surprised she's this calm. She was just attacked—again—by a knife-wielding notorious psycho, and she fought her way out of a room with three adversaries.

"You saved me again," I point out.

"I put you in danger in the first place," she replies.

"Where we at? In saving each other, I mean. We should be even by now, right?"

"I stopped counting a while ago," she says, her voice lively now.

I chuckle.

"You should get another CAT scan," she says softly. Her hand touches my scar.

"If we go back to the ER, they'll probably report us to the police," I say, looking at her now.

She shakes her head dismissively. "Under what charges? Getting hurt too much? Is that a crime?"

I imagine running into baby-doctor once again. "I wonder if the hospital has a frequent customer punch card," I say.

"Hits to the head are serious, Drake."

"Tell you what, once the bump goes away, I'll make a return appointment. I can tell them I've been having headaches. This ought to get me another scan."

"Deal."

The silence comes back, resilient this time. Only when I'm almost finishing up, Skye mumbles, "I feel sorry for her."

I stop the improvised surgery. "You've got to be kidding me."

She gives me a pained look. "We broke into her house. I attacked her. I hurt her."

"Awesome," I say. "I couldn't care less about her. Well, maybe I could, if I tried really hard…"

"Come on, Drake. You're better than this. What if I hurt her?"

I drop the tweezers and hug her. "You didn't, Skye. *She* tried to kill you. Don't forget it."

After I break our embrace, she nods, unconvincingly. She motions for me to resume the operation. I remove another shard, and Skye grimaces.

"We made a mistake," she says after a while. I don't contradict her. "Many mistakes. This is getting way out of control."

"Well, if they had let me go after I broke in—into what I thought was an empty house, by the way—nobody would be hurt. Including me."

"The same applies if we didn't break into her house to begin with," Skye says.

"Good point. Useless now, but good. Hindsight is a bitch." Something else bothers me. "Who were those guys? How did she get them to work for her?"

Skye shrugs. "If she's really a Night witch, I'm guessing they work for potions, sex, or money. Even drugs: some of us can brew powerful hallucinogens. A few Sisters actually make a living of it."

"I loved what you did with the potions," I say. "But you should have told me before. I'd recommend using a Super Soaker: much more effective."

She chuckles, but her expression is still pensive.

"Do you think Jane is calling the police right now?" I ask.

"I've been thinking—Ouch!" Oops. I made a mistake and pushed

226

a shard of glass even deeper. She removes her hand, blows a little on the wound, and then says, "I've been thinking about that. I don't know. Many things are hard to explain. Why would we go to her house? What is all that glass and strange liquid all over the place?"

I take an involuntary look at the bloodied glass I've been depositing on the dresser. "She doesn't have to explain anything. Actually, she just has to tell the truth. Because we acted like criminals. And she has our blood in her house. And someone might have seen my plates—not that are many caramel-colored Volvos in the city."

"I can think of only one reason," Skye says, raising the index finger on her good hand, "that would stop her. The Veil."

"Does she care?"

"If she does, she must belong to a coven. And that would be an even bigger problem."

Chapter 48: Skye

Jane doesn't show up at school the next day. Nor do the police.

I'm wearing long sleeves and knitted gloves. When I look at my wounds, the word that comes to my mind is "evidence." If Jane wanted to get us in trouble, it would be too easy.

But no sirens and no calls to the principal's office mean we get a reprieve. At least for today.

Today I'm glad I got my Jane alarm. Drake, however, has no True Sight. He's so uneasy. Jumpy, really. It's odd seeing him so subdued.

"What's wrong?" I ask after we make out. "I mean, besides…" I let my voice trail.

We're at Priscilla's—now Drake's and mine—hidden picnic table behind the building.

"I'm not worried about you," he says. "I mean, you can detect Jane, and you showed me you can take care of yourself. But I wonder if she will go after me, you know?"

"After you? She already went after you."

"After my family. It's the oldest trick in the bad guy's handbook, right? And it would be easy. Dad is so trusting, and Mona is already hanging out with crazy people."

I don't know what to say.

Chapter 49: Drake

At night, I get to sleep really late, concerned about Jane, the human wrecking ball, and all the other weird stuff. I wake up so tired that I don't have the energy to be worried. My body just drags itself downstairs.

When I arrive at the kitchen, I see Dad drinking coffee. He sets the mug on the table deliberately. A big grin lights up his face.

"No work today?" I ask.

"No," he says.

I'm too sleepy to investigate further. I just pour myself some coffee and munch on an Eggo (a habit I retain from my toddler years).

Sounds come from upstairs. Mona is up, and she's probably rummaging through her drawers. Doors are opened and closed, faucets turned on and off. I sip my coffee and notice some neatly stacked sheets of paper on the kitchen island. My brain is too sluggish to register their meaning, though.

Mona finally comes to the kitchen. She's as surprised as me when she sees Dad at home.

"What are you doing here, Dad?" she asks.

"Well, I live here," he says, still grinning. What's up with him?

"Aren't you supposed to be in Renton by now?" Mona asks while she steals half of the Eggo from my plate. I'm too slow to react.

"I'm going to Vegas today," Dad says, and we can tell he's been dying to say it for a while. He glances from me to Mona and back, scrutinizing our reaction.

I finally feel strong enough to get back to the world of the living. "Are we that deep in debt? Are you trying to gamble your way now?"

Nothing fazes him and his (rare) grin.

"We have an IT convention in Las Vegas," Dad says. "Tom was supposed to go, but he came down with the flu, and the company gave his spot to me." Dad seems very satisfied with the arrangement.

Mona leans back on the counter. "Really? Because this sounds like an elaborate story."

Dad goes on the defensive. "No, I really have to go to Las Vegas. I'm a vendor. Look, I have the badge and everything." Beaming, he shows us a fancy name card with the company's name and the convention logo. I decide to have some fun

"'Shopped!" I say.

"What?" my father asks, confused.

"I don't even work with computers and I can create a better Photoshop than that," I explain, handing him back the badge.

He snatches it from my hands. "You two are impossible," he mumbles.

"Come on, Dad. It's a joke…"

"Go have fun!" Mona says.

"Yeah!" I say. "Just don't come back married, okay? I don't want an exotic dancer as a stepmother."

He chuckles, but his expression becomes solemn again. He points to the papers on the counter. "I printed the hotel information and the whole schedule so you guys can find me if you need me. There's an envelope with money for expenses, but only use it if you really need it. The bills are paid, the fridge stocked." He stares at us, and I recognize the same look he gave me when I was six and he left me at the kindergarten for the first time. "Are you going to be okay? I have to stay there until Friday, but I'll call every night."

"Don't you guys go out after the convention?" I ask. Dad is reluctant to reply, so I go on, "Don't worry about us. If we need something, we'll call you. Just enjoy the trip."

He nods, grateful, and turns to Mona. "I'll be back with plenty of time for your birthday, sweetie. Any ideas for gifts?"

"A year in Europe?" She raises her eyebrows. I can't even tell if she's serious about it.

"I can bring you a replica of the Eiffel Tower, what do you say?"

"A replica of a replica? No, thanks," Mona replies. She eats the last piece of Eggo. *My* piece.

"I'll surprise you, then," Dad says.

I can't shut up. "You already did."

***

After I tell Skye about my Dad's impromptu trip, her blue eyes sparkle.

"What about your sister?" she asks.

"Mona, the Queen of Dramaland, informed me this morning she'll be staying over at Pain's—her friend. Sleepover."

"Interesting…" Skye says. "So, you're going to be home alone?"

I grin. "Yes…"

She slides her index finger down my chest. "I thought about something we could do."

"I thought about it too," I manage to say. It's hard to speak while

231

holding my breath.

"Cool. We need a good plan for the search," she says, excitedly.

I feel like someone poured icy water on me. "What?"

Skye withdraws her wandering finger. "What? Isn't it what you were thinking?"

"No. Not even close," I say.

She bursts out laughing. When she sees my annoyed face, she stops. Unwillingly. She touches my face with her hands, holding my head between her palms and staring into my eyes. "Now that you mention it—not that you actually mentioned it—I understand what you mean."

I nod slowly, my head still captive in her hands.

"It's not a bad idea," she says.

I hope I heard her right. "You mean it?" I whisper.

But there it is, a slight hesitancy. In a flash, I feel hopeful, crushed, and guilty about our exchange. I don't want to put pressure on her. Well, I'm not a monk, and I'd prefer not to wait forever, but the last thing I want is to leave her in an uncomfortable spot.

"Why—why don't you come over? I'll cook something, we can watch a stupid movie, and just, you know, be together," I say. "No expectations," I add, after a pause.

She shows me a sunny smile: an absolute, joyous smile.

Then she moves closer and kisses me. This kiss—an enticing, lush display of passion—is nothing like we had ever had. It tastes like a juicy fruit, a scrumptious, fleshy delicacy. She pulls me to her as if afraid she might lose me. For some reason, this feeling of being desired puts it over the top for me.

The kiss moves instantaneously to the top spot of my "best kisses ever" list. Fortunately, an ever-expanding list.

Chapter 50: Skye

Drake picks me up at home, under the suspicious glares of Aunt Gemma. Feigning innocence, I wave goodbye. I had mentioned to her that I might arrive home late, if not at all, and we had a nasty discussion.

He doesn't speak much on our way over. It's weird going to spend the night, with the sun still up. Dusk won't be upon us until around seven o'clock.

He makes a point of opening the door for me and letting me in first.

The house is neat—or maybe Drake slaved all afternoon to make it more presentable. We go through the kitchen to the deck.

"I hope you like barbecue," he says.

He must see my eyebrows raising, because he adds, "I wanted to cook for you, but I don't know how. Barbecue is a no-brainer." He shrugs. "Don't worry, I know you don't eat meat."

"I love grilled veggies," I say. He beams and proceeds to turn on the gas grill.

I look for an MP3 player of some kind. When I ask Drake about it, he blushes a bit and points to a small pile of CDs by the home theater system. I browse through the plastic cases: it's mostly emo and goth bands, and some indie rock. I smile: almost all the indie bands are from the UK. Dirty Pretty Things, the Arctic Monkeys. The last remnants of our old empire.

"Are all of those yours?" I ask, raising my voice so he can hear me from the deck.

"Only the *music* CDs. The downer bands are all Mona's," he yells back. He seems to be struggling with the vegetables he intends to grill.

So, Drake is a rocker—an endangered species. I still know so little about him... Franz Ferdinand is my choice. I skip to the third track. Through the patio door, I see Drake smiling softly when he hears the first riffs of "Take Me Out." I'll leave the more romantic soundtrack for later; now I want to inject some life into the house.

I come to him and embrace him from behind. He leans back slightly, making the contact between our bodies more intimate, but he carries on with his cooking.

"What are you making?" I ask.

"I'm wrapping corn in aluminum foil, so it doesn't burn. We're also having broccoli on the grill. I'll cook your boca burgers and my *real* burgers later."

I give him a soft kiss on the back of his neck. "Mind if I look around?" I ask.

He hesitates for the tiniest of seconds, but points to the inside of the house with his barbecue tongs. "Go ahead," he says.

Going back inside, I really look at the house for the first time. It looks modest, put together more for functionality than anything else. The flat screen TV is new, but everything else, couch, curtains, tables, are worn and about at the end of their life. The kitchen cabinets are white, refinished. The walls are painted in bright colors, giving the house a cozy and happy vibe.

At the bottom of the stairs, I see the garage door to my right, but I don't go there. Instead, I move upstairs, where I find three rooms. The master has a small bathroom and white walls, and it is even barer than the living room. I pass another small shared bathroom in the hallway. The next bedroom is Drake's. He tried to hide the pigstyishness of it, with no success. The closet door opened, probably by itself, and now reveals a pile of dirty clothes crumpled in a heap. On the desk, a computer, some energy bar wrappers, and an empty Vitamin Water bottle. His school books are stacked on a small bookshelf above the desk.

I sit on his bed. Fortunately the cover is a geometric, abstract pattern. I was afraid of finding Disney characters. I bounce on it, and then I giggle: am I unconsciously test-driving it for later in the evening? It *is* a good-sized queen bed, I notice.

"Come on, Skye," I whisper to myself. I set the thought aside.

On the wall, I see a massive Jimi Hendrix poster. Drake is old school indeed.

The poster makes my mind itchy. Something's wrong, and I can't pinpoint what. Then it strikes me. I go back to the hallway and glance to Mr. Hunter's bedroom and to the stairs at my feet. Except for the Hendrix poster, no paintings or pictures hang anywhere on this floor. I can't recall seeing any downstairs either.

Mona's bedroom door stares at me—a purple door. I like her already.

I want to see if she has paintings on the walls. I shrug and open the door. There, I find the life in the house.

Her bedroom is a collage. The walls are covered with small posters and magazine cutouts. Blockbuster fantasy movies and indie cult flicks share the wall's real estate equally. Top models of both genders mingle with Madre Teresa, Che, Obama, and other iconic figures. I see an Aztec mask hanging on the wall. Kanji characters are stenciled below it. Mona uses the walls as white boards, sketching and writing stuff in every gap between the pictures.

The room smells of lotus flowers. I see an incense burner on her dresser. I smile; Mona is a kindred spirit.

The dresser is the only organized space of her bedroom. A huge mirror dominates the area above the dresser. It has little lights that remind me of Mum's dressing rooms. But Mona's dresser is personal, with small pictures framing the mirror, like a miniature version of the walls around me. She has an interesting collection of make-up, including every color imaginable of lipsticks, mascara, and even some hair paint.

The smell of Drake's cooking invades the bedroom and fights the lotus scent. It snaps me out of my journey to this strange land. I regret to leave.

On my way out, I notice the walls have no bookshelves, but piles of books litter the floor. I'd like to take a look at some of them, but Drake yells from below.

"Skye, would you make us something to drink?"

I give a last glance to Mona's sanctuary and leave, closing the door. I go down two steps at a time, feeling good about myself, about Drake, about our evening together.

Then I see him waiting for me. He's wearing a black apron with huge white block letters reading "Kiss the cook."

I feel that, as a guest, I must oblige.

***

Our (virgin) piña coladas sit on the floor. We cuddle on the carpet lazily. Drake is propped on some pillows, embracing me from behind while we watch college football on the telly.

"It's like rugby, but with helmets and steroids," he whispers in my ear.

"I've lived half of my life in the States," I reply, showing off my American accent. "I know baseball too!"

"That's 'airborne cricket' for you. Why do you use an American accent?"

I've never mentioned it to anyone before. "To blend in. I don't want to attract attention."

He snorts. "Good luck with that. Have you *seen* you? Or your eyes?"

My hand goes behind him and slaps the back of his head, softly. "You're so silly."

"Hey," he says, his voice playfully malicious. "You're not in a position to be calling me names." He tightens his embrace.

As an answer, I lounge further back, and mold my body into his. I grin at his muscles stiffening.

His hands caress the front of my neck, a touch not soft enough to tickle me, nor too firm. Just perfect.

I want him badly, but this simmering is so nice. We have the whole night, and I'm waiting for darkness to envelop us. It just feels right.

He kisses the nape of my neck. A dry, soft touching of his lips to my skin. It gives me goose bumps, and I let out an involuntary, soft moan.

I lay the back of my head on one of his shoulders, elevating my chin, giving him access to my slightly parted lips. He takes the initiative.

Making out with him is sooo good. My hand goes behind his neck, pushing his head down toward mine, making our kiss more intense.

A primal urge takes over me. I turn around and lie on top of him. Even I am surprised by my eagerness. I push the pillows away. My hands reach for his wrists, and I pin them against the carpet, leaving him at my mercy. He doesn't fight it. I can't stop kissing him.

We lose track of time. In one of the rare moments when I let our lips separate, he whispers softly, "We should come up for some air."

"Air is overrated," I whisper back, and we resume our session.

He turns the tables on me, rotating our bodies so he emerges on top. He's the one holding my arms gently against the carpet now, my wrists above my head.

I'm lost in this different world. No worries. No rush. Nothing, just the two of us. I even feel a slight vibration as if a low-voltage electric current flows through the skin of my back. It's pleasing, and I notice its intensity is increasing. Drake's lips explore my neck.

"The ground is shaking," I say, dreamily.

He gives a soft chuckle. "Already?" he whispers. Drake doesn't stop kissing my neck.

A tingling. Pleasant, stimulating at first, but—

Magical energy. A Sister is close to us. But I never felt it like this, so sparsely. It's always a wave. This thin veil of energy is delicate, almost ethereal. And what's up with the vibration?

"Something's wrong," I say. My eyes open. Knickknacks on the mantle are vibrating.

"What?" he asks softly. "Am I…"

He doesn't need to finish the question. The whole house shakes. Drake's eyes bulge, and he leaps to his feet.

"Earthquake!" My voice quivers as he helps me up.

His eyes scan the house in a blaze, and soon he's dragging me to the front door. He opens it and pushes me against the frame. He takes his place in front of me.

He holds my hand, trying to soothe me. "It's a strong beam!" Drake yells over the otherworldly noise.

The house shaking is surreal, but what distresses me is the energy I feel. It gets stronger and stronger, as if an electric shock permeates me. The tingling overwhelms me, saturates my body, and soon I'm shaking too.

The trembling—*my* trembling—becomes uncontrollable, and I feel like fainting, my eyes losing focus.

Drake notices it and gets a hold of me. He hugs me hard, trying to subdue my spasms.

We hear an ever-increasing rumbling sound. The noise of squeaky metal is terrorizing. The knickknacks tremble to the edge of the mantle and plunge to the floor, like mindless lemmings. The TV follows suit and falls from the stand, crashing onto the floor where we were just seconds ago.

I'm regaining control of my body. My shaking weakens, but not the shaking around us.

Drake feels my body relax. "Are you okay?" he yells over the noise.

I nod to him, and he lets me go slowly. The tingling is still there, but now it's a steady flow. Still, it's the strongest signature I've ever felt.

It's got to be the Singularity.

Car alarms set off, and their blaring makes us turn our attention to the outside. It's bizarre. Cars shake from side to side in a macabre jig, and the street itself seems to pulsate. I'm unsure if everything is vibrating that hard, or my own quivering makes it all blurry.

I look back to Drake, who tries to reassure me with a friendly grin. But I can see the uneasiness behind the smile.

For some reason I think of Mona's neatly arranged dresser upstairs. In the midst of the panic, the image of all her make-up and jewelry knocked over and her delicate belongings shattered makes me sad.

We hear glass breaking in the distance, some cries. A few neighbors imitate us and find shelter by their front doors. On the street, I see a young boy skateboarding fast, pointlessly trying to run away from all of it.

Drake notices him, too. "Come here!" he yells above the mayhem. "Now!"

The boy jumps off his skateboard in a seamless movement, abandoning it on the sidewalk, and runs to us. He positions himself between Drake and me. Drake puts his left hand on the boy's shoulder, who nods gratefully, but says nothing. Drake's right hand still holds mine.

The rumbling subsides. The screeching sound of metal on metal goes away. The noise of destruction, inside and outside, fades. Except for the car alarms. When I tune that out, the remaining silence is eerie.

I'm still shaking, but I think now it's mostly my legs.

Drake's nervous smile regains some confidence. The boy between us, despite his cocksure skull t-shirt, smiles sweetly to me. He turns to Drake and reaches for the hand on his shoulder. They fist-bump without uttering a word, and the boy dashes to his skateboard, left overturned on the curb.

"I know him," Drake explains. "He lives down the street."

His words awaken me from my terror spell. I take a deep breath, but my knees stumble, and I almost fall. As always, Drake is there for me, and he catches me.

"Easy," he says. "You okay?"

I'm embarrassed to show weakness, and I straighten up quickly.

"I think so. But I felt magical energy—"

My cell rings.

"Skye!" Gemma's panicked voice greets me. "Are you hurt?"

"No! I'm fine. Drake's here with me. How about you?"

Drake watches me for a second, and then runs inside.

"I'm okay. I hid under the table," she says. Thank Goddess for the massive dining room table. "Do you need me to pick you up?"

"No, I'm fine," I say. I see Drake going upstairs.

"All right. I'm on my way to Linda's. I'm worried about her." Linda is our elderly neighbor, who lives alone. I hope she's safe.

"Sure. Don't worry about me," I say. "I love you," I add. It surprises even me.

After a beat, Gemma answers. "I love you too, dear. Take care. Call me often."

"Sure thing," I say. I hang up, moving inside to go after Drake. Just then I see him running down the stairs, two steps at a time, his cell glued to his ear.

"Mona is not answering," he says, worried. "What are you doing? Go back to the door." He grabs my arm with a strong, rough grip, and drags me back to where we were before. "Aftershock," he says as a way of an apology.

While we wait for Mona to pick up, I scan the street. People are coming out of their houses to examine the damage, turn their car

241

alarms off, and assist their neighbors. It's about dinnertime and most families are home. A couple emerges from the house in front of us. The woman carries a surprisingly quiet baby and the man yells at us, "You guys okay?"

"Yeah," Drake answers, cell still pressed into his ear. "You?"

The man nods and points to his baby, "Little Kevin was laughing the whole time. He thinks we were playing some game. Kids…"

Drake gives him a half-smile and points to his cell. "I can't find Mona. I'll go to her friend's house. If we miss each other and she shows—"

"I'll let her know," the man interrupts. "She can stay with us until you're back."

Drake just lifts his hand in a thanking gesture. The man waves goodbye and goes check on his family. Drake turns to me. "Is Gemma okay?"

I nod. "Do you think we should drive now? I mean, the aftershocks."

"I need to *know* that Mona is okay," he says. His voice is breaking. "My dad left her with me."

I remember his pain over the fire incident. He doesn't need to explain. "Sure," I say. "Let's go."

My cell tinkles again. Connor.

"Did you feel that?" he asks.

No how-are-yous. Again. "Of course I felt it, you twit!"

"She's right in front of our eyes, Skye. Can you track her?"

"No, it went away," I say, ever the dutiful Sister.

"Come on, Skye, find her. Don't screw this up!"

I look at Drake's desperate expression. "I need to do something else now," I tell Connor before hanging up.

Chapter 51: Drake

I fear the worst when neither Mona nor Pain answers the phone. And I don't have Pain's landline number anywhere. Stupid new cell phone.

Damn earthquake. The last one I can remember hit when I was a kid. It was much weaker than this. Pain's house is not far away. I decide to run there with Skye.

We hold hands and negotiate our way through the people crowding the streets. They're still disoriented, looking behind their backs as if an aftershock might sneak up on them. Fortunately, very few are bleeding. Small groups sit curbside, maybe afraid to get back into the buildings. Businesses are handing out plastic cups of water.

Traffic is slow. A few cars are left in the middle of the road. Going on foot was a good idea.

An antique shop owner examines the damage inside. Some houses and stores have broken windows. Debris and bricks litter the sidewalk, and at least one parapet fell—judging by the lack of blood, not hitting anyone.

I see small fissures on the side of the buildings. The sidewalks are uneven and cracked. Across the street from us, a water leak goes unchecked.

Skye grabs my arm. She has a frightened look on her face. "What?" I ask.

"I sense another Sister," she says, quietly. She looks around. "Not too close."

"Do you—"

"No," she says, "Never mind. Let's go find Mona." But she looks over her shoulder one more time.

We run the last block. When I turn Pain's street corner, my heart sinks. They are not outside like everybody else.

Skye says, "Take it easy, Drake."

I let go of her hand and run to Pain's. While ringing the doorbell, I look through the window. It's a split-level. Only the foyer is visible from the outside. Nobody answers, so I go around the house, quickly looking through the windows. I reach the backyard and climb the stairs to the second-level deck. Mona and Pain are just lying on the floor inside. Still.

I yell, "Mona!" I try the door handle, bang on the glass door.

Skye joins me, peeks inside, and picks up a heavy plant pot. "Get out of the way," she commands.

She hits the bottom of the pot near the door handle, breaking the glass door. Mona and Pain are far enough away. They aren't hit by the shards.

Some glass still clings to the frame, so I sneak my hand inside, unlocking the door. When I slide the frame open, more pieces of glass fall. I don't care. "Mona!" I yell again.

Skye is dialing 911. I go inside and kneel next to my sister, ready to start CPR. I saved Skye. I can save Mona.

But Mona is still breathing. A quick check tells me Pain breathes too.

I shake my sister gently. No response. Mona just lays on the floor, still.

No visible wounds, no blood. On either of them. It actually makes me more anxious, not knowing where they are hurt, or how much.

A sorrow the size of the world overcomes me.

***

When the paramedics put Mona on the gurney, I almost lose it. I feel like I'm about to cry. Skye tries to console me.

Mona is stable, but unresponsive.

"They're secured," the paramedic says. I pull myself together. I'll ride with Mona and Pain in the ambulance, and Skye will drive my car to the hospital.

Skye points to the ambulance and whispers, "Just go. I'll be with you soon."

***

I called Dad after the paramedics arrived. He said he'd be on the first flight out of Vegas, but they told him they're still assessing the conditions at Sea-Tac, and the airport is closed. I try to calm him down, to no avail.

"It's all my fault. I shouldn't have left you guys alone. I'm sorry," he says. He doesn't sound like he's about to cry. He just looks defeated.

Promising him I'll call with news, I hang up.

Neighbors called Pain's parents, who were having a night out. They too are on their way to the hospital.

***

They took Mona for exams. The anxiety is killing me.

She looked so peaceful when I saw her. Rested. Actually, I've never seen her so beautiful, so... glowing. It made me even sadder, how she looked like a little princess.

But my sister is no little kid. She is a tough, tough girl.

That's the only reason I let them take her away from me. If it were up only to me, she wouldn't leave my sight. It may take a couple of hours so I wander around the hospital, drifting like so many others tonight.

The TV in the ER waiting area catches my attention. Many people with small injuries await triage, and we're all glued to the news. The earthquake wasn't catastrophic. No fatal injuries have been reported so far, but many are in the hospital, and the material damage is significant. The report says some people are having trouble locating family and friends. They are careful not to use the word "missing." Everything is chaotic, a few cell towers are down, and they don't want to cause panic.

The seismologists are surprised by the absence of aftershocks, especially when the earthquake was so close to the surface. They can't understand how an earthquake was produced at such shallow focal depth, whatever that is. They say the city of Seattle was unlucky, because the epicenter was right inside the city limits. On the other hand, it was a minor event, only a 5.0.

Boulder and Sean call from Eugene to check on me. Their families are okay, but they are coming back anyway.

I realize there's nobody else I need to contact. Or that needs to call me. The Hunters are a small, isolated family. When bad things happen, I feel even lonelier.

The atmosphere in the waiting areas of the hospital is one of solidarity, though. The common cause to our misfortunes brings us together, and we share the apprehension about our close ones.

Some people look more anxious than others. A lady can't stop crying, but five or six people surround her—maybe her family. A big guy about my age seems shell-shocked, tentative, looking completely out of place next to the elevators.

Suddenly he stiffens up and looks at the elevator doors. His sudden reaction makes me follow his gaze. When the doors open, Skye is inside, looking straight at the guy. She has a glint of recognition in her eyes.

Chapter 52: Skye

Before I leave, I call Priscilla. We assure each other we're okay. I tell her about Mona, and she asks me to send her best wishes to Drake. I end the call and drive to the hospital.

The parking lot is full, but I squeeze Drake's Volvo between two SUVs. As I'm leaving the car, I sense the tingling. A Sister is around.

Judging by the low intensity, it's somewhere in the hospital. I get in the elevator with other people. As we move up, the tingling intensifies.

It's odd. I felt it before, every time Judi and Mum were together close to me. It's coming from two sources upstairs. And increasing.

The elevator door opens. After everybody leaves, I see Connor staring at me from the waiting room.

When the doors begin to move again, I come out of my stupor, and extend my arm to stop them from closing. I get out and march to Connor.

He doesn't even let me ask. "Jane listed me as her emergency contact. I didn't even know about it."

"What happened to her?" I ask. A myriad of questions swirl in my mind. Is this another one of Jane's ploys? Is she here because of our break-in? Is Connor with her?

Now, why would the last one come to mind?

"Motorbike accident. Apparently she was riding when the quake hit," he says.

I nod, trying to piece the puzzle together in my head.

"Did you see her?"

"I did, but she's unconscious. The doctors didn't find anything too worrisome in their tests. But she has a few bruises, even cuts on her face. She doesn't look good."

Goddess, the guilt is sudden and overwhelming. Yes, she tried to kill me, amongst other lesser attacks. Still, it's not like I want to kill her. I *did* want to harm her at her house, and self-defense was only an excuse then. I'll never tell Connor I've been there. I don't want him judging me, or reporting me to the Mothers.

Once again, I feel this is going too far. It wasn't supposed to go like this.

"Are you kidding me?" Drake's voice behind me makes me jump out of my skin.

"Drake!" I say. "I..." I point to me. "Connor..." I say, pointing to my ex. It's too much to process, and I sound stupid.

"I've been listening to you two for a while," Drake says with a menacing tone totally not his own. He turns to Connor. "So, you're the idiot who cannot control Jane."

Connor is unfazed by Drake's barbs. His eyes dart between Drake and me.

"Excuse us," Drake says to Connor. "I need to talk to Skye." When Connor doesn't move, Drake yells, "Now!"

The waiting room crowd glances at our group. Connor, ever the Veil protector, looks around nervously and walks to the nurse's station.

The thoughts in my head are a little more organized now. "Listen, Drake," I say, "I didn't know he was here." I have no idea why I feel compelled to explain it to Drake. It's not like I did something wrong.

"I've heard you. I saw you. I know you were both surprised," Drake says, calmer now.

"Are we okay?"

For a moment he seems about to lose it, but he sighs deeply. His voice is bitter. "No, Skye. We're not okay. I'm not. Mona isn't either. I couldn't protect my sister. I can't protect you. And everything is conspiring to pull you and that... guy together. Oh, yeah, and the witch thing."

Connor is coming back to us. He clearly overheard Drake.

"You broke the Veil?" Connor whispers to me, sizing Drake up.

Drake steps in. "*I* broke it, man. As you three just prove over and over, you witches are not that smart."

Connor must have Teflon ears, because his priority is clear. "Lower your bloody voice," he says in a growl.

"I need to see Jane," I say.

This finally breaks their staring contest.

"What?" Drake asks.

"Why?" Connor asks.

"I just need to do it." My eyes seek Drake's approval.

"Is it about the search?" Connor whispers.

"Does it matter?" I say.

***

Somehow Connor agrees, and somehow he makes the staff let me visit Jane (his Trust Charm is handy) in her private room.

The tingling is intense so close to her.

Does she feel my presence? Even when I'm sleeping, I can sense the physical sensation if a Sister is nearby, but the tingling might not bother witches that don't possess True Sight. Mum and I have rooms away from each other in part because I can't sleep with her magical energy so close to me, but she has no problem with mine. Sleeping next to Connor was equally impossible.

I shake the thought from my mind.

I stay by the door, hesitant. Afraid of seeing what permanent damage my attack caused to her good looks. Guilty about unhinging her so thoroughly that she crashed her bike.

And yes, I'm concerned that she'd snap out of her coma and attack me, Carrie-style.

I get closer to her bed. She's still, breathing with no help from machines. A blanket covers her, except for the arms. I see deep red and black wounds on her left forearm and elbow.

When I'm close, I dare to look at her face. There it is.

Her left cheek has two big gashes where I hit her with the flask. Several minor cuts adorn her once lovely face. All of them caused by me.

I expected a serene look, but her eyebrows are wrinkled with a crease of concern. Even when she's blacked out, Jane's personality surfaces on her harsh expression.

It doesn't stop me from, in a kindhearted moment, touching her face tenderly with the back of my hand. I feel for her.

I caress her face with my fingertips. I want her to feel it, to know that she's not alone. That we call each other Sisters for a reason.

My hand stops at those two big gashes. The rough tactile sensation of the wounds makes me sad. Her face is ruined.

Then I see tiny green sparkles coming off my fingertips. A small, visible electric current flows from my hand to Jane's face.

Startled, I withdraw my hand. I'm not sure of what I just saw.

It had no effect on Jane's sleep. The wounds on her face, though, glow a light pink.

What is that? I dare to reach my hand out again, mimicking its previous position.

There it is, the electric current. It begins with tiny sparkles, but as I leave my hand over the wound, the flow increases. Not much. It reaches a stable stream.

The scabs turn a darker shade of pink and start to vanish. Fascinated, I put my hand over her other cuts. Soon they disappear.

The scabs are gone now, and the two sides of one of the gashes slowly close the cut's gap, creating new flesh, new skin out of the green stream of magic.

Yes, magic. What else could it be?

But it wasn't supposed to work like that. It's never visible.

And I'm sure I don't have a Healing Charm.

Nevertheless, I let Jane use my magical energy to heal herself. *She* is doing this. But I let her.

I owe it to her.

The second big gash is gone. Her face is perfect. Out of curiosity, I still leave my hands close to her face. The green flow is steadfast.

Color comes to her face. I look closer. A very thin patch of facial hair over her lips disappears.

I remove my hands in horror. I realize what is going on.

I rush to the bathroom and look at my reflection in the mirror. Only it's not me I see. Or, rather, it's not the prom queen version of me.

What I see is what I should have looked like all my life. Not gorgeous, no-imperfections-Skye. The real Skye. A plain British girl.

Jane has just stolen my Allure Charm.

Chapter 53: Drake

Mr. Darcy and I are waiting for Skye. At least we're on opposites sides of the waiting room. I'm not that modern of a boyfriend.

I should stop calling him Mr. Darcy. It's a bad omen. Mr. Darcy *always* gets the girl.

The jerk suddenly looks around, confused. His eyes stop on me, but after a while, he goes to the patient's room area.

He's not beating me up there. He probably wants to talk to Skye alone. I start to move, but my cell dings. Frowny faces look at me; I forgot to turn it off. It's Skye.

"Take the elevator and come down to meet me," she says in a rushed voice. "I'm at P2, waiting for you. Don't ask."

I've been through enough with Skye. I know that if she could, she would have said more. I do as told. Connor doesn't notice me sneaking out.

When I arrive at P2, Skye is in my Volvo, the motor running, parked right in front of the elevator. I sneak a quick glance to the cargo area of my car before jumping into the passenger's seat. After I close my door, I look at the back seat.

We leave in a hurry. Skye asks me, "What are you looking for?"

"For a moment, I thought we were kidnapping Jane," I answer, finally seeing her up close. She's different. "Wow, was it rough in there? You look like hell."

We took the ramp up out of the parking lot. Her eyes are on the driveway. We reach daylight, and I take a closer look.

Her face is different. What is going on?

She goes four blocks without a word, maneuvers around a piece of road blocked by the earthquake debris, and then parks in a strip mall's lot. She turns to me.

Skye looks like she just got out of bed after a rough night. Her eyes are puffy. Her skin's dry.

It's weird. She is still beautiful, but she lost that gloss, that sparkle. It's like seeing a movie star without make-up and flattering lighting.

It doesn't matter to me. "What happened?" I ask.

She stares at me, no doubt looking for clues, but she finally relents. "I'm not sure," she says. Her voice becomes throaty once again. "I think Jane might have stolen my Allure Charm."

This is one weird sentence. I try to wrap my mind around it.

"Is that even possible?" I ask "Wait, wasn't she in a coma?"

A frayed Skye shakes her head. "I don't know what's possible anymore."

She tells me how green sparks flew from her hand and healed Jane's face. She points to her face when she explains all the signs of Allure left her.

I laugh.

She gets mad.

"Sorry," I say. "But... This is just insane." She turns her back to me, staring out of her window. "Try to see it through my eyes. Imagine you weren't trained since you were a kid to see magic as natural." I want to touch her, make her turn to face me, but I just talk. "To me, it's easy to accept when we're talking about potions and… and… feelings. It's unlikely, but it's somewhere between, I don't know, homeopathy—to me, very plausible—and horoscopes."

"Is that how you see me? A New Age weirdo?" Her voice quivers.

No sense hiding it. "In the beginning, a little, yes. I mean, can you blame me? Since then I've seen enough to believe in you. But now we're entering the realm of special effects."

She turns to me. "Look at me," she says, tears streaking her face. "Look at me!"

I stare into her eyes.

She takes a long time. "I'm changed. Can't you see it? Can't you accept it?"

"You look different," I say, wiping a tear from her cheek. "But you're still Skye."

She tries to back away from me, but my hand cradles her face. My other hand reaches behind the back of her neck, and I pull her gently toward my chest.

She lets out a few hiccupy sobs. "I'm not vain," she says without moving, her voice muffled. "I'm not one of those girls. I know it's easy to say this when I never had to worry about it, really. But I'm not shallow. I'm not."

It's not a question. I want to give her some reassurance. "I know," I say.

After a long pause, she becomes less agitated. She says, "It's just that she took away something that's been a part of me forever."

I nod. I understand her pain now, but she can't see me.

"I've never seen anyone do it, Drake. It can't be done." She moves away from me, wiping her face with her sleeve.

She's a mess, yes, but at the same time she looks so… real, so much like a person, and not someone supernatural. Vulnerable. I didn't know it was possible to want her more.

"It can't be done, Drake," she repeats.

"What do you mean?"

She untangles herself from my embrace and faces me. "She must be the Singularity. Can you imagine Jane with all that power?"

Chapter 54: Skye

After I share my suspicions with Drake, he stares at me, speechless.

"Do you understand?" I ask.

"I do," he says. "But you're wrong. Jane told me she was twenty. The witch you're looking for should be seventeen, right? Or even a boy."

I shake my head. "Jane could be lying. Or maybe the Singularity operates differently, maybe her Daybreak comes at a different age. The Singularity does have magical shields up, and that's unheard of."

He sighs. "There's also the logical explanation. If she were the Singularity, she would have used her power against us. She wouldn't hang around Mr. Stuffy, who's searching for her. Or she would've been gone, doing whatever it is almighty witches do."

Drake has a point. It still doesn't explain how she stole my Allure. I point that out to him.

"Can't you ask someone? Maybe it *is* possible and you just didn't learn it yet," he says. "Your mother would know, wouldn't she? Or your ex?" Drake adds, reluctantly. "Why didn't you tell him about it? Why did we have to run away?"

My mouth creases. I'm ashamed of myself. "Because it's Jane. All the Sisters will worship the Singularity. She would have extraordinary power." I stare at him. "*Jane.*"

He puts his palms up in a helpless gesture. "But what can you do? If she is the queen of magic, she is. There's nothing you can do about it."

I lower my eyes. "I thought about… preventing it." I wouldn't say it aloud to anyone else.

As I expected, he looks at me with surprise, his mouth agape. But he recovers quickly. "Sorry, Skye," he says with a soothing voice. "That's not who you are. I know you."

"But isn't it the right thing to do?"

His voice is firm. "No, it isn't. Sometimes we just have to let things play out."

***

I call Mum in England. It's morning there. She doesn't answer. Nor does Judi. I leave a message for each of them to call me back ASAP.

Drake convinces me to go back to the hospital. I call Connor and ask him to meet me at the outside parking lot. It's on the far side of the hospital, opposite the ER, but we need some privacy to discuss things under the Veil.

While Drake goes check on Mona and talk to her doctor, I will tell Connor the news.

When Connor first sees me, he can't hide his shock. Apparently, my former good looks were important to him. He wants to know what happened, but I ask him to answer some vital questions first. I try to shake off his magical energy signature so I can focus on our conversation.

An ambulance siren catches my attention—another one. I look

259

around the full lot, so many injured people coming to the ER.

Focus, Skye.

"Connor, when you were with Jane, was anything different?"

His expression darkens. "Skye, are you sure you want to go there? Again?"

"Don't be a smart ass. I'm not talking about being horny. Was anything different? With your magical energy?"

"What do you mean?"

I search for the right words. "Did you feel, I don't know, a disconnection of some sort? Magical energy flowing?"

He looks at me startled. "Yes. Yes, I did. I mean, I sensed her and all, but sometimes I felt like a decrease of my personal magic... I thought it was just this generic bad vibe she had." He shrugs.

That's when I tell him about the Jane incident, my Allure, and my suspicion.

"No, it's not possible," he says, calm. "She can't be the Singularity. It doesn't make sense."

"But how did she steal my Allure?" I point out.

His brow furrows. "I've heard of that. My parents like to talk about the old days, and I remember them mentioning a Charm that could absorb magical energy. It might be something like this."

"This must be it then!"

"No, no..." Connor says. "The Sister could only absorb magical energy when the source was dying."

I remember what Mum told me about the magic being part of oneself. Indivisible. Unless, it seems, if you die. Then the energy abandons you—

I grab Connor's arm. "She was doing a ritual while I drowned!" I yell.

Connor becomes livid, not because of my revelation, but worried about the Veil. He looks around nervously even though we are in a sea of cars with no one within hearing distance.

"Tell me that again," he asks.

"That's what Jane was doing to me! That's why she didn't stab me with her knife: she needed me to live for a little bit while she absorbed my energy!"

Connor's eyes twitch when he makes the connection.

"Let's see her," he says, pulling my arm so I follow him. I have flashbacks from when we were together. His commands and his hands-on attitude.

I shake his hands off, but I say, "Let's."

We enter the hospital, cross the lobby, go up the escalators. In some hallways we pass gurneys with people. Those are the minor victims of the earthquake—the lucky ones.

When we are halfway to the ER, I see Drake running toward us.

"Mona is gone!" he says out of breath. "I mean, not in her room. They took her for exams but now nobody knows where she is!"

I'm unable to process the information. I look at Connor, who only says, "Let's see Jane."

The three of us rush through the hospital, back to the ER, toward Jane's room on the other side of the huge building. When we enter the ER waiting area, I already know the truth. I can't feel anyone besides Connor. We cross the area, ignoring the protests coming from the nurse's station.

Connor arrives first at her room and swings the door open.

Jane's gone.

Chapter 55: Drake

I thought my brain would be murky, numbed by Mona's disappearance. Instead, what I get is a clear mind. I turn to the nurse who came complaining after us.

"You've got two patients missing! Do something! Lock down the hospital."

The nurse is as shocked as we are and mumbles, "I'm not sure we can—"

"Do it! Now!" I yell at her. Nurses have always been scary to me. Not anymore. She must have seen something in my eyes, because she goes running back to her station.

I point to Connor. "You, make sure they close the hospital."

To Skye, I say, "Call 911, and then search this floor. Maybe they're still around."

They say something back, but I'm too busy running to the stairs. I rush down, reach the garage, and frantically look around.

The traffic in the garage is heavy; many people are coming in with earthquake-related injuries. I run to the main exit and walk backwards from there, scanning cars and faces.

The sounds I'm expecting don't come. Where are the sirens, the clang of heavy steel doors closing? Why is it taking so long?

After a few minutes, I see my search is fruitless. And they still are letting everybody come and go! I rush back up to the ER.

As soon as I open the stairwell's door I see Connor at the station, talking to the nurse. "Why aren't we in lockdown?" I yell at him. I couldn't care less about the shushing sounds from staff.

He comes to me. "They can't do it. Because of the earthquake. Too many people need access to the hospital. Besides, they close it only if a baby is missing, or a nutter is on the loose."

"Jane qualifies!" I say.

He shakes his head. "Not to them, she doesn't. They told me they lock it down if there's a shooting, or an escaped convict or something like that. But they sent some staff to look around. They *are* concerned patients might be missing. But they think they're just misplaced. It's been a busy day."

Skye comes to us. "Didn't find them," she says out of breath. "911 took my call, but the woman said they have their hands full now, and we're low priority."

"She's a kid! Missing!" I say. I don't know what to do. My fingers go through my hair repeatedly. This is not happening.

"The police said they might be in the hospital, somewhere, lost in the chaos."

I look around the waiting room, and I see many other desperate faces. I'm not the only one concerned about a loved one tonight.

"Okay," I say, trying to compose myself. "The three of us *know* Jane took Mona. Right?" I glare at Connor, challenging him to contradict me, but he just nods. "Let the staff look for them here at the hospital. But Jane took Mona *somewhere*."

"Her house?" Skye asks.

Connor says, "You mean her condo? In Fremont?"

Skye and I exchange glances. "She's got another place," I say. "Connor, go to this Fremont condo. Skye and I will go back to Greenwood. That way we have witch radars on both places."

Connor looks at me sternly, but says nothing.

We spend a few minutes exchanging phone numbers with the hospital staff.

"Are you calling your father?" Skye asks.

Dad! What am I going to tell Dad? "Not now," I say. He can't do anything right now.

Chapter 56: Skye

Drake is driving like a madman, daring any police officer to stop us.

"Do you trust Connor?" he asks. "He'll help us, right?"

I don't understand. "He *is* helping us."

"I mean, doesn't he have a hidden agenda? He won't make a deal with Jane or something like that, right?" Drake takes his eyes off the road for a second. "Do you trust him?"

I remember Connor's second Charm is Trust. People tend to believe him. Drake asking me this means he doesn't trust Connor—at all.

My answer is not direct. "He'll do the right thing." He will, because the most important thing to him is finding the Singularity.

Drake keeps silent while overtaking two cars using the right lane.

He looks at me twice. "Your looks are coming back," he says with a frown.

"What?" I look for the vanity mirror. He's right. My old face is returning.

"Was it temporary, then?" Drake asks.

This is weird. Okay, I think I got it. "It seems Jane can absorb magical energy, including Charms. But it's temporary unless she absorbs the magical energy leaving the body of a Sister."

"Leaving the body?"

"When a Sister dies," I say. I explain to him that's probably what Jane tried to do to me at the pool.

"I get why Jane fled the hospital," I add. "All Sisters felt the energy during the earthquake, and Jane might think she has a chance of identifying the Singularity."

"Really? Even if you didn't?"

"Maybe Jane was close to the Singularity when the quake hit."

"But why would she take Mona? Does she want to get back at me?" he asks me.

"It can't be just that. It would accomplish nothing."

Something is nagging me, and I can't put my finger on it. It's an idea bouncing inside my head.

"Mona is a tough cookie," Drake says. "When she awakens, she'll fight back. She may escape from Jane."

I think Drake is just giving himself a pep talk, but I humor him. "Yeah. She might do that. Where would she go then? Who'd she call?"

"I don't know. Me, I hope. Or Pain."

Here comes that idea again. And again it flutters away.

Drake stops the car in front of Jane's house. All the lights are out. The whole street looks dark.

"Do you feel anything?" Drake asks.

I shake my head. "What now?"

"Call Connor," Drake says. I've never seen him so serious.

While I call him, I look at the abandoned house. I shiver when I recall the violence there. What if those two guys are waiting for us again? Jane must be weak after the injury. She probably knows we are coming. She must become stronger.

"Unless Jane wants to get more energy," I say, my words forming almost at the same time as my thoughts.

"What?" Drake asks.

But Connor picks up. "Hey, Skye. No luck. Jane's not here. I've talked to a neighbor who said she hasn't seen anyone today. What about you?"

"Same here," I say, hurried. I put him on the speaker so Drake can hear him too. "Listen, do you know where Jane had the accident?"

"Yeah, they gave me the address; her bike is still there. Do you think she might go back to get the bike?"

"Just give me the address!" I say.

"Hold on," he says. I imagine he's searching his pockets. "Corner of 45th St and Queen Anne Avenue." I look at Drake.

He says, "Connor. Can you think of any other place Jane might take Mona?"

"No," comes the answer. "I'm drawing a blank."

Drake says in a nice way, "Please go back to the hospital then. Help them search. Can you do that?"

Connor sounds puzzled. "Really? Don't you want me—"

"Thanks, man," Drake says, turning off the cell.

"What was that about?" I ask.

"The address. That's like two blocks from Pain's," Drake says.

The realization hits me. "Jane was there. Or close to them." I turn to him. "Why did you hang up?"

His face is inscrutable. "Still don't trust him."

"What happened at Pain's? I mean, don't you think it's odd, the two of them unconscious with no visible wounds? And how did Jane get knocked out?"

Drake looks rattled. "What do you mean?"

"Think about it! Three of them passed out with no injuries!"

He mumbles, "Jane had injuries…"

"She got hurt falling from the bike, and the rest was my doing the other day. Actually, Jane probably fell down when she felt the energy. She must have been close to the source."

Suddenly Drake's eyes bulge, and his face goes livid.

"Mona!" he says. "She was looking fantastic when I saw her at the hospital."

"And?" I can't see why this is relevant.

Drake is frantic. "Skye, she was looking *magically* fantastic." He points at me. "Like you."

In my head, all the puzzle pieces fall into place. "Allure," I say. "Mona has Allure. Mona is a Sister."

Chapter 57: Drake

We went through an earthquake and a kidnapping today, but this one revelation is what shocks me the most.

"How? How can Mona be a witch?" I ask. I can't even comprehend the words I'm speaking.

"She could be," Skye says. She's thinking hard, putting things together. Good, because I'm in no condition to do that. "It's not hereditary—not necessarily. Your mother could even be a Sister."

I really don't need more information; I can't handle it. My head is spilling facts and conjecture. "Let's focus on Mona right now," I say, almost pleading. "Can she be the one you are looking for?"

She nods. "Whoever the Singularity is, I'm pretty sure she created the earthquake. It's too much of a coincidence with the quake and the release of magical energy happening at the same time. If Mona is a Sister, she would be releasing a signature—unless she is the Singularity."

"This is not happening…"

"And even if Mona isn't the Singularity, even if she's a regular Sister, Jane probably wants to get Mona's energy." She utters the last few words in an increasingly low voice, looking at me expectantly and putting a hand on my shoulder.

I make an effort to hide my anger and focus on the practical side. "Where are they? Can you turn on your radar or something?"

She shakes her head. "We'd be wasting time if we just rode around hoping to catch Jane's signature. Where else could Jane go and have some privacy?"

"Brianna's!" I say.

"Good!" Skye says. "Let's go!"

***

I drive even faster than before. The police are probably too busy with the quake emergencies to bother with a speeding old car. I try to map the fastest route in my head. I could really use a GPS right now.

Brianna lives close to I-5, on Corliss Avenue. Our school's street, the 92nd, is the straightest path there. When we're about five blocks from Brianna's house, Skye grabs my arm.

"I'm sensing her!"

"How many?" I ask.

"Just one," she says. "But it's getting strong quickly." She bites her lip.

It takes me a while to put it together in my mind. Jane is probably already absorbing more energy. Which means…

I can't put it in words. I just hope I'm wrong.

We speed past our school grounds, and I glance briefly to my left, seeing the school's pool, *my* pool. A thought zaps through my head: I want to go swimming, forget the world, forget all this.

"It's too strong!" Skye says.

I hit the gas harder.

"Wait!" she says. "It's weaker now!"

Something clicks inside my head. I slow down and hit the brakes.

"What?" Skye asks.

I put it in reverse and back up, guiding myself through the rearview mirror.

"It's getting stronger again," Skye says, looking at me.

"Jane is inside the school," I say, my teeth clenched.

I reach the lot's entrance, put the car in gear again, and cross the lot without slowing down. The Volvo hits the curb and goes airborne for a second. I cross the grass and paths in front of school, avoiding trees, and I stop short of the entrance stairs.

Skye and I leave the car at the same time, climbing the steps two at a time, but by the large door, she pulls my arm.

"We're too close," she says. "Jane is sensing I'm here. She can feel me."

"Screw her. When I'm done with her, she won't feel anything," I reply.

The door is locked. Without thinking, I kick its glass part, hard, harder than I've ever hit anything. It's all a blur to me, but a few more kicks create an opening big enough for me to slide my hand inside and open the bolt from the other side.

We reach the dark hallway. I turn to Skye. "Where?"

She points to the other side of the building. The gym. We run there.

When I turn a corner, I see a blurry shape moving toward me. I duck instinctively, slowing down. Skye is right behind me, though, and something hits her before I have a chance to warn her.

She lets out a yelp and tumbles to the floor. I see another shadow, this time a person running away from us. Even in the dark corridor, I recognize Brianna.

I turn to Skye. She's unconscious. Breathing steadily.

She's sleeping!

Crap.

I shake her a few times and even give her one hard slap. Nothing.

I leave her there and start toward the gym. I'm more cautious now, aware of the danger of thrown potions.

Jane must have sensed Skye and sent Brianna to attack us.

Skye would have sensed where Jane is. But I don't have this radar, and either Jane or Brianna—or even those two guys from the house—can surprise me.

But nobody ambushes me. I stop by the gym's closed doors and look through the glass. The door is close to one of the corners. From where I stand, I can't see the whole basketball court.

But I see enough. In the center circle, Mona lays down on the half-court line, still wearing her hospital gown. I can't see her face.

Kneeling next to her is Brianna, searching for something inside a backpack. She has a numb, happy expression on her face, like a peaceful zombie. It's creepy.

But Jane's nowhere to be seen.

I glance over my shoulder—maybe she's coming from behind me—but nobody's there. I don't know what to do.

Brianna makes the decision for me.

She removes a handcrafted, ancient-looking black knife from the backpack. Then she looks straight at me.

I pull my hood over my head, squint my eyes, and take a deep breath. I have no idea how these potions work, but I'll try to minimize contact with them if someone throws one at me. I open the door, expecting the worst.

Then I rush inside, half-ducking, just in case Jane is in my blind spot ready to attack me.

She isn't, but Brianna yells, "Stop!" Brianna pulls Mona's inert head up and holds the knife's blade close to my sister's throat.

I halt right underneath the backboard.

Jane is in the other corner of the court, the one I couldn't see from the door. She sits cross-legged, with closed eyes and hands resting on her knees: the same pose she used when she tried to kill Skye in the pool. A ritual pose. Since she doesn't move, I turn to Brianna.

"Please let my sister go, Brianna," I say in a calm and soothing voice. "She's a kid."

Brianna looks at me as if I'm mad. "A kid? Have you seen what she did? She created an earthquake!"

"Don't hurt her. It'll accomplish nothing," I say. Things just come out of my mouth. How do you reason with a person willing to commit murder? How do you think straight when your sister's life is on the line?

Jane starts chanting. She's in a trance-like state, and I wonder if she can even hear us. Taking a cautious step forward, I point to Jane. "Jane wants her power. Jane would be the one creating earthquakes then. Mona didn't know what she was doing."

"That's the point, idiot," Brianna says. "Jane will know what to do; she can control all this power." Brianna doesn't move the blade even an inch away. She's stalling. Why?

I step ahead again. "What's it to you, Brianna?"

"Jane will turn me into a Sister."

Another step. I'm about at the free-throw line now. "No, she won't. It can't be done. Skye told me."

"The Singularity can do anything," Brianna replies. Not a shred of doubt in her voice.

Crap, crap, crap.

Brianna is in this to the end. I have to stop her. But it will work only if Brianna understands what she's doing. How much does she know? Only one way to find out.

"I know you can't kill Mona until Jane is ready to absorb the energy. You're bluffing."

Brianna's response is to force the blade into Mona's throat, almost to the point of piercing it. I let out a gasp, but I don't dare to move.

Brianna smiles. "Jane told me the energy lingers for a while. Jane's got a window. It doesn't need to be at the exact moment. So, I can kill your sister anytime I want."

Is she bluffing *now*? If she can do it any time, what's stopping her? My mind whirls. Jane is still in a trance. The determined look in Brianna's eyes terrorize me.

Is Brianna trying to hurt me too? Another desperate thought comes to me.

"I've loved you, Brianna," I say, trying to make the lie stick.

She chuckles and shakes her head. "Well, I didn't love you, Drake. It's not about *you*."

When I realize I'm out of ideas, reality hits me. My sister is going to die.

How do you think straight when your sister's life is on the line?

You don't.

Chapter 58: Skye

I open my eyes, but it's still dark. Where...?

The hallway. Somebody threw something at me. A potion.

A Sleep potion.

The tingling. A Sister is around. Jane.

It's all fuzzy. My head feels like scrambled eggs.

I prop myself on my elbows. The morning cleansing potions I've been taking and my protection rituals are paying off right now. If not for them, I'd be asleep for hours.

Have I been? I look at my cell. The numbers are blurry. Squinting, I see I slept for about five minutes only.

Where's Drake? The gym!

Dizzy, I pull myself up, the cell still in my hand. Call for help. Connor.

I stagger toward the gym while speed-dialing Connor with one hand and steadying myself on the wall with the other. No! Don't call him! Drake doesn't trust Connor. I hang up before the call is completed. I turn off the phone for good measure.

I'm already feeling better when I reach the gym's door. I see Drake talking to Brianna, who's about thirty feet away from him. She's holding a knife—a black athame, the mark of the Night

Sisters—to Mona's throat.

My tingling sense tells me that Jane is inside, somewhere to my right, but I can't see her. Does she sense me too?

I grab the gym's doorknobs, ready to intervene.

Suddenly, Drake lunges forward. Brianna presses the knife into Mona's throat.

Before Drake can reach them, Mona opens her eyes. I can see blood trickling down her neck.

A lot of things happen at the same time, and my jelly mind has trouble comprehending it all. At first, a tsunami of magical energy hits me at once, paralyzing me. It's unlike anything I've ever felt, a humongous jolt of pure magical energy. I grab the door's handles to avoid being knocked back.

Simultaneously, a fireball erupts where Mona and Brianna were just a second ago. Its shockwave throws Drake backward, hurtling him toward the gym wall.

Brianna and Mona are a mass of fire. The gym is instantly ablaze, the fire spreading rapidly. Exercise mats are burning. Posters and signs blacken and crumble.

The energy wave is suddenly gone. After I recover the control of my muscles, I push the doors open with all my strength. Hair-raising screams fill the gym.

While removing my jacket, I rush toward Mona and Brianna, who are still on fire. In my peripheral vision, I see Jane in the corner of the court, thrashing around.

I'm about to use the jacket as a blanket to quell the fire, when I see Mona stepping back from the orange and yellow flames, staring in horror at Brianna's burning body.

Mona is completely unharmed.

Brianna is flailing and screaming. I try to wrap her with my jacket, but she spreads herself on the floor and starts to roll over. I use the jacket like a matador then, flapping it over her, helping her extinguish the flames. Why aren't the sprinklers on?

The wooden floor is catching fire quickly, and the smoke becomes thick. I see Mona step right over a high flame, and she doesn't even acknowledge it. Not even her hospital gown burns. Behind her, flames lick the walls.

Still helping Brianna, I yell to Mona, "Drake! Check him!"

This brings Mona out of her stupor. She rushes to Drake.

Brianna stops moving and just lies there, face down. But at least she's not on fire anymore. When I turn her, a scarred, grimy face greets me.

She's breathing, barely. And she's badly burned. The smoke will do her in soon.

"We've got to get out of here!" I yell. "Now!" I grab Brianna under her armpits and drag her toward the door. I cough and look around, but I don't see Jane anywhere.

"I can't carry him!" Mona yells.

"Drag him!" I reply.

"He's too heavy!"

I lay Brianna down on the floor. "Let's switch!"

We do that. Mona clutches Brianna's left arm and drags her. I carry Drake, grabbing him by the armpits. He's facing away from me, but I can tell he's not burned as badly as Brianna.

Mona and I maneuver to avoid the flames. My cough gets worse, but Mona is unaffected. When she opens the door, the hallway's clean air is a blessing.

The sprinklers still aren't working. Mona closes the door, and we look through the glass. The gym is completely consumed by fire. Paint starts to bubble up on the smoldering walls on our side. The door is scorching.

I look at Mona's hand. She has just touched the handles. Not a single burn.

Kneeling down, I examine Drake's wounds. He's breathing in gasps, his face covered in soot, and he's got a few burn marks, but he's not hurt as badly as Brianna.

"The fire is spreading," I say, turning to Mona. "We've got to move them."

"Call 911!" Mona says.

Thinking fast, I search Brianna's pockets and find a phone. "Call them on this. Tell them your name is Brianna. I have an idea. I'll be right back."

The cafeteria is right next to the gym. I rush there and find a pair of busing trolleys. I come back with them.

"The dispatcher told me they're overwhelmed. They will send someone as soon as they can," Mona says while we hoist Drake and lay him down on a trolley.

We move to do the same with Brianna. "What about the firemen?"

"Same thing," says Mona. "What are we going to do?"

We begin to roll them back to the entrance, away from the inferno. I say, "About the school? It's no use. They'll never be here on time. Let it burn," I say.

"What about them?" Mona asks, nodding in the direction of Drake and Brianna.

"I have another idea," I say. "But we have to move fast."

***

"Okay, don't ask me anything," I say. "We don't have much time."

The gym is in the school's central building, and I don't think the neighbors have seen the fire yet. We have a small window before they notice the smoke and call for help. And maybe the firemen will still be busy with the quake.

After Mona nods, I continue, "We're doing a circle of prayer. I can't use your energy, and you don't know how to perform a healing ritual, but the both of us can pool our strengths and make it happen."

Maybe, I think. But I don't say it.

We're standing up, holding hands. Drake and Brianna lie side-by-side on the ground, at our feet, still unconscious.

To her credit, Mona doesn't question anything. She just nods, her eyes small plates of awe.

"You only have to do one thing. Do not freak out. Relax. Let the energy flow. Slowly."

"The energy?" she asks.

"Don't worry. You'll feel it."

She starts to shake and takes her hands away. "I can't do it..."

I grab her hands. "Drake told me tonight you're a tough girl." She looks at me. "Drake," I repeat, nodding in his direction.

She looks at him and nods to me, but her hands still shake.

"You can do it," I say. "You *will* do it."

We close our eyes. I start the chanting I did in the woods the day I met Drake. I already traced the bloody runes on their five points. We're going to have make do with a makeshift commune. At least we're outdoors, in contact with dirt and grass, and an enormous bonfire burns next to us.

Please Goddess, allow it to work.

I invoke *my* magical energy, but since we're communing, Mona's energy comes into the energy pool. I feel it, a rush of power. Mona's body jerks back, but I expect it and grab her hands firmly.

My biggest fear is Mona creating another disaster when she releases her energy. But she understands a little bit now, expects it, and that makes a difference. Other Sisters will feel her energy too, but it's going to be much less intense than when she created the earthquake or the inferno. I hope.

Her energy flow increases, and I push these thoughts from my mind. I breathe steady, visualizing Drake and Brianna's healed bodies, invoking ancient powers of nature.

Mona and I become one. Her energy is overwhelming, and, for a moment, I feel like she's holding back, trying not to overpower either of us. It's working.

She learns fast.

My chanting gets more intense, and I start to feel our energy flowing toward Brianna and Drake.

***

When the ambulance finally arrives, Mona and I are in the Volvo parked next to the pool. Drake is coming in and out of consciousness, resting on the floor of the large cargo area.

The school is beyond help. The paramedics get out and see Brianna lying on the grass, alive but still unconscious.

I turn to Mona, and she smiles at me.

Chapter 59: Drake

I'm thinking about wearing a helmet everywhere I go. Seriously, how many times can you be knocked out without suffering a massive brain injury?

At least I didn't get burned in the fire. The shockwave threw me away from the flames. And I've got the world's greatest nurse by my side.

Skye leans over me and kisses me fully on the lips.

"Hello, nurse," I say.

***

We had many bases to cover, and Skye came up with a solution for each of them.

First, we had to explain Mona's disappearance from the hospital. That was easy, but it required a lot of acting on Mona's part. She just said she woke up in the hospital disoriented and called the nurses several times before leaving her room.

The hospital staff and the police were skeptical at first, but they had had a number of machine glitches on the day of the earthquake. The confusion and the crowd also made it plausible that a patient would wander around the hospital attracting little attention.

After the fire in the gym, Skye dropped Mona off at the hospital's garage, where she was conveniently found by an orderly after a few minutes. She acted the part, sounding disoriented and making little sense. The police, busy with more pressing matters, gladly swallowed the explanation. The hospital also was awfully happy we weren't pressing charges. Misplacing a patient is not good PR.

Well, officially, they *did* misplace Jane. Police are still looking for her, since she hasn't been seen since she disappeared from the hospital. Also, there's the small matter of her school burning down. The police's only clue about the fire is Brianna, who is in a coma.

Mona and Skye's voodoo worked well for me and spectacularly for Brianna. They actually saved Brianna's life. They even reverted almost all of her burn wounds. When she wakes up, which Skye tells me it should be soon, she'll be able to live a normal life.

Well, as normal as a wannabe murderer can live.

Police also asked us why we accused Jane of kidnapping Mona. After they interviewed some of Greenwood High school students and staff, the police understood our suspicion. Jane's bad reputation saved us from more questioning.

And the school is gone.

Really, things couldn't have worked out better. I mean, considering.

Chapter 60: Skye

I feel Connor's signature and prepare for our meeting. Or rather, for our confrontation. He didn't sound pleased on the phone. I wouldn't care—not anymore—but I need him to be happy. He must believe my story.

I chose a neutral ground for the talk: the International Fountain at Seattle Center, which is turned off. I sit at the raised edge of the sunken half-dome. When he arrives, I stand up and give him one of my best smiles. I'm glad my Allure is back. It makes things easier.

"Why so chuffed?" he asks me, already suspicious.

"I've got good news," I say. I do, but I'm going to tell him a whole other set of good news, completely fabricated.

He looks around. A guy eating his brown-bagged lunch is at the fountain, but he's sitting on the opposite edge of the dome, away from us. A woman with a stroller crosses the Seattle Center boulevard. It's too chilly for tourists. Connor waits until the woman is gone and asks, "Do you know where Jane is?"

I'm taken aback. "Is that what you're worried about?"

His face gets heavier. This is not going well. "Don't start with this again, Skye. Either you're over me or you aren't."

Damn, he's right. Let it go, Skye. "I'm over you."

"So, it's about Jane? I'm asking because she's missing, and she would only disappear if she had found the Singularity."

Ooh, I'm going to relish this.

"She did," I say.

The look on Connor's face is priceless. Unfortunately, he recovers fast. "No more games, Skye. Tell me the truth."

I remind myself to resist his Trust Charm so I don't babble the truth by mistake. "Actually, the Singularity found Jane."

He shoots me an exasperated look, and I try not to enjoy it too much.

A middle-aged couple holding hands arrive and sit a few yards from us. She rests her head on his shoulders while she drinks from a Tully's cup. Connor looks at them uncomfortably, and I don't know if he's worried about the Veil or the display of intimacy. Either way, I need him happy and relaxed today.

"Come with me," I whisper while going into the dry fountain area. I climb down the half-dome, careful not to slip. He follows me, and we stop by the water spouts. I hope nobody turns them on while we're here.

"Who is she? *Where* is she?" His voice is cold.

"Her name is Brianna Jenkins. Right now, she's in the hospital in a coma."

"Brianna?"

"Do you know her?" I'm afraid of the answer, the only unaccounted item of my lie.

"I remember Jane mentioned something about a Brianna. Wait, she goes to Greenwood!"

I nod.

Connor asks, "But how come Jane never detected her? How

come *you* didn't either?"

Here I sprinkle a little bit of truth to make the lie more palatable. "The Singularity works differently. She is special. We were right: she has natural defenses. Magical shields, and they are always up, even at close range, even when we touch her. But we can sense her when she uses her magic and loses control of it. Only she doesn't only use it, she *unleashes* it."

"The earthquake," he says.

I nod again. "She caused it. I still don't know if she did it on purpose or if she lost control somehow while testing her powers."

Connor shakes his head. No doubt he's imagining the consequences.

"What does Jane have to do with it?"

I hope the story sticks. "My guess is that Brianna sensed Jane, identified her as a Sister, and befriended her. Brianna doesn't come from a witch family, so I think she had no other way of learning about magic unless she posed as a Knowing, doing whatever Jane asked her to do. Brianna was the one who gave me the Blinding potion at school."

"It makes sense," Connor says, more to himself.

Yes!

He looks at me with a hint of suspicion. "But how do you know that? And what about the school fire?"

"I think Jane saw Brianna releasing her energy, but Jane was knocked down by the earthquake. When Jane woke up in the hospital, she realized who Brianna was and went after her." I stop there, waiting for him to make the connection.

Connor grabs my arm. "Jane can absorb energy!"

"And Charms," I say. I look at my arm, still held by him, and he lets it go. I decide to be graceful. "Remember how she stole my Allure? She probably hijacked your Trust Charm too. I imagine that's how she got you to spill the beans about the Singularity's location." I'm not so sure about that part, but I want his sympathy.

He nods. "Yes, it might have been that. She steals energy. She wanted to steal the Singularity's energy! Wow," he says. "Just... wow."

"Indeed. Brianna fought back when Jane attacked her and— intentionally or not—created the fire that razed the school."

Some kind of classical music starts to play. I look around, confused. The woman drinking coffee makes a beckoning gesture. "They're turning the fountain on," she yells.

We thank her and climb up to the promenade. The water ballet starts.

Connor watches it for a minute and then says, "Wait a minute. And what about your boyfriend's sister? Why did Jane take her away?"

It's so weird hearing Connor, of all people, refer to Drake as my boyfriend. Anyway, that's not why I'm here.

Mona's involvement is the part of the story I have most trouble with. "I have no idea. Maybe Jane wanted a hostage? I really don't know. I think Jane changed her mind and gave Mona a Forget potion. When they found Mona in the hospital garage, she didn't know how she got there."

He looks at me for a long time, before saying, "It does sound like Jane."

I refrain from sighing in relief.

Connor continues, "I'll let the Mothers know at once. We'll keep an eye on this Brianna."

He turns to me with grateful eyes I've never seen before. "Thank you, Skye. You found her! I owe you. All the Sisters owe you," he says. He shakes his head. "You actually found her! You're amazing…" He moves to hug me, and I think his Trust Charm is working, because I let him. I even hug him back.

He was never so warm, so open, so… vulnerable.

But it's too late now, Connor. You are two years too late.

***

"Darling, you must come at once!" Mum says on the phone. "The Mothers want to thank you."

"Mum, enough about that," I say. "How are you?"

"Wonderful. I've never felt better. My daughter is the pride of the Sisterhood."

"I mean your health."

She gives a little, very *proper*, chuckle. "Oh, *me*. I'm fine. The doctors are astounded by my recovery. Of course, they don't know I've been having some help on the side. When are you coming back?"

I think of Drake—and also of the few loose ends left to tie up.

"It might be a while," I say.

Chapter 61: Drake

So, here I am, not only dating a witch, but also the brother of the most powerful witch in the world. Mona always thought she was a freak. Now she knows it for sure.

I have no idea how this is going to play out.

I try to imagine what will happen when Brianna wakes up. They have her on the scene of the arson, with burn wounds. Her car was there too, at the gym's back entrance, and the call to 911 came from her cell.

Also, it seems a horde of witches will be watching her forever now.

Brianna not only is a Knowing, but she also knows Mona is the Singularity. Skye is thinking of slipping a Forget potion in Brianna's IV drop, but Skye doesn't know how potent it can be, nor if it could be absorbed that way.

I always forget Skye didn't finish her witch studies or whatever they're called. Do they have a college for that? There's so much I don't know yet. And Mona is even more of a beginner.

Now it's time for the Big Talk. Not the one I was afraid to have with Skye a while ago.

This is about Mona, Skye, and me discussing our options. Mona will walk us through what went down on the day of the earthquake.

For the first time in years I'm allowed in Mona's room. Well, I've been here from time to time. I just wasn't allowed to.

Dad is downstairs. He's just glad we're all okay. But I think he'll never travel without us again. Ever.

Since Mona's Allure kicked in, she looks gorgeous and radiant. She didn't lose an ounce or an inch, nor has she changed her slouched posture, but she exudes a glow of beauty. Which so doesn't match her emo wardrobe.

Mona starts. "Pain and I were just hanging out when that bitch— "

"Jane," I say, trying to help.

Mona shoots me a threatening stare. "That *bitch*," she continues, "knocked at the door. At first, she said she was Drake's friend. But I think she saw our candles and our Wiccan props in the basement before knocking on Pain's door."

"Why do you think that?" I ask.

"She started asking questions," Mona says, "very specific questions about the Craft. Now, Pain is not one to be pushed around, and she told this Jane character to piss off. Jane just stood there, asking more and more questions, being scary nosy, until Pain slammed the door in her face. We watched Jane linger around on the street for a while. Then she climbed on her bike and left. That's when Pain said she thought Jane knew about me."

I ask, "What about you? Did you know about the… witchcraft?"

"I've got to tell you something, Drake…" Mona says and lowers her eyes. "I'm sorry."

"About what?" I ask.

Mona doesn't answer right away. She looks at her stuff on the dresser, all back after being knocked out by the quake. I wait patiently.

When I'm about to open my mouth, Skye jumps in. "About the fire," Skye says.

"Hey, it's just school," I say, trying to lighten up the mood.

Mona looks at me with pleading eyes. "Skye means… our old house."

My stare shifts from one to the other.

Oh!

Mona's words come in a hurry. "I'm sorry that you thought you had caused the fire. It took me a while to understand—to accept—what had really happened. But then I couldn't tell anyone. Who would have believed me?"

I'm having mixed feelings about this. Sure, I'm glad it turned out I'm not guilty of ruining our lives, but Mona could've told me before. At least make up a story.

I don't want to think about it. I ask Skye, "How did you know that?"

Skye shrugs. "I had a hunch. Because of the school fire. This morning I asked your father the date your house burned down. Same day the Singularity's energy was released."

My mind reluctantly accepts the logic. "Yeah, about that: wasn't she supposed to flip the switch at fifteen?" I ask.

Skye nods. "She did. It was the earthquake. The first outburst she had, at thirteen—I'm guessing—was just a pre-release. Like a valve letting steam off because of too much pressure. I've never heard of a pre-release before, but now we know Mona's magic doesn't follow the old rules. Her true powers, like the Allure Charm, didn't manifest until she had her Daybreak."

The unblemished, beautiful new face of my sister catches my

attention. It's just one of the many things that changed.

"What happened that day, Mona?" I ask.

Mona's tone is timid. "I just felt this burning inside, like my body was in flames. I remember the curtains catching fire before I passed out." She looks away.

"Now we know fire can't harm her," Skye says with admiration. "This is a new Charm, as far as I know."

"After the fire," Mona continues, "I was lost. I couldn't tell anyone, and I didn't know what had happened. I read a lot of books about mysticism and magic, but only Wicca had something that remotely made sense. So I started practicing it, and Pain got interested too. When I felt I could trust her, I told her everything. She's been helping me figure this out ever since."

For two years she held that secret. Wow. My sister *is* tough.

She goes on. "When Jane showed up talking as if she knew about me, I panicked. Pain tried to calm me down, but I was so out of whack! I wouldn't listen. Then I felt the burning inside, the same burning that had started it all. I couldn't control it and control my nerves at the same time. I was so freaked out I couldn't even explain to Pain what was happening."

Mona's eyes become wet, and she reaches for a tissue from the dresser. Skye moves to sit by her side and puts her arm around my sister.

"It was bubbling up, and I thought of the fire, and I yelled to Pain to get away from me… It was a mess of screams and pain, until I felt something…" She doesn't finish.

"Horrible?" I ask.

"Wonderful," Mona says.

Skye shows a knowing smile.

Mona's voice almost chokes. "It was like I was detached from reality, soaring above the ground. I felt a wave of happiness inside me. I can't..." Mona looks at Skye. "I can't explain."

"Nobody can," Skye whispers, nodding her head.

I'm feeling very, very left out. "And?" I ask.

"I was just wishing it—whatever *it* was—didn't cause a fire. It was all very confusing, but I tried to hold it in. Then... poof. I remember waking up at the gym. That's it." Mona's expression seems to ask for forgiveness.

I stare at Skye.

"What?" she asks.

"What do you mean, 'what'?" I say. "Fill in the blanks."

My girlfriend sighs. "Jane probably got suspicious when she saw your sister dabbling in magic without emitting a signature. Maybe she confused the Wiccan stuff," Skye says, pointing to some books scattered on the floor, "with the real thing. Then the quake hit, and Jane had a bike accident. At first I thought she fell because of the quake, but it wasn't that violent at the beginning, remember? Jane's a good biker; she wouldn't just fall for no reason."

"Maybe a car hit her bike?" I suggest.

But Skye shakes her head. "I think she fell because of the impact of the Singularity's energy hitting her. I sensed it from here, and I almost fainted. It must have been overwhelming to Jane, since she was so close to ground zero. When Jane woke up, she called Brianna to ask about Mona. Brianna found out that Mona was at the hospital and brought her car over, helped Jane kidnap Mona, and they drove to school."

I can see where things fit. It would be hard for Jane to take Mona away without help, or transportation. That's why Brianna's car was at

Greenwood High.

"But why was Jane at Pain's?" Mona asks.

I raise my hand, "I know this one." I ignore Skye's chuckle and continue before any of them takes away my moment of glory. "Jane knew Skye could sense her, so she tried to get back at me by going after you. She must have followed you to Pain's. She might even have been spying through the windows before knocking on the door." I look at Skye, who nods her approval. Pride invades me.

"We *were* praying right before Jane showed up," Mona says.

I give a 'See?' look at Skye, but she just rolls her eyes.

She turns to Mona. "Okay. Now we have a problem. Jane and Brianna both know you're the Singularity. We don't have to worry about Brianna for now."

"But she'll talk when she wakes up," Mona argues.

Skye answers her. "She'll be busy with her own problems. First, she'll have to defend the arson changes. And she won't dare to mention magic to police or to her family. Who would believe her?"

"What about the covens?" I ask

"I told the Mothers that Brianna was the Singularity. There's no way to disprove my claim. Or to *prove* it." Skye is very happy with herself. "It's a catch-22, really. The Singularity only emits a signature when using her powers—the Sisters believed that because of the supposed Daybreak, two years ago, and the earthquake. But Brianna can't use magic, since she doesn't have any."

Mona says, "Still, at some point she'll tell them I'm the one they're looking for."

Skye shrugs. "They'll think Brianna is just trying to deflect attention from herself. They won't believe her. Remember, her credibility is not at an all-time high right now. I think the Mothers will stay away until the arson incident is cleared up. They'll watch her, for sure. They'll never let her disappear."

She gives Mona a meaningful look and rests her hands on Mona's shoulders. "And that's why I'm not telling them about you. You have to understand this: once the Mothers find out about you, your life is over."

Skye's voice has never sounded harsher. Mona is looking straight at her.

"They can't afford to let you loose. They believe the type of magic you can do is so conspicuous that the Veil will be compromised forever. So far, we've been lucky you had the outbreaks in private spaces, with only Sisters or Knowings around. If you had one in a public place, where an army of phone users can tweet about it and post pics and videos online, the Veil would be history."

"I would be outed, but the other witches... Can't they hide?" Mona asks, her voice quivering.

"It's much easier to hide when nobody is looking for you," Skye says. "If the Veil is broken, anyone suspected of using magic will be subjected to an unprecedented level of scrutiny. Like paparazzi times a thousand. Imagine how much People magazine would pay for a witch tell-all?"

"Can't the magazines do that now?" I ask.

"Now they'd be laughed off. After Mona produces a bonfire out of thin air around her, *everybody* is going to see it on YouTube and believe in magic. But that's not the worst part. People are afraid of what they don't understand. Minorities are always persecuted. And we witches have a history of being executed."

"At least Mona can't burn on a stake," I say, thinking out loud.

The two most important women in my life look at me with

disdain in their eyes.

Sisters, indeed.

"Drake," Mona says with a grave voice. "Shut up."

Chapter 62: Skye

The sun plays hide-and-seek behind the buildings while Drake drives us to Boulder's house. I had forgotten about it. The sun, I mean. I'm even wearing short sleeves. The scar Jane's knife left on my arm is almost gone.

Before we go to Boulder's, we stop at the 7-Eleven for paper plates.

"What about Jane?" Drake asks when we're back in the car.

I hate it that Jane is permanently on our minds. "I'm not sure," I say. "She must be burned from the gym fire, and I'm pretty sure she can't heal herself."

He shakes his head. "No, I mean, what is she going to do?"

I shrug. "I know Connor is looking for her. Remember, Connor believes Jane is after Brianna, not Mona."

"But Mona is in danger," he says.

"She is, but I gave her a few little somethings she can use to defend herself. I'll perform morning cleanse and shielding rituals on her—when I'm sure her magic will not get out of control. Also, Mona has started to sense magical energy. She can only feel it when a Sister is close, but with her power she could even have a stronger sensibility than I do."

"How is she?"

"She's *your* sister," I say.

"Now she's yours too," he replies.

I'm taken aback, until I realize he's not implying I'm family. He means she's my *Sister*, capital S.

I chuckle. "You two still didn't have a *talk*, did you?"

"The last one didn't go well." He doesn't smile.

"She feels guilty about the earthquake. I told her she shouldn't: it wasn't her fault, and nobody died. Pain supported me."

"Is Pain out of the hospital already? And is she a Knowing now?"

"Well, technically, she's been a Knowing for some time," I tell him. "Anyway, I think Pain and I convinced Mona." I glance at him. "You're taking this pretty well."

"What can I do? I've seen enough to accept it." He shows me a crooked smile.

Something else must be said. "Drake, you've got to understand: this will never go away."

He looks at me, serious.

"There might come a day when the Mothers come knocking."

Drake puts on a brave face. "We'll deal with it."

"That's not all. Mona's magical abilities will increase. It'll take a while for her to use magic, at least in a controlled and discreet way. Things will get weirder and weirder."

"I seriously doubt that," he says.

"Be warned. So far Mona showed Allure and this fire immunity I've never seen before. She doesn't play by the old rules. She might have more than two Charms. Unheard-of powers. And things can get nasty."

His eyes flicker between the road and me. "What do you mean?"

There's no easy way to say it. "Jane is not the only rogue Sister.

We know others are out there, hidden. She might even belong to a renegade coven. I mean, her bike, her houses—someone probably pays for that. And she wouldn't learn Night magic by herself. A Night coven must be supporting her."

"But they already knew about the Singularity, right? What changed?"

"The earthquake. They knew *of* her. Now they know what she can do. *And* Jane might tell them who she is."

Drake goes silent. I respect his privacy. I just stare at him while he drives. Not even his somber expression can mask his good looks.

Pushing all the trouble aside, I smile, just happy to be with him. Looking outside, I notice the city. It kind of sparkles in the sun.

Seattle is not such a bad place after all.

I love the irregular, patched-up sidewalks, the always-wet alleyways. The ever-present greenery. The unique vibe and the positive attitude.

I love that the city can be mellow or rock and roll.

I even love the gray skies that make the sunny days—like today— much more special.

And I love it all even more because Drake is here.

Chapter 63: Drake

"D-man, you're here! And you brought the wife!" Sean speaks *and* chuckles at the same time. I wonder if he's a witch. Maybe that's his special Charm.

Forget about magic. I came here to have fun. The last month had the record of "weirdest moments of my life" toppled over and over. I crave some normalcy.

Sean takes the bag with paper plates from my hand and leads us to the backyard through the side of the house. The windows have plastic covers, a common sight in the city trying to rebuild itself.

Boulder and Priscilla are on the deck. Judging by her body language, not as a couple.

"Hey! Welcome to our small barbecue gathering!" Boulder says aloud. "We're lighting a fire in homage of the fire in school. Clever, huh?"

"Not as much as you'd think," Priscilla says.

"Oh come on, the school burned. Let's burn some meat," he replies, giving her a one-armed hug.

"Let's *cook* the meat, not burn it, please," I say.

Priscilla is not amused. She pushes Boulder's arm away. "It's not all fun and games, you know? My dad mentioned they'll probably spread us among the other schools in the district while they rebuild Greenwood High. We may end up in different schools."

"Thank you, mood killer," Sean says. He brings us a beer and a soda, and gives me the latter. "Here's your kid's drink." He looks at Skye.

"I'll take the grown-up drink," Skye says. Sean hands her the beer can, and I can see that with that line, she earned his everlasting respect.

Boulder turns to Skye, "How do you like it, Skye? Medium-rare good enough for you?"

"I'm a vegetarian," she says. I can almost feel Sean's disappointment.

Boulder arches his eyebrows. "Really? Well, D-Man here is crap-tarian. But you still make a good couple."

He's clearly a few beers ahead of the rest of us. He puts a hand on my shoulder, as a big brother would do. "You with a girlfriend, Drake... I always believed you'd grow into a man."

I'm speechless by his backhanded compliment. His eyes show some pride. Or maybe it's too much alcohol. Of course, he's not done.

"I still do," he deadpans, slapping me hard on the back. Sean laughs.

Wiping laughing tears from his face, Boulder continues, "Now, seriously, I'm glad. Hey, we could double-date. Are you up to it, Priscilla?"

This is unexpected. We all stop to look at Priscilla.

She gazes at her soda for a while, and then she answers. "Sorry, gorgeous. I promised myself I'd date all the guys in the world—and I already did you."

Boulder's smile is gone for a second, but comes back soon, this time softer.

"To tell you the truth, I don't really like your decision. But I'm understanding. I can wait. So how about I'm the first one on your second go-round?"

We all stare back at Priscilla. Who blushes. The Predator *blushes*.

This is one of the most awkward moments ever. Thankfully, my girlfriend restores order. Skye grabs my arm with both hands and moves closer to me. "Sorry, Boulder, but Drake and I need a date for ourselves." She stares into my eyes. "Our first date."

I like the sound of that. And her eyes. The blue in her eyes is the exact same color of the cloudless sky above. I need to ask her what this shade is called. Maybe later. Now I have a more pressing question. "Are we finally going on a date? A *real* date?"

"And I give you my word this one will have a happy ending," she whispers to me, her voice full of promise, her blue eyes full of mischief.

Excuse me while I kiss Skye.

###

AUTHOR'S NOTE

Thank you for reading this book. Writing a novel is a blast, but no easy task. Knowing that you got a few hours of entertainment out of this story makes it all worth it.

For updates on the next book in this series and to be the first to hear about other new releases, sign up for my newsletter: http://bit.ly/fabiobuenoemail (your email will never be shared, and you can unsubscribe at any time).

I hope you enjoyed reading WICKED SENSE. Please let your friends know about it! Word-of-mouth is vital for an author to succeed. If you enjoyed the book, please leave a review on the book retailer websites, even if it's just a sentence or two. Your review makes a difference and would be much appreciated.

I'd love to hear from you. Connect with me on my website (FabioBueno.com), Facebook (Facebook.com/FabioBuenoAuthor), Twitter (@_FabioBueno_), or email me at fabio@fabiobueno.com.

All the best,
Fabio

BROKEN SPELL

BROKEN SPELL, the second book in the Singularity series, is now available!

Be careful what you wish for.

Skye wanted to find the Singularity. She got what she sought, but to protect the most powerful witch alive, Skye had to betray her coven. Now she regrets entangling her boyfriend Drake in her hidden world.

Drake yearned for Skye, but now he finds out that getting the girl is just the beginning: keeping the girl is the hard part. When tragedy strikes, Drake faces an impossible choice that could destroy his family and his shot at love.

The vicious Night covens seek retribution at all costs. Wicked Jane has returned, scarred from her last confrontation with Drake and Skye, and holding a baffling secret that may change everything.

Dangerous alliances arise. The Veil is about to be broken.

Falling in love has never been harder.

ACKNOWLEDGMENTS

Having just one name on the cover is deceptive. Many people were involved in the creation of WICKED SENSE, and I'd like to thank them.

I'm forever grateful to the Writers in The Rain: Angela Orlowski-Peart, Suma Subramaniam, Eileen Riccio, Martina Elise Dalton, and Brenda Beem. Your friendship, expertise, and advice have changed my life. Reading your novels has been an absolute pleasure. Here's to many more fries- and commas-filled Thursday nights.

Destiny Makers and Wanatribe: you are some of the most generous and talented people I've ever met.

Thanks to graphic designer Martina Elise Dalton for the perfect cover. To Grammar-Hero Alyssa Linn Palmer, the line editor of this book. And to Eagle-Eyed Amanda Shofner, copyeditor.

Great friends and great readers Carlos, Flavia, Jose, and Lucio: I couldn't have done it without your support.

My family and in-laws: thank you for never looking at me funny when I said I wanted to write.

My loving and patient kids: thanks for putting up with my long hours at the computer. You're my own fantasy world.

Jana aka Wonder Wife: I didn't know the meaning of "love" or "life" until I met you. Thanks for teaching me.

ABOUT THE AUTHOR

Fabio resides in the Pacific Northwest with his wife and kids. When not writing or reading, he geeks out with family and friends, solidifies his reputation as the world's slowest runner, and acts very snobbish about movies. He loves to hear from readers and hangs out here:

@_FabioBueno_

FabioBueno.com

Facebook.com/FabioBuenoAuthor